3 1252 01519 2560

DISCARDED
SPARTANBURG COUNTY PUBLIC LIBRARIES

M MEEK
Meek, M. R. D.   l s
If you go down to the woods

medlock

SPARTANBURG

OCT 0 2 2001

DEMCO

IF YOU GO DOWN
TO THE WOODS

A Selection of Recent Titles from M. R. D. Meek

POSTSCRIPT TO MURDER
THIS BLESSED PLOT
TOUCH AND GO
A HOUSE TO DIE FOR*

* *published by Severn House*

IF YOU GO DOWN TO THE WOODS

M. R. D. Meek

Spartanburg County Public Libraries
151 S. Church Street
Spartanburg, SC 29306-3241

This first world edition published in Great Britain 2001 by
SEVERN HOUSE PUBLISHERS LTD of
9–15 High Street, Sutton, Surrey SM1 1DF.
This first world edition published in the USA 2001 by
SEVERN HOUSE PUBLISHERS INC. of
595 Madison Avenue, New York, NY 10022.

Copyright © 2001 by Margaret Meek
All rights reserved.
The moral right of the author has been asserted.

British Library Cataloguing in Publication Data

Meek, M. R. D
  If you go down to the woods – (A Lennox Kemp mystery)
  1. Kemp, Lennox (Fictitious character) – Fiction
  2. Lawyers – Fiction
  3. Detective and mystery stories
  I. Title
  823.9′14 [F]   3 1252 01519 2560

ISBN 0–7278–5647–2

All situations in this publication are fictitious and
any resemblance to living persons is purely coincidental.

Typeset by Palimpsest Book Production Limited,
Polmont, Stirlingshire, Scotland.
Printed and bound in Great Britain by
MPG Books Ltd, Bodmin, Cornwall.

M Meek
Meek, M. R. D.
If you go down to the woods

One

The girl shown into Frank Davey's office first thing on Monday morning had a spiky look about her. Perhaps it was the arrangement of her hair, which not only stuck out from the top of her head but also managed to do the same thing at shoulder level. She wore kitten heels, but they were kittens with claws and marked the carpet as she slouched over to his desk and flung herself into the visitors' chair. Even sitting down she was all edges, elbows sticking out sharply from the sleeves of her leather jacket as if it was still on its coat hanger.

Frank had half risen, half held out a hand, but withdrew it hastily when he could see she wasn't there for the civilities. As she thrust a familiar piece of paper at him, he almost flinched – so near had come the red fingernail to stabbing him in the chest.

"Says it's a summons," she said in a tone which seemed to doubt the universe.

"Yes," said Frank. At least he'd seen summonses before. Studying this one would give him a breather. For Miss Lillian Egerton, the name on the paper, was not only his first client of the day, she was his first client ever . . . Although he had been articled to the senior partner at Gillorns, Solicitors of Newtown, he had spent three years in the pleasant pastures of Equity before returning to the firm as assistant solicitor. He was a member of a profession, but felt like an amateur; he hoped it didn't show.

Lillian Egerton was nineteen, and she was charged with malicious damage and theft from premises at 14 Bolton Street, Newtown, on the night of Saturday the eleventh of February. That was just over a week ago. The local police had wasted no time.

1

He lined up the summons carefully on his blotter and spoke to his client with what he considered to be proper gravity.

"If you would simply tell me in your own words, Miss Egerton—"

"Lily," she snapped at him.

"Er . . . Lily . . . About the circumstances on the night of—"

"Well, for a start I wasn't there, was I? Not near the place . . ."

"But you know the premises in question?" Frank knew them and probably so did most of the people in Newtown: 14 Bolton Street was the health centre, a beacon of hope to some, for others the doorway to doubt and despair.

"I have to know the place, don't I?" His client was continuing in her own interrogatory style. "It's that Dr Parfitt I see when I go for my pills. He's OK. But he wouldn't be there that time of night . . . Stands to reason . . ."

"What time of night would that be?"

She wore so much mascara that her eyes looked fenced in but when she turned them full on to him he caught a flash of green. "You trying to catch me out? The time they said – around midnight. I weren't anywhere near Bolton Street by then."

"Would you tell me just what your movements were that night, Miss Egerton . . . er . . . Lily." Frank liked to think of his voice as low and persuasive without realising that sometimes it was barely audible.

"Eh? What you saying?"

She leant forward and the lapels of her jacket fell open revealing enticing slopes of snowy flesh which were a lot less angular than the rest of her.

Frank cleared his throat. "Just tell me where you were, Lily, when all this happened."

She hitched her chair nearer to the desk and leant her arms on it, giving him the benefit of a closer intimacy. There was a perfume from her hair that made him think of the bowl of hyacinths in his girlfriend's flat. The flowers had stayed fresh for weeks, then suddenly they'd changed colour

2

and faded, but the scent still hung about, too heavy, too sweet.

"Being a Saturday, like," Lily Egerton was saying, "I was down the pub with my mates and when it come to half-ten we were leaving, see, when this bloke comes over and offers to buy me a drink. My friends, they weren't for staying on, like, but, me, I wasn't that anxious to get home . . ."

"You say this was about half-past ten in the evening . . ." Frank was aware how stilted and pedantic he sounded after the girl's narrative flow, which had its own rhythm.

"It were long before closing-time it that's what you mean, and there was still lots going on."

"Did you know this man who offered you a drink?"

"Not from Adam. Never seen him before, and I know most of the regulars down at the Cabbage White on a Saturday night. So I says to him, I says: 'Why should I have a drink with you, you might be up to no good?' We had a bit of a laugh about that with my friends, like, but they wouldn't stay, so I thought why not, he's not a bad-looking guy, talks nice an' all, so I let him buy me another vodka and soda. I'd been on them earlier and when I'm out I like to stick to the same . . . And in case you're asking, no, I wasn't drunk." She broke off and gave Frank that green stare again.

"Like I said I wasn't drunk, I'd only had a couple before that – you can ask my friends . . . Anyway, he sits down and we have a bit of a chat. He says he likes my style, the way I dress and that. I know I dress smart, gets you noticed it does, away from the herd. I could tell he was a gentleman the way he spoke, like, and that he appreciated my looks. Well, I was wearing this halter-neck thing, it's dead cool, black with sequins, and my tan leather skirt, the one with the fringe, the one I gave the earth for . . ."

"Were you still in the Cabbage White at closing-time?"

"We mighta had another drink by then. This guy – told me his name was Brad, short for Bradley – said would I like a run in his car, no funny business, just a look at the moonlight, he says. He seemed OK to me, we'd been getting on just great and I could see he liked me a lot, so I thought what the hell.

3

Don't get me wrong, I've been out with plenty of men in cars, you gotta be careful but, like I said, he was OK so I says yes, and when we gets to the car-park, boy am I glad. He's got this great white Merc . . ."

"A white Mercedes?" Well that shouldn't be too hard to find. Frank had been following her story as if it was on television.

And right on cue she crooned a few bars of the song in a voice made as husky and seductive as the original. When she stopped she showed the little white points of her teeth in a comradely grin. Frank couldn't help himself; he grinned back.

"Want to know where we went?"

He nodded.

"Out Emberton Woods way, a place I'd been scores of times but never in a car like that. And there was moonlight just as Brad said, but Jesus was it cold! I wasn't for getting out of the car so we just stayed there, larking about with the music on his stereo, and smoking a few fags. He didn't come on to me, if that's what you're thinking, just a bit of fun, like, then he drives me home."

"What time would that be?"

"Must've been around two, I 'spose. There's a clock on his dashboard, says it's half-one when we're on the road outta the wood. I tells him where I live and, like the proper gent he is, he stops at the end of my street. I gets out and he says 'see you around' and drives off. Reckon he's a salesman of some sort but posh with it, high-class cars, that'd be it."

"When you were arrested," said Frank, carefully, "did you tell the police where you had been on that Saturday night?"

"Course I did, but that lot weren't for believing me, were they? Out to stitch me up they were. That Sergeant Hopkirk, he watches me like a hawk."

"How do you mean?"

"Lives opposite, don't he – and a right peeping Tom he is too. There's nights I'd like to leave the curtains wide open and give him and that starchy wife of his a real eyeful, do a striptease for them, like." She gave a short scream of a laugh, pushed back her chair and lifted one leg over the other to give

Frank a taste of it. Her legs were skinny but shapely, and they seemed to go a long way up. "You know the trouble with that Harry Hopkirk," she went on, "he fancies me rotten. Has done for yonks. Kept asking me out, he did, and when I wouldn't – well who'd go out with such an ugly-looking sod? – he starts picking on me for things I never done, like this . . ."

Suddenly she jumped to her feet. "Can I use your toilet?"

"Of course." Frank got up and opened the door to his secretary's office. "Joan? Can you spare a minute to show my client where the washroom is?"

Back at his desk, and glad to have a moment to himself, he went through his scribbled notes. They didn't seem to have caught the essence of the interview; the full flavour of Lily Egerton was not to be snared and caged in words.

He noted her address was 24 Marshall Avenue, which was in a cluster of housing devised by Newtown's Development Council as an example of social cohesion, providing council houses, private residencies and police housing in the hope they would all live happily together . . . It had seemed a good idea at the time.

Frank had known Sergeant Hopkirk slightly, and quite liked him but he agreed with Lily Egerton that Hopkirk had not been favoured when faces were being given out.

He reached for the Legal Aid forms – better get one filled in before she came back. He was just finishing it when the door opened, and she slid into the room and stood in front of his desk. He fiddled around for a pen. "If you'll sign it here, Lily . . ."

"I have to get back to work. I asked for time off but I must not take the whole morning."

Work? He hadn't associated her with something so mundane. "And my name is Lillian Egerton," she said.

"Oh, that's all right. I'll alter it." Only then did he look up. Something in her voice had set him wondering.

For one crazy second, he thought that Joan had returned him the wrong client. But that was absurd for the jacket was the same and so were the long skinny legs. As for the rest of her it was as if someone had taken a fresh oil portrait and wiped it savagely with a cloth dipped in strong spirit. Hair that had been a bright mass of coppery wires now hung limply around a face scrubbed clear of make-up. Only greyish smudges on the skin showed where eyeliner had been sponged away leaving the eyes themselves, still green but without the sparkle, pale as weed in a shallow pond.

Frank was sure that the girl who'd come in originally had cared for her appearance and knew the impact her personality made. The woman before him now – and she seemed more woman than girl despite her given age – left no impression. In a crowd she would merit no more than a passing glance, lank hair, a downcast look and sallow skin, the end of her peaky little nose damply pink, shoulders that drooped, it all spelled dowdy and, in a teenager, social death.

He had been conscious that he had been staring, possibly rudely, and that he had been silent. He rushed into speech: "Work? I'm sorry. I didn't realise. I won't keep you much longer. If you will just sign the form." She did it without fuss, and stepped away from the desk, regarding him without expression. Frank felt she was deliberately putting him at a disadvantage, and ploughed on: "I shall have to see you again before the case comes up before the magistrates." He looked down at the notes. "That's in . . . er . . . ten days' time. I shall be making enquiries, and of course getting the tapes and witness's statements from the police. Shall we say a week today, and at the same time, if that's all right with you?"

"It means another morning off work." Her voice was flat, and what she was saying noticeably un-cooperative.

"Oh, yes, your work. I didn't ask you before. Where do you work?"

"I'm at Bernes. On the industrial estate. I told the foreman I'd be out this morning. Next Monday, nine thirty? I shall be here." She was very precise. She turned her back on him and walked over to the door. Somehow her skirt seemed longer than when she had come in, it trailed its hem on the back of her calves giving her an untidy look. She closed the door quietly behind her, leaving him staring at it and trying to collect his thoughts.

Joan came in with papers to sign and to tell him his next client had arrived.

"Give me a few minutes of your valuable time," said Frank. The way to a wider view at Gillorns was to note the perceptions of the clerical staff whose minds were not necessarily clogged up with law. "What did you make of that girl?"

"Miss Egerton? Very rum. Used half a box of our tissues in there and left them all over the floor of the loo. Badly brought up, I'd say."

"What did she want to take off all her make-up for? If I didn't seduce her with it on, I'm hardly likely to do it when it's off."

Joan shrugged. "Told me she had to get back to work. Maybe she's at some place where they don't like it."

"She's only at Bernes, that's the Swiss firm on the estate, I think they make optics. It's hardly a training school for nuns. But it wasn't only the lack of make-up that changed her . . . She looked smart enough when she came in, she left as if she was something that had been trodden on."

"It's the devastating effect you have on all us poor females." Joan had been with the firm long enough to have known Frank in his salad days. "So, I make a file on her?"

"Yes. And would you ring Sergeant Cobbins at the police station and see if they've got the tapes and witness's statements ready on the case. Tell him I'll pick them up at lunchtime. That'll make them get their skates on."

"Will do. Now are you ready for Mr McCann and his thumb?"

Frank groaned. It was an industrial injury case he'd taken over from a colleague. McCann worked at the sawmill and there had been a slip-up. The result was not life threatening, but grisly all the same.

"Just as long as he keeps the bandage on it. He insisted on Mr Cantley seeing it the first time he came in and it quite put him off his lunch."

"Well, Mr Cantley's in court today, so it's your turn."

"All right, Joan, wheel him in."

7

Two

Later that morning Frank Davey telephoned Bernes. In the past he had done some work for them in connection with contracts of employment.

"Is Mr Bexby still the personnel officer?"

"That's right. I'll put you through."

"Glad to hear you're back with the old firm, Mr Davey. What can I do for you?"

"A Miss Egerton. Lillian Egerton. She has been to see me, and I understand she's one of your employees."

"I know Lillian, yes. She told the foreman she'd need time off today to go to the solicitor's. She did the right thing coming to you." He chuckled.

"Did she say what it was about?"

"Oh, yes. It's happened before, of course, but never been taken to this length. I don't know what the local police think they're up to."

"What do you mean, it's happened before?"

"This kind of bother with the police. They keep mixing Lillian Egerton up with some gang on the Thornton Estate. As if our Lillian would have anything to do with that lot of riff-raff. Hope you get it sorted out before it goes any further."

All this vague talk was only confusing Frank. He thought it was time to be more direct.

"How long has Miss Egerton worked for your firm?"

"Let me check. She's been here nearly three years, she came to us straight from school, started on one of the benches, now she's a supervisor."

"Is she a good employee?"

"The best we've ever had. She's never off sick, never late,

she's quiet and gets on well with the work. It's fiddly stuff, you have to be dead accurate so it needs concentration. Lillian never lets us down."

Frank wondered if they were talking about the same girl. "Lives at 24 Marshall Avenue?"

"That's right. I believe the house belonged to her grand-parents who'd bought it from the council. When they died she took it on and lets out a couple of rooms. She's careful with money. I know all this because she asked financial advice about taking on the place from our accountant, Mr Bradley—"

"Mr who?" Frank interrupted.

"Howard Bradley. He gave her some very good advice about letting."

"Could there possibly be anything between them?"

"Are you out of your mind? Sorry, but it's such a prepos-terous idea. Howard's on the verge of retirement, and as for Lillian – well, you've met her. A nice enough girl but she's hardly got the looks for a teenage mantrap!"

Which was exactly how Frank had seen her. He made no comment, however; after all she was his client.

Alex Bexby was still speaking: " . . . and if you need a character reference for the court we'd be happy to oblige, Mr Davey."

"Thanks. It could be useful when the case comes before the magistrates, particularly when it's from a local employer. We may well need something – this is a serious charge against a young girl."

"Lot of nonsense in my view. I don't see it getting as far as the court. They'll drop it like they did those other times. But, just in case, I'll let you have a letter showing our confidence in Miss Egerton."

Alex Bexby talked about her as if she was some kind of mascot at Bernes, a shining light on the shop-floor and harmless as a purring pussy-cat.

Was she having an affair with Alex? Had she got him so smitten with her that he wasn't seeing straight? Frank knew the personnel officer to be hard-headed – and he needed to be for the firm, by the nature of its work, employed many young

9

local girls. It was seen as an easy berth for school-leavers uncertain of their futures when it was unlikely they were going to be academics. Bernes paid decent wages while they sorted themselves out between choices: early motherhood, wedding bells or casual sex and loose pragmatic partnerships in the modern manner.

No, Frank decided, Bexby was unlikely to have succumbed to any lure that Lillian Egerton might have had, and for the time being he must accept that officer's view of her as genuine.

When Frank went into Newtown Police Station after lunch it was Sergeant Cobbins who had the papers on the Egerton case ready for him. The two men had known each other for years as Cobbins had been a police constable when Franklyn Davey was first articled to Gillorns.

Unfortunately, in Frank's opinion, he had never been allowed to forget it and now, despite being a Solicitor of the Supreme Court, as soon as he stepped into the doors of Newtown Police Station, he was treated as if he was still in nappies. Today was no exception.

"Hullo, young Mr Davey, so you're back with us then. Pity you got landed with this one for your first. It is your first, isn't it?" He had the bundle marked "Egerton" but gave no indication that he was about to hand it over. He was shaking his head solemnly so that the mat of grey curls that topped it bounced up and down. Frank would like to have taken the whole head and bounced it along the floor.

Sergeant Cobbins came out from behind the desk and led Frank off into another room as if they were conspirators. "I can give you mebbe a wee hint or two," he said. Cobbins was a countryman and had never lost the thick accent of the old rural villages. Frank thought it was high time he was put out to grass – perhaps being made desk sergeant was nearly the equivalent; he couldn't have many years left in the force.

"I'd be obliged to you," he said, stiffly, not meaning a word of it; he had no intention of putting himself under any obligation to the Newtown police. When he had first been articled, his principal, Lennox Kemp, was still acting for them in local prosecutions, but now that there was the Crown Prosecution Service this practice had long died out.

The sergeant put the folder down on the table, but kept his finger on it as if reluctant to let go of a tasty morsel. "She'll not get away with it this time, we've got her by the short and curlies."

"Am I to understand that Miss Egerton has been in trouble before?"

"She never said? Wanted to give you a good impression I suppose. She's done that with a lot of folk."

"Precisely what sort of trouble has she been in?"

"It's all in the record, Mr Davey. She's with that hell-raising gang that's the terror of the Thornton Estate. Breaking windows, burning fences, scrawling graffiti on garage doors, threatening old folk, using foul language . . ." Cobbins tut-tutted like an outraged matron. "And there's been talk of drugs," he finished, darkly.

He's a bit of an old woman himself, thought Davey, and decided he'd better get to the nub of it. "Has Miss Egerton ever been charged with any of these offences?"

"We never had the evidence. You got to know what it's like policing an estate like that. Plenty of complaints made but when it comes to using the law there's no one backing them up. We've given her a caution scores of times."

"Formal caution?"

"Well, no." Cobbins was reluctant to admit it. Then he perked up. "But now she's gone too far, trying to nick drugs out of the health centre. Caught in the act by the very best possible witness."

The sergeant was dying to tell him the name – it was evident in his eager eyes – but Frank wasn't going to give him that satisfaction. It would be all in the file anyway.

He put his briefcase squarely on the table, opened it, and prised the bundle from under Cobbins' calloused thumb. He shuffled the papers together so that they were neatly in a file along with what was obviously a tape, and stowed the lot away in his case.

But Sergeant Cobbins wasn't giving up easily.

"You'll see for yourself, Mr Davey, it's open and shut. Reckon me and Harry Hopkirk'll have a drink on this one when it's over. He's been after that girl for months."

"Really? Sergeant Hopkirk fancies her, then?" He couldn't resist the gibe.

Cobbins was flustered. "Course I didn't mean it that way. Just that he's been trying to nab her, that's all. And it's Inspector Hopkirk now – he's got a promotion."

"Bully for him. Now I must get back to the office, Sergeant. Looks as if I've got quite a task ahead of me." He tapped the briefcase.

"You can say that again." Cobbins stood back to let him out of the room. "Did she spin you the tale of the white Merc?" Seeing Frank's look, he chuckled. "She's tried that one on us before. Emberton Woods, the moonlight and the white Mercedes Benz." He rolled his eyes. "Sounds like a fairy tale, doesn't it? And that, you'll find, is just what it is. Can't think why she uses the same story over and over again, you'd think with an imagination like hers she'd come up with something new."

By this time the sergeant was back in position behind his desk. His commiseration for Frank Davey might even be genuine.

"Good day to you," was all the young solicitor could manage, and a mutter of thanks as he swung the door shut behind him. For the police, through Sergeant Cobbins, to vouchsafe him all this information and deliver it with such glee could only mean one thing: they were certain that Lillian Egerton was about to be convicted.

Once back in his office and having gone through the not particularly heavy file, and listened once again to Lily's fanciful attempt at an alibi – which was almost word perfect to the account she had given to him – his spirits dropped even further because Cobbins' hint of a reliable witness was all too accurate. It was Dr Gerald Parfitt who had seen his own patient, Lillian Egerton, throw a brick through his surgery window at a quarter to twelve on that Saturday night, and minutes later chased her out of the building.

In the face of that kind of evidence it would take more than a white Merc to get her off; it would need an armoured knight on a white charger . . . Franklyn Davey didn't give much for his chances.

Three

When Alys de Lisle telephoned the Kemps on the following Sunday evening, she interrupted a discussion Lennox and Mary were having about parents – their own. Such a subject could hardly be a serious one for these two people who had come together in their middle years and had already lost most of their kin had it not been that they were expecting their first child. Both were thinking of the event with various degrees of trepidation.

"It's the genes we should be knowing about," Mary had said after some thoughts of her own. "So that we've got some idea what it'll get from us."

"Apart from a brand-new nursery, a comfy cot and five or six meals a day?" But he realised she was in earnest and must be taken that way. "Well, your mother was Irish, how about your father?"

"I reckon he'd be the same. She told me he'd died before they could get married so she emigrated to the States." Mary sighed. "She was a great one for putting the gloss on things . . . Being unmarried and pregnant in Ireland at that time probably meant she got thrown out, had me under a hedge somewhere, then managed to get the money for a steerage class passage."

"Did she not tell you anything about your father?"

"By the time I was old enough to listen she was married to that drunken stevedore, Smith. Reckon the likes of him were on the dock when immigrants from Ireland landed, on the look-out for country girls with no sense. And him with the ready fist if ever she mentioned what had happened back there." Later when Madeleine Blane had talked of such things she was weak and wandering in mind and body so that her tales of the "auld" country were too infused with myth and legend to satisfy her down-to-earth daughter.

"A bit of mystery's no bad thing when it comes to the genes," Kemp assured her. "You could be descended from the High Kings of Tara, and here's me with mere Anglo-Saxon blood and plebeian at that."

"But your mother gave you her family name of Lennox so she must have thought it meant something?"

"My mother considered herself a gentlewoman as she'd never had to work in her life but that was only because her father was a licensed grocer in Manchester. She was very genteel, my Mama, a not altogether rare example of the type who can believe anything once they set their minds on it. She was under the illusion that she belonged to the Lennoxes who went back to the days of Mary, Queen of Scots."

"Hardly a success story. Whose side were they on?"

"I think they played both sides against the middle like most folk. One of them was spying for Henry the Eighth, which didn't endear him to his fellow Scots."

"You tell me that now? Well if there's a cynical gene going it certainly got through to you."

"Not any more," said Kemp, fervently, "this idea of an off-spring has knocked that right out of me. I feel all soft and gooey one minute then I get in a sort of panic thinking of the terrible responsibility, having to bring up a child – To teach it what's right and wrong when you're in doubts yourself."

Mary stretched herself. "Why can't children be born already mature, their mouths full of teeth and their heads full of brains? It's this awful rearing that's the problem. I don't actually mind having the baby, it's the bit in between that and their leaving school. If you believe the half of what you read you could be harming the poor mite from the moment it's born by feeding it with a genetically modified plastic spoon, or not saying three hail Marys at its first cough. Why can't they be born grown-up and manageable?"

"Ready to sit the Law Society finals, and take over the office so that I can retire?"

Mary threw a cushion at him which he ducked as the phone rang.

It was going to be a long time before either of them was to feel so light-hearted again.

Kemp was standing by the table in the hall where there was one of their telephones. The others were in the study and the kitchen but he was averse to having one in the sitting-room, feeling they must have some space free from intrusion.

He barely recognised the voice. "Is it you, Alys? I can hardly hear you. That's better. What can I do for you?"

Alys de Lisle was sobbing. "Please come, Lennox. I have to talk to someone."

"You want me to come now? Yes, yes . . . Hush, hush, Alys. Calm down . . . What is wrong?"

"It's Elinor. She's missing. Oh, Lennox, I don't know what to do." There was a high wailing sort of noise as Kemp spoke calmly over it, asking questions, soothing the distraught mother. "We shall both come, Alys, we shall be with you shortly."

Mary looked at his face as he came slowly back into the sitting-room. Her own had turned pale. "What's wrong, Lennox?"

"Alys de Lisle. She sounds in a terrible state. Elinor has been missing for nearly twenty-four hours."

"Has she told the police?"

"Apparently not. There are all kinds of reason, she says. She's rather incoherent. George is away at some international conference in Toronto."

"Does he know?"

Kemp shook his head. "She says no one knows. There could be a perfectly simple explanation."

"But she's had the time to go over all those," said Mary. "Look, I'll drive, Lennox. I've not been drinking, and you had most of that bottle of claret at supper, and a glass of brandy. Besides, it sounds as if Alys could do with a woman there. I'll get my coat. We can talk in the car."

But they found little to say. Instead they each followed their own line of thought about the de Lisle family.

16

When Kemp had come to Newtown over ten years ago it was his first job after being reinstated by the Law Society, and he had owed it to Archie Gillorn, then head of the firm, that he was being given the chance to climb back into the profession. He had been struck off for six years for taking trust funds in order to pay the gambling debts of his first wife, Muriel. To repay the monies Kemp had sold everything, and was practically penniless. Archie Gillorn had introduced him to George de Lisle, then one of the local bank managers who had provided financial help in what, for Kemp, was a tricky time. The two men had become friends and remained so, even though George had risen rapidly in banking circles and was now based in the City. Kemp found it surprising that the de Lisles had not moved to London for George was constantly travelling abroad and could only spend a little time at home. But he had married a local woman so perhaps it was Alys who did not want to leave Newtown. She had been married before and had the child, Elinor, who was now thirteen.

Mary was thinking about Alys. They had met about a year ago and continued to find themselves in the same charity groups, helping out at jumble sales, arranging coffee mornings, ferrying the elderly or the disabled to meetings or classes. This was not at all Mary Kemp's cup of tea but as she was fond of saying to her husband: "What else can you do in England when you're the lady wife and it's expected of you?"

He might laugh but he realised how irked she was by her situation; after thirty-five years of running about (mostly at the behest of other people) she had been yanked to a standstill by the twin reins of marriage and pregnancy. She was also in, for her, an alien country. Perhaps it was their very differences that had drawn together Mary Kemp and Alys de Lisle.

Whereas Alys had grown up in Newtown, Mary Blane, now Kemp, had grown up in Vineland, Pennsylvania. Alys' people had not been rich but neither had they been poor, certainly never on the level of Mary's family of siblings, brought down by sheer drunken pigheadedness – and to be in abject poverty in the richest country in the world was to fall off the bottom of the map altogether. But Mary herself had been a survivor, picking

17

herself from the bottom heap by whatever means available; Alys had never really been put to the test – until now.

Mary had learned early in her life that appearances are everything, but even this truism was of no help to her. She was small for her age – the nourishment of infants not being high on the priority list of her Smith stepfather whose own off-spring could at least benefit from an inheritance of beef and brawn – she was colourless as to hair, eyes and complexion, dumpy as to figure, and all in all a fairly inconspicuous nonentity. Mary had found it expedient to go along with this view of her personality until she was old enough to use her mind which had nothing to do with the way she looked. She had always found it fascinating to see how people did try to live up to what they saw in their mirrors every day – particularly if they were that rare thing, stunningly beautiful.

And that was Alys de Lisle. Wherever she went, the comment would be made: "What a pretty woman!" And she was so pretty. Her fair hair, which she wore long on her shoulders or tied into a plait at the back of her perfectly poised head, her fine skin, ivory and rose, her long almond-shaped eyes of a shade between blue and violet, her features so perfectly drawn it was as if the artist had just lifted his pencil . . . Yet she seemed to have no vanity. She rarely used make-up – of course it could be said she didn't need to, looks like hers required no enhancement – and it was as if she never really noticed that the measurements of brow to chin, cheekbone to cheekbone, and the length of her nose were the stuff of rare classic perfection. Pretty woman, people said of her and she was quite unaffected by it; she had grown up with these looks and she seemed to be completely unaware of the effect they had on other people.

Her name was pretty, too. Mary, who had been taking classes in literature at the local college, thought it had a medieval sound as though Alys should be a high-born lady in a wimple but, when she mentioned this to Mavis Chard, the woman who now came to the Kemps twice a week to do the cleaning, Mrs Chard had sniffed.

"She was plain Alice Hobbs when we were at school together, and she was plain Alice when she married Charlie

Hawkins. Not that it did her much good, her marrying Charlie even if they were the best-looking couple that year they got wed. Everyone thought of him as the great catch – more fools they . . ."

Mary found Mavis Chard a goldmine when she wanted any information on Newtown families of whatever layer in the hierarchy. It was some recompense for the fact that she had never wanted a cleaning lady – as they were called in this strange country of circumlocution. Mary was a good listener, and her years as a live-in nurse had sharpened her perceptive faculties to such a degree that she was particularly sensitive in the area of servant relationships, and with what delicate precision they should be treated.

Mrs Chard had only recently taken cleaning jobs because her husband was out of work – only temporarily, she insisted, until something turned up for him – but she considered Mrs Kemp as the best of her ladies. For one thing, she was a foreigner. Irish-American, and not too proud to talk in the kitchen over a cup of tea, for another she could be a real help, like when she went herself and confronted those sourpusses down at the benefits office to make sure they gave Mavis Chard her rightful dues.

"What happened to the Hawkins marriage, then?" Mary had asked her.

"Fell apart, didn't it? He were never no good, that Charlie Hawkins, for all his looks. His father had the garage, right? Well, what does Charlie do but get into stolen cars and all that racket, hoping to get rich quick. So it's either a spell in jail or . . . He hops it. Divorced, dead or gone to Australia . . . ?"

"Come on, Mrs Chard. Which was it?"

"Well, there was a divorce, and then he does go to Australia. Alice, she doesn't come out of it all that badly. She'd always been a bit ahead of the rest of us at school." Mavis tried not to be too grudging on this. "So she gets a job in the bank. Afore long, there she is married to Mr de Lisle and he takes over her and the little girl, Elinor."

Mary noted the respect Mrs Chard showed in that Mr de

19

Lisle did not have a forename she'd use; bank managers, doctors and even lawyers were, at the time of which she was speaking, still sacrosanct.

It was fitting that the de Lisles should live on one of Newtown's highest points. Such points were few in a town which had developed along the line of the Lea Valley – the reason for the original railway – to use up a string of worked-out gravel pits, but the contours of the land did indeed rise slightly towards Emberton Woods and the edge of the green belt. There the developers had put their only prestige project, a clutch of four and five-bedroomed houses set in spreading lawns. At first they had been slow to sell but with the prosperous nineties they had become highly esteemed, and priced accordingly. It was perhaps something of a drawback that you had to traverse the entire Thornton Estate and pass both its primary and comprehensive schools in order to drive to the station, but you didn't have to look out of the car windows if you weren't altogether in favour of the social mix the council had intended.

29 Coverley Drive had been named – without too much imagination – Fairlawn, and it certainly had that. Like its neighbours it was built in the neo-Georgian style, red brick with white trim, a town house rather out of its element.

As the Kemps' car turned into the driveway, lights sprang out from unexpected corners of the shrubberies till the façade of the house itself looked like a miniature fortress; burglars, prowlers and even stray cats would be properly discouraged by the glare.

When she got out of the car Mary glanced into the darkness beyond the house. Only the width of a field separated its back garden from the woods, a long black line of trees silhouetted against the starry sky to the North like an army waiting the word to advance. Mary had enjoyed Emberton Woods in the summer and autumn but now on a cold winter night their very stillness was a menace.

Lennox was going up the steps ahead of her when the front door opened, and Alys threw herself at Mary after giving him a hasty greeting.

"Go in," she said, "go in." Then she was sobbing on Mary's shoulder. "I don't know what to do . . . I can't talk to anyone . . . Evelyn's here . . ."

Mary partly understood. Evelyn de Lisle was the mother-in-law without parallel, a formidable lady who normally resided in one of the best parts of Chelsea, where it was Alys's fervent wish she would remain.

"It just happened to be one of her visits," she told Mary, grimly, "and then this awful thing happened. I can't face her . . . I can't talk to her." Alys was crying now, noisily, without inhibition. She clung to Mary who tried to guide her back to the steps. "Hush now, my dear, you just let Lennox deal with Evelyn. But come you away in – you're shivering with the cold already."

But it wasn't the cold that caused Alys to draw breath in long shuddering sighs. Even when they had reached the hall and she half turned to Mary at the open door of the sitting-room, the look on her beautiful face was one of stark unashamed terror. Mary held back and only slowly followed into the glare of two great chandeliers shedding their light into every corner of a room, furnished in the minimalist style, where nothing could look out of place.

Certainly Evelyn de Lisle was very much its centre. She was at one end of a blonde leather sofa, her elegant legs stretched out to the warmth of glowing electric logs, the only spot of colour in a decor devoted, it seemed, to only the palest of pastels. A setting for Alys as for Evelyn, the place was perfect but tonight the effect was ghastly.

Kemp had been standing beside the arched stone fireplace but now he came over and took hold of Alys's fluttering hands. He put her into an armchair as far from her mother-in-law as the furniture arrangements allowed. He drew up a chair beside her and sat down.

Taking the hint, Mary seated herself on the sofa, and observed what a terrible thing it was to have happened, but there would be a rational explanation for it all, she knew Elinor was a sensible girl. Mary spoke in her softest, most soothing voice, drawing the elder Mrs de Lisle's attention away from

21

Kemp and Alys. Her strategy was not altogether successful, so determined was Evelyn to hear what was being said across the room.

She made an impatient movement – only just short of rudeness – for Mary to be quiet. She had probably never in her life told someone to "shut up" and didn't know how to go about it even now.

"Take me slowly through it again," Kemp was saying. "Just tell me once more where Elinor was going yesterday, what time she left, and what time you expected her back."

"I've already told Mr Kemp all that, Alys dear." Evelyn de Lisle had the kind of voice that never needs to be raised, it could cut the air like the tone that breaks glassware. "I couldn't do otherwise," she went on, "now that you'd brought him here, and Mary as well. The one thing we didn't want – all these people coming round."

Alys put her hands together between her knees and squeezed them tightly. She had no tears left, and now she couldn't speak. Kemp said, without turning round: "Mary. Do you think you could find us all some tea or coffee in the kitchen? I'm sure Mrs de Lisle would be pleased to help."

To have ignored his plea would have been the height of discourtesy. Evelyn de Lisle was a lady, she had no option but to obey. She rose and without a murmur led Mary from the room.

Alys needs a respite, thought Mary, as she fiddled with cups and saucers under the eye of the mother-in-law, all the while keeping up a patter of small talk. She was good at it. It was a semi-professional habit dishing out soft pabulum, nurses used it, the filling-in of silences not to be borne, the trivial round, the common task thinly spread over the unspeakable.

Someone had once told her that in hot-springs country, a geyser was something bubbling away and sending up small fountains of liquid mud, but if you could gaze down one of those vents when they stopped there was a black hole going all the way to the centre of the earth. The geyser had been only the merest hint . . .

People were like that. All you got was a hint, the depths

were not to be measured. Evelyn de Lisle was not the kind even to hint that her feelings were being racked. She spoke about George and the conference.

"He's travelling with the Prime Minister, of course. He has his ear." There was no impression of boasting, she simply accepted that George would be equal to the job. "The important days are Monday and Tuesday, that's why he must not be disturbed, he mustn't be told about this. I've watched those awful scenes on the television when children are missing . . ." She clutched Mary's hand. "That must not happen," she said fiercely.

"Indeed it will not, Mrs de Lisle. The media won't be involved, you can trust Lennox there, and he's just the man George would have chosen to handle it. Tell me now, when is George expected back?"

"Wednesday morning – an overnight flight. But, surely by that time—"

"Yes, by then we will have better news." Mary prayed silently that it might be so. She led the older woman to talk of Elinor, which she did eagerly as if words alone might conjure up the figure of the missing girl.

It appeared that when George married Alys some eight years ago Elinor had been an enchanting child of five. They must have been a picture – the beautiful mother and her angelic little girl – and one that even the most difficult mother-in-law would have accepted.

"George could not have children of his own." Mrs de Lisle stolidly acknowledged this flaw in her side of the family. "He had mumps at an unfortunate time in his youth, but he adored children. He absolutely doted on little Elinor . . ."

Behind her back Mary switched off the kettle. Give Lennox and Alys longer to talk. Mrs de Lisle hadn't noticed. Sitting upright in a kitchen chair, her hands were arranging and rearranging cups on the tray but as if the movements had nothing to do with her. All Mary had to do was listen – another thing she was good at – and put in the occasional sympathetic word.

The marriage of Alys and George had, surprisingly, worked;

if the elder Mrs de Lisle could have found fault with her daughter-in-law, she would have done so, but she had failed despite a certain stubbornness in the upbringing of Elinor, and even there she made allowances.

"Of course I understood – Elinor is her child. And Alys herself is Newtown . . . But it would have been so much more suitable if they had moved to London . . . I had even found the perfect house for them in Islington. Not too close to me . . . I had no wish to be at their beck and call nor expect them to entertain me often . . . I have my own social circle, Mrs Kemp . . ."

"I am sure of that," said Mary. "A lady like you. But of course you would have seen more of George."

"George is very attentive. He visits me when he has to be overnight in the City. And it was he who suggested I keep Alys company this weekend while he was in Canada. For the first time she was not enthusiastic, she wondered if I was fit enough after a recent cataract operation, but I assured her it was no trouble. And now this . . ." The present suddenly impinged upon her talk and she made a small helpless gesture with her hands. Then, suddenly, sharply she asked: "Hasn't that kettle boiled yet?"

Mary switched it back on. "Just about," she said. "Would Elinor have liked a move to London?" she asked.

Evelyn shook her head. "It was she who was most against it. Can't think why."

"Perhaps because her school friends were here?"

"It was her schooling that went all wrong," said Evelyn, decisively. "If only there had been a nearby private school for her, but it meant going almost to Cambridge to get one. You see, she started in a nice little private place here in Newtown but that was only up to ten . . . That's when they should have come up to London and Elinor could have continued in the private sector. But, oh no, Elinor wanted to go to Thornton Comprehensive where all her chums go." Mrs de Lisle gave a shudder of distaste. "It's a terrible school, Mrs Kemp, you mark my words. Ah, you've made coffee . . . Do you mind carrying the tray?"

Four

M ary felt that she was bringing more than a tray out of the de Lisles' kitchen; from Evelyn's talk she had gained some insight into the lives of the family who used it.

She was ready to share that knowledge with her husband as they drove down from Fairlawn, but first she wanted to know what Alys had told him.

"She said enough to make me decide to see John Upshire tonight, rather than wait till morning. A telephone call won't do. I know it's the other side of town . . ."

"I don't mind the driving. I just hope they're still up on a Sunday night. Remember, Lennox, they've not been that long married."

"It is a missing child. He'll understand, and so will his wife. I'll give you the facts on the way. That'll help to straighten them out in my own mind."

Alys de Lisle had told him that her husband had left on Saturday morning, and by the arrangement made earlier in the week with her mother-in-law she had picked up Evelyn from Newtown station at midday. The three of them – Alys, Evelyn and Elinor – had lunch together and talked about the timetable for the evening. It had seemed simple enough. Alys herself had been invited to play bridge with friends who, knowing George was away and her mother-in-law in residence, had made up a table specially for her. Elinor was going to the local youth club on the estate where she usually went on Saturday nights with school friends to play table tennis, sit around listening to music and drink Coke. Alys left at half-past six as it was a good forty minutes' drive to where the Finlays lived at Ember Village, and bridge was to start at seven thirty.

Evelyn de Lisle told Kemp that just before seven Elinor's friend Monica had arrived at the house and the two girls left for the youth club. Monica told Mrs de Lisle that her mother would pick them up before ten o'clock and bring Elinor back. Some time before ten, however, Mrs de Lisle took a telephone call from Mrs Hodge who asked if it would be all right if Elinor "slept over" with Monica that night. Mrs de Lisle, who knew and approved of both Mrs Hodge and her daughter, said it would be perfectly all right, and when Alys arrived home some time later she was told and was happy with the arrangement. Both ladies retired to bed secure in the knowledge that Elinor was with the Hodges.

On Sunday morning George phoned and chatted to Alys as was his normal habit when abroad. He would have liked to speak to Elinor but Alys explained she was at a friend's house. When she had not returned by lunchtime Alys called Mrs Hodge to thank her for having Elinor, saying she would drive the short distance and collect her.

"And that was when panic set in," Kemp finished.

"I gather Alys didn't let on to the Hodges that she'd no idea where Elinor was?"

"They don't do things the simple way in this house. Alys covered up . . . There'd been a mix-up, Mrs de Lisle had misunderstood . . . it was another friend Elinor was with. Alys did, however, learn two things from Mrs Hodge: first, there had not been any call from their house the previous night, and when Mrs Hodge had arrived at the youth club before ten only Monica was waiting for her – and in a temper because, she said, Elinor had dumped her and gone off with someone else earlier in the evening."

"That I can well believe," said Mary. "Elinor can't stand Monica Hodge."

"How do you know that?"

"It was a conversation I had with Alys at one of our ladies' meetings. We were talking about young girls and she said Elinor had this friend – she called her a 'cling-on' who'd latched on to her ever since they were at that private school. And if Monica is the kind of nice girl that Evelyn de Lisle

26

approves of, then I'm not surprised Elinor finds her a drag. She'd be the last person Elinor would want to have a sleep-over with, as they call it."

"Hmm, that's interesting. Because there was a row on Saturday about Monica. Earlier in the week George and Alys – who keep a pretty sharp eye on Elinor – found out that there was going to be an event at the old Drill Hall, some music groups coming down from London, there were posters stuck up all over the town. It was a ticket-only affair but some of the boys from Thornton Comprehensive knew some of the performers in the various gigs, and it wouldn't be difficult to get in. Well, apparently at lunchtime on Saturday Elinor said she had been asked to go by one of the sixth-form boys. Alys, knowing that it would also be George's decision, absolutely forbade her to go. Evelyn, who believes in direct action, immediately phoned Mrs Hodge and made the definite arrangement that Monica would see that Elinor went to the youth club and nowhere else, and that Mrs Hodge would pick up both girls before ten."

"I bet young Elinor was over the moon about having her evening mapped out for her. I'm not surprised she bunked off."

"We don't know that she did bunk off," said Kemp, carefully, "but now we know she was in a temper there is all the more reason for hope."

Mary sighed. "Those poor women. The undercurrents you feel in that house . . . That last hour we had with them was too terrible altogether."

They were both silent, Mary concentrating on her driving as they had reached the arterial road that circled the town, Kemp going over in his mind every aspect of the scene in the de Lisle drawing-room under its pitiless white lights. He had found in his dealings with clients that, no matter the circumstances, no matter their assertions of complete candour, people always hid something. More often than not it was unimportant, though perhaps not to them, but there were times when it could have set the mortar of the building bricks in a case a lot sooner if there had been absolute disclosure.

27

He had done his best to calm Alys as he drew the facts from her. He had asked to see Elinor's room but its surface told him nothing and it was too soon to pry. Upstairs, with Mrs de Lisle safely in the kitchen with Mary – and he was grateful to her for that – Alys opened out a little on the subject of her mother-in-law. "She doesn't understand that Elinor is no longer a child, she's a teenager with a strong will of her own."

Mrs de Lisle's decision to co-opt Mrs Hodge into Elinor's Saturday-night arrangement was typical, she was treating the girl like a five-year-old, and naturally it was resented. But Elinor had assured Alys when she went to her room before her mother went to her bridge party that it was OK, she would go with Monica to the youth club, and agreed to be picked up by Mrs Hodge later. "I think that was all said just for my benefit," Alys told him, sadly. "I think if she was determined to go to this thing at the Drill Hall, she would have gone."

"And that's one of the reasons why I'm going to have a quiet word with Superintendent Upshire, Alys. He's an old friend, and I'm not making an official enquiry. Please assure Mrs de Lisle that Upshire's men will be discreet. It's not uncommon, you know, for the police to be involved with teenagers who run off without there even needing to be a record when the kids are found alive and well . . ."

"I feel so guilty," Alys kept saying. "I shouldn't have gone out."

"You've nothing to feel guilty about," Kemp had told her, firmly. "Elinor's grandmother was there. There was no reason why you should not have gone out."

"Alys carries guilt around with her like a shopping bag," Mary was saying as she drew up at traffic lights. "She would have felt equally guilty if she'd let her bridge friends down at the last minute because her daughter was having a tantrum."

"Evelyn, on the other hand, feels no guilt at all," Kemp mused. "It's just not in her nature."

"Well, I think you let her off far too easily. That phone call, she was much too vague about it. She couldn't say what time it came, or even if it was Mrs Hodge's voice."

"That's because she now knows that it wasn't. She genuinely

thought it was at the time. Ladies like Evelyn de Lisle don't expect to receive bogus phone calls, or be lied to."

"Certainly not by the likes of Mrs Hodge. She patronises that poor mother of Monica as if she was some kind of upper servant. 'A very decent kind of woman' she called her as if she'd been asked for a testimonial. Did she hear any background noises during the call?"

Kemp had questioned Mrs de Lisle closely. "She *thinks* there may have been music, and giggling. She says she took it that it was the girls in the background. But she's very vague about the timing of the call. She might have been asleep and doesn't want to admit it."

"She's a bit muddled about a lot of things on Saturday night," said Mary, briskly. "What was Elinor's mood when she left, what time did the call come in, and how much later did Alys return . . . I think I found the reason in the kitchen bin."

"Go on, surprise me."

"An empty bottle of gin, and several tonics. Not that I blame her, of course, there's nothing nicer for an elderly lady than a comfortable chair, a few gin and tonics and nothing much on the telly."

"It would certainly account for the vagueness about time, and if it was Elinor herself making that call, she'd have no difficulty in persuading her grandmother that it was Mrs Hodge on the line. I'm beginning to think this is more than likely to be simply a schoolgirl prank."

"I certainly hope so," said Mary fervently as she drew up outside the house of Superintendent John Upshire. "There's a light on downstairs, so at least you don't have to wake them up. You don't want me, do you?"

"No, you go on home, Mary. I can walk from here when I've had a word with John. I do feel I will sleep easier if I've at least put in hand the minimum of enquiries – particularly about that musical event at the Drill Hall. There's bound to have been a police presence, the local force is always scared witless that London's drug scene will contaminate our innocent borough through the eardrums of its hapless youth."

Five

O n Monday morning Frank Davey stopped at the coffee
dispenser on his way into his office; he needed the
stimulus before facing his first appointment, Lillian Egerton.

He pulled the file towards him. It was still a lightweight.
In the week that had passed he felt he had fulfilled any duty
he may have had towards her, but he'd been unable to find
anything to put flesh on its bare bones, certainly nothing in
her favour.

The barman in the Cabbage White couldn't remember seeing
her in the pub the Saturday night in question, though he knew
her. "Right little go-er when she's in the mood . . ." He winked
at Frank. "Comes in with her gang. If they gets noisy we chuck
'em out. Nah, there weren't no trouble that Saturday and I never
saw no stranger. A white Merc? You've gotta be joking . . . If
there'd been one of them in our car-park we could've sold
tickets to view."

Frank had taken a walk up Marshall Avenue, and looked
over the broken-down walls of number 24. It was a corner property a little larger than the others of its type and he remembered
Bexby saying she let rooms. Certainly Lily Egerton herself
could not have owned all the rusted cars, vans, motor bikes
and pedal cycles with which the place was littered. With hardly
a blade of grass showing number 24 was an eyesore, and one
directly in front of number 21 which Frank knew to be the
home of Sergeant, now Inspector, Harry Hopkirk. Perhaps his
recent elevation might enable him to move to a better address
where the outlook was less sordid?

Frank would have liked to have had a word with his client's
doctor but as Dr Parfitt was the chief witness for the other

30

side, such a move would have been unwise. All the same he was interested in those pills she said she got from the doctor; were they so essential to her that she was prepared to burgle the surgery at midnight to get hold of them? He would have to ask her.

"What's making you so glum this morning?" Joan had come dancing in with his mail.

"Do stop jigging about. You make my head ache. And I'm not feeling very cheerful at having to see Miss Egerton in ten minutes."

"Ah, but you haven't—"

"Why's that? I've got her down for nine thirty."

"But I've got your mail. The case is off . . . dropped . . . taken out . . . whatever you like to call it."

"You're winding me up. Here, let me see."

There it was in black and white: addressed to Franklyn Davey and sent by Inspector Hopkirk of Newtown's finest . . .

"And I confirmed it with the Clerk of the Court," said Joan. "The case of Lillian Egerton has been removed from the list."

"Whoopee!" Frank got up from his seat and grabbed Joan round the waist. "Shall we dance?"

"I knew you'd be pleased." She extricated herself, put the rest of the mail on his desk and waltzed off into the corridor. Within minutes she was back.

"Miss Egerton's in the waiting room."

"Shit. I bet they sent her a letter by second-class post. Oh, well, we'd better have her in."

This morning Lily Egerton was evenly clad all over in creased black leather which suited her, and she knew it. She banged her crash helmet down on top of the steel filing cabinet with a satisfactory clang, ran her fingers through the bright mesh of her red-gold hair and sat down on the visitor's chair which she pulled up close to the desk. Her nails flashed scarlet and her green eyes glittered at him alarmingly through their barricades of black. It was like getting too near to a set of traffic lights – and much too early in the day for Frank to be thinking in similes.

31

"You came on your bike, then?" It was all he could manage to say while he tried to keep his mind in neutral.

"Yeah, just the Honda."

"Not the white Mercedes?" He hadn't been able to stop himself; a sense of euphoria had taken over any attempt to be serious.

A movement behind her eyes before she blinked it away; he could have sworn it was an instant's puzzlement. Then, as if recognising that a joke had been intended, she tried a more stilted one. "The Honda's nearest the door, like, or I'd have used the Rolls."

Frank cleared his throat, and became professional. "I'm sorry, Miss Egerton – er Lily – that you've been given the trouble of coming in here today, but the police have withdrawn your case. They have dropped the charges against you."

She thumped on the desk with her little fists. "Yippee!" she shouted, "I told you, didn't I? Bet that Harry Hopkirk's sick as a parrot."

"At this stage I have been given no reason for the withdrawal of the case," Frank began, cautiously, but it was clear that Lily was not listening.

"I told yah, didn't I?" she said again. "It was Hopkirk who's out to get me. All he ever wanted was to get his leg over, and I'm not having that with his sort – lousy policeman." She paused. "You drinking that stuff?" She nodded at the polystyrene cup.

"It's not very nice," he admitted.

"I wouldn't mind some if it's not against the rules or anything."

Joan was only expected to provide coffee when Frank had elderly affluent ladies changing their wills for the fourth time, but so taken aback was he that his finger was on the buzzer almost without volition.

"Er . . . Joan? Could you possibly manage a cup of coffee for my client?"

"The bone china on the silver salver or is Madame more accustomed to plastic?"

"The latter, I think, thank you. And would you get me Inspector Hopkirk at Newtown CID, please."

"Has he bloody well got a promotion? The sleazy bastard. Anyway, what d'ya want him for?" Lily Egerton didn't miss a trick.

"I've a couple of things I need to ask him."

There were more than a couple of things Frank would have liked to ask his client: the names of her friends in this gang that had been spoken about, why did she keep using this ridiculous fable of the white Mercedes, and what was the medication she was receiving from her medical practioner – and did it have any bearing on her erratic behaviour . . . ? He now had no legitimate reason to ask these questions, and he felt balked. But at least he could get a few answers from Hopkirk.

Lillian Egerton had got up and was moving restlessly round the room. She stopped in front of a beaky lawyer in a high collar and white stock.

"That's the way you should look, Franklyn Davey, not in a bloody pin-stripe like any City gent. Now, he's cute . . . Any relation?"

"No way," Frank hastily repudiated any connection. The print had been on the walls of Gillorns for over twenty years and probably came with the premises.

Joan came in with two more cups of coffee. From behind Lillian's head she gave her special monkey grin – the one she used when she'd summarised a client as being phoney from the feet up. "I have Inspector Hopkirk on the line. Shall I put him through?" Joan's raised eyebrows enquired whether he was up to dealing with the call in front of his client.

Frank frowned at her. "Of course, Joan. I want to talk to him straight away."

Hopkirk was gruff. "You want to talk to me, Mr Davey? I presume it's about the Egerton case. I was told you act for her."

"You presume correctly." Frank was only too aware that his performance – and he could call it nothing less – was geared to his audience. "Am I right that all charges against Miss Egerton have been dropped?"

"Yes." A monosyllable, telling him nothing except that Hopkirk was a very growly bear with a very sore head.

"Well, Inspector, you have to understand that my client has been put to a great deal of distress and personal inconvenience in this matter."

"She's bloody lucky to get away with it if you ask me, and I don't care whether this is off the record or not."

"Yes, I *am* asking you, Inspector. I understand this is not the first time my client has suffered harassment at the hands of the local police force."

"If she's calling it harassment, then she's a liar, Mr Davey. And I would warn you to be very careful."

"I'm perfectly capable of assessing the legal implications in this matter, Inspector Hopkirk. Before I can close my file there are some things I have to get straight. Have you in the past ever charged Miss Egerton with any offence?"

A long hesitation. Then: "No."

"Thank you. One more question, why have these present charges against Miss Egerton been dropped?"

"I don't see that I have to answer that. As I said, she's lucky to get away with it."

"Not satisfactory, Inspector. My client has been under great stress, she's had to take time off work . . . We could be talking malicious prosecution here . . . As her legal representative I should be failing in duty if I didn't enquire as to the reason the case has been withdrawn."

Frank was not absolutely sure of his grounds but just across his desk his client was leaning her chin on upturned palms and gazing at him with glowing emerald eyes. It was enough to make the most punctilious lawyer ignore the hurdles of procedure and protocol.

And it paid off.

"It was our chief witness," Hopkirk admitted, reluctantly, "he refused to testify. Once we told the CPS they advised dropping the case."

"You mean *that* Dr Parfitt who said he'd actually seen her?"

But Hopkirk had had enough; as a seasoned police officer

he knew that, when it came to words, lawyers won every time. He rang off.

Like an Olympic hero Franklyn Davey turned on the podium to receive the plaudits of the crowd; Lily clapped her hands softly together. "You weren't half good," she breathed. "That told him off good and proper. Sucks to you, Harry Hopkirk." She raised her coffee cup and drained it to the dregs. "The gang, they're gonna love this."

"Is that what you call the mates you go around with?"

"The Dick Turpins, yeah . . . Silly name. It got started when we were all at the comp. The first intake, they called us. Made us special, like."

"Your parents moved out from London into what they called Newtown, is that right?"

"Hey, it were me grandparents. But I guess you know your what-do-you call it, sociology? Anyway, some teacher took us out into the woods, supposed to make us learn about the place. There was this Dick Turpin's Cave. We took the name from there, and it sorta stuck."

She went suddenly quiet as if those childhood days stood in her mind like a challenge. When she spoke again it was in a lower tone.

"It couldn't have been easy for them," she said, "they were used to the East End where they were all close. They'd have the bombing an' all, down there night after night in the Blackwall Tunnel." She shuddered. "I couldn't have stood it but they did and never talked about it much 'cept mebbe when they'd had a few, Christmas, like. Then they were chucked out here to make the best of it, bloody acres of green fields and folks as didn't care . . ." She suddenly looked across at Frank as if accusing him of conjuring up things she didn't want to talk about. "Hey, you put something in this coffee?"

He was saved from making a stupid reply to a stupid question by his buzzer.

"Your next appointment is here," Joan was warning him in a tone which showed that she was irritated about the time he was spending with Miss Egerton, who had already been written off as a client.

"Sorry – er, Lily – much as I'd like to go on talking to you—"

"Yeah, I know . . . The paying customers are waiting." She got up and walked over once again to the nineteenth-century lawyer. "D'you ever get asked to trace missing persons? You know, like you see on *Crimewatch*?"

"Well, not exactly like that. But it does come into our work sometimes to have to find people that go missing. Fathers who're being chased for maintenance in matrimonial cases, that kind of thing."

"What about kids that go missing? Would you know where to look for them?"

She had her back to him and had dropped her voice so low he had difficulty in hearing what she'd said.

"Do you mean children?" he asked.

"Well, you know, teenagers, like." She was peering intently at the signature on the print as if she was thinking of buying it.

"If a child goes missing, then the police should be called in."

She turned a serious face to him, and frowned.

"That's the last thing a kid would want . . . Why'd it have to be the police?"

"For one thing, a child is vulnerable. If an adult chooses to disappear there'd be no need for police, it's taken for granted grown-ups can look after themselves, and it might be an invasion of their privacy to go after them. But with a child, or even a young person, it's different. They might be in danger, they might have been injured. Besides, the police can question people, discreetly if that's necessary."

"How'd they go about it, then?" She had come over, picked up her helmet and put it under her arm. She was looking steadily at him but there was a change in her attitude, and the sparkiness had gone from her eyes. He had the impression that some essential energy was draining from her. He wondered about drugs . . . So early in the day?

He tried to answer her, for her question seemed to have been in earnest. "Well, the police can go into places of employment,

36

schools and colleges, where missing youngsters are concerned, and there's always the social services."

But he might as well have been reading it all out of a rather dull textbook; he had lost her interest.

"I'd better be getting back to work. I took time off this morning. I told the foreman . . ." The words she used were almost the same as the last time, and delivered in the same, flat, toneless voice. Frank wanted to shake her. He tried to find a way of doing so.

"Have you any idea, Lillian, why Dr Parfitt should say he saw you that Saturday night at the surgery, and then withdraw his statement?" She stood irresolute for a moment, cradling her crash helmet. "I've no idea," she said, "he's a very good doctor. I like him. Is it all right if I go now?"

Frank got up and held out his hand but she didn't even see it, she was by now halfway to the door, and she didn't look round. Her smart boots somewhat incongruously stumbled on the rug whereas when she had come in she had been as sure-footed as a young deer stepping lightly on the forest floor.

Frank chided himself for the extravagant thought but the notion of a woodland creature had been in his mind more than once in the last twenty minutes. Now he felt he had let something escape; he had not been quick enough to grasp it.

Six

L ike its counterparts all over the country the Drill Hall at Newtown was a creation of the military, and so of unsurpassed ugliness. Built starkly with an arched roof of sub-standard concrete, it should have been pulled down years ago but in the flush of development it was somehow overlooked and finally ignored altogether. Being loosely in the Green Belt and on common land close to a tongue of Emberton Woods it was of no interest to builders, so it remained, an eyesore to the higher residents of Thornton but still a popular venue for events staged for the benefit of youngsters on the lower council estate. They preferred it to the youth club when they got old enough to discriminate between what was provided for them by the powers-that-be and what could be discovered for themselves.

The Drill Hall was sometimes favoured by entrepreneurs from London as a try-out place for pop concerts not quite up to having big names, and for tricky ventures in jazz and folk because it was cheap and up till now, trouble-free. A rumour from the depths of the drug-dealing underworld that Newtown police, being out in the sticks, wouldn't know cocaine from cornflour was in fact quite untrue, but did no harm to pulling in an audience.

"You can have PC Andrews," Sergeant Cobbins told Kemp grudgingly on Monday morning, "he's new and don't know the area yet, but he's learning. More to the point, he was on duty there Saturday night."

"Thank you very much," said Kemp, and meant it. The word passed round discreetly by Superintendant Upshire seemed to have opened doors without incurring too much curiosity.

38

Nevertheless, Cobbins was an old hand. He had known Kemp in the days when he had been more private investigator than respectable solicitor, and he thought there must be more in this visit to the Drill Hall than met the eye. Kemp must be up to something.

"Come on, then, Constable Andrews," said Kemp. He'd already shown the photograph of Elinor de Lisle to him, but without success. "There were hundreds of them there on Saturday, little 'uns and big 'uns, nearly all of them from the school. Anyway, it was the London lot I was to keep an eye out for. Inspector Hopkirk told me the locals weren't likely to be any trouble, he'd made sure of that."

"How did he manage that?" asked Kemp as they got into his car.

"Well, he's got this council estate gang well sewn up. And they didn't get any tickets for the Saturday night rave-up."

"I see." It sounded as if the newly promoted Hopkirk believed that prevention was better than crime; he wondered if the members of this so-called gang agreed.

"It's the only way to deal with these young criminals," the constable was going on, earnestly. "Inspector Hopkirk, he had a word with the head of the comprehensive. There was an allocation of tickets, right? The chap from London that's running the show, he lets the school have a batch at discount and the school's happy because the sixth-form have a band of their own and want to get a foot in the London clubs, see?"

"Not entirely." But Kemp didn't think it mattered. "So the local audience would be mainly from the school?"

"Right. And that kept out the troublemakers, like the Dick Turpins. It's what they call themselves, sir."

"And you had no trouble at the Saturday night concert, then?"

"Peaceful as a Sunday school picnic," said the young man, piously. "You have to hand it to Inspector Hopkirk, sir, he knows what he's doing. That mob from the council estate, they'd have wrecked the show, and mebbe brought in drugs . . ." he finished, darkly.

"You called them young criminals; have any of them act-ually been convicted of anything?"

PC Andrews did go red. "Not to my knowledge. I haven't been here very long, but there's been criminals in their families long before they moved out from the East End. That's what Inspector Hopkirk says, and he should know."

Kemp was finding Constable Andrews a bit of a prig and his enthusiasm for his inspector too sycophantic for the young man's future health. Kemp didn't know Hopkirk personally, had only heard of him as a well-conducted officer, diligent in pursuit of wrongdoing and keen to get ahead in the force. As he also lacked the two qualities which might hinder his upward progress – humour and imagination – in Kemp's opinion there would be no stopping him. Perhaps PC Andrews was right to hitch his wagon to this particular star.

They were approaching the slight knoll on top of which stood the Drill Hall with the dark wood behind it and on either side as if anxious to get a grip on the building. Kemp was reminded of what his wife had said as they were leaving Fairlawn last night: "Those trees are like an army – and they're closer than when we arrived."

It was true that what was left of the ancient forest stood its ground darkly against the sky, giving the impression of black battalions or at the very least defensive outposts. Looking at the trees now as the road curved up to them, Kemp thought that taken individually they were no more than trunks and branches. Like people they could be still as stone till a wind rose and moved them so that they waved their arms or wrung their hands. It was when they drew together when a storm was coming that they became implacable. In any case they were indifferent to the comings-and-goings of people who walked their paths or plunged deeply into their under-growths.

Kemp sighed. He liked his trees to be individuals not mustered against humans. Each one on its own was like some tall, gangling boy, tossing shaggy hair and stretching long limbs, but when they closed their ranks against some imagined slight, or found themselves bandied about by other folks' word of mouth, then like that line of woods they could look dangerous . . .

He knew his thoughts were the outcome of a troubled mind. When he had telephoned the de Lisle house early that morning there was no news. Alys sounded drained of tears, her voice dry and cracked. She was adamant that when George called later in the day he must still not be told. Kemp suspected that Evelyn had had her say in that decision.

"He has an important speech to give today, and another tomorrow. After that . . ." Alys had stopped.

After that, thought Kemp grimly, the hunt is on in earnest.

He didn't know what story Sergeant Cobbins had told the young constable about this visit to the Drill Hall. The sergeant himself had simply been informed that Kemp, as a friend of her parents, was making an enquiry as to whether or not Elinor de Lisle was in the audience at Saturday's musical event. There was nothing official about the visit, Kemp was just hoping that someone might remember seeing her. It might look as though doubtful parents were checking up on the girl's own story as to where she was on Saturday because they thought she might be lying. It didn't matter what was thought; all that mattered was to clutch at any straw. Besides, Kemp wanted to look at the place: how close was it to the woods, how easy was it for someone to slip away from the crowd and disappear?

All the hours since he first spoke to Alys de Lisle he had been aware of a terrible apprehension and every step he had taken was in the same sequence, following a path already mapped out; all police officers knew the process, the early stages of a murder investigation. Of course, he told himself, blindly, it would not come to that. There was still hope.

He hadn't expected any reaction to the photograph; as Mr Lewis, the man in charge of the clearing-up operation at the Hall, said after one look at it: "There were too many of them and the lighting's peculiar – all flashy inside and out here it's dead dark. Well, you were around," with a nod at PC Andrews, "you know what it was like."

But one of his assistants, a burly little man who was shifting chairs about, stopped and took the photograph over to a window. "That one, now I do remember her . . . Asked me for change for the payphone in the passage."

"You're sure?" asked Kemp.

"Sure I'm sure. For one thing she was polite – that's not something you can say of the rest of them. I give her change of her pound and she said, thank you. Now them's not words you hear often from that lot. Nah, I never saw her inside the Hall, this would be in the interval for it wasn't so noisy then, otherwise I'd never have heard her. It was out in that passage over there between the loos and the phones. Nah, I can't say if she was with anyone. Hold on a minute . . . Other girls it had to be, there was a lot of giggling going on as I remember it. Mebbe they were in the ladies', there'd be a bit of a queue, it being the interval, like. Sorry I can't help you further, mate, I don't think I caught a sight of her again that night."

Kemp thanked him and went outside where Lewis and Andrews were discussing Saturday night's event in self-congratulatory tones.

"It were quieter than other times," Lewis was saying, "I'd got a good relationship with the London chap running the gigs and he knew we wanted no trouble if he was up for a future fixture. But look at the mess they leave! It's allus the same with these Londoners, they leave the place like their own street markets on a Sunday morning. Reckon it's the way they live, everything on the floor. They're supposed to leave the Hall tidy but do they heck. At least this time you didn't have to make any arrests, did you, Constable? If there were any drugs going they kept them under their hats!"

"That was because my inspector took the precaution of keeping out the rowdies," said Andrews, stiffly. "He knows where they're coming from."

Kemp didn't think he could stand another paean of praise to Hopkirk and neither it seemed could Lewis. "Well, if that's all, Constable, I'll be getting back to work. We've got band practice here tonight and I've got to get the place shipshape."

Driving downhill to the police station where he could deposit Constable Andrews still shiny new and as yet undamaged, Kemp asked a few questions of his own.

"You say they call themselves the Dick Turpins, this group on the council estate, have you had anything to do with any of them individually?"

"I've run into a couple . . . Right cocky little bastards they are, too. Jeff Coyne and Kevin Williams – both nineteen and unemployed. Between jobs, they call it." He sneered lightly, but it was a sneer all the same. "Caught them spraying graffiti on the doors of the youth club . . . Made them clean it off or be taken down to the nick." Andrews smirked, savouring this small moment of triumph. "But it's a girl that's the worst. She's the ringleader, she's the one Inspector Hopkirk's out to get."

"Oh? What's her name?"

"I dunno. She lives on the estate in one of the bigger council properties, and that's where they all hang out when they're planning things. The inspector keeps a close eye on her but he don't want her name to get out. He's only waiting, see, to get something on her that'll stick. That's what CID's all about, isn't it? You have to get something that's watertight else those lawyers stitch you up in court." His voice sank somewhat and he stared straight ahead at the road. The silence that lay between them was palpable but Kemp was in no hurry to remove it. Give the youngster time to think about what he had just said, let him sweat it out.

At last PC Andrews gulped. "Sorry, sir." he managed. "I didn't mean—"

"I'm sure you didn't." Kemp smiled. "Anyway, I don't even know her name."

He thought of giving the young man a few words of advice. For example, if his ambition was to get into the CID, then he'd have to learn to watch his mouth, there would be times when it might be wise to keep it shut. Also, no matter his own opinions or his admiration for his seniors, a less positive approach might bring greater rewards. Softly, softly, catchee monkey, Kemp wanted to tell him but why should he bother? Let the force look after its own . . .

He drove the long way round to Fairlawn while he thought out his strategy, which he had to admit was limited by the constraint put upon it out of the need for discretion. However, the visit to the Drill Hall had confirmed one thing: that call on Saturday night had come from Elinor herself.

In the cold light of the white sitting-room he told Alys what he had discovered.

"So, it was really Elinor, that phone call?"

"I think so," said Kemp. "I don't know whether that's good or bad. At least if it was her she was a free agent."

Alys gazed straight ahead, her face like the model for a statue. Even under stress, and in extreme tiredness – for Kemp was sure she had not slept – her beauty was undiminished, the purple shadows round her eyes making them more luminous, the skin of her forehead more fragile.

"She'd meant all along to go to that concert," she said, wearily, "and I can't say I'm surprised. She had a will of her own and she would always do the opposite of what her grandmother wanted. She was careful with George and me, but when it showed . . ." Alys stopped, and put her head in her hands so that her words were muffled. "All my fault. I should have known . . . I should never have gone out."

"You can't blame yourself, Alys. She would probably have done it despite you, found some excuse. Girls of that age . . ." He began, then stopped helplessly. What did he know about girls of that age, anyway? His thoughts turned savage. If he was to be any use here then he must think in terms of routine, like a policeman.

"There's something I want you to do for me, Alys, if you can bring yourself to it. Will you ring Monica's mother and find out a little more about how the girls got parted on Saturday night? I understand Monica wasn't pleased because Elinor went off with someone else. It would be a help to know who that someone was. At this stage we can't question Monica herself. But if you had a chat with her mother we might learn something. Could you do that – even if it means lying?"

"Oh, I'm getting used to doing that." There was a new bitterness in her voice. "You should hear me talking to George when he calls. But I think I know what you want." She crossed over to the telephone on the desk, and dialled.

"Mrs Hodge? Estelle . . . Alys, here. I just wanted to

apologise for that mix-up Saturday night. It was a silly mistake and Mrs de Lisle is ever so sorry." Alys listened for a moment. "Well, that's very nice of you, I'll tell her. And I'm sorry I bothered you on Sunday."

She paused, and Kemp could hear Mrs Hodge's voice, for it had a high, penetrating quality, but not what she was saying. Half turned away from him Kemp saw Alys draw her brows together, frowning. "No, I didn't know that," she said, "she didn't tell me . . . I'm sure she didn't mean it, girls do have their little tiffs . . . Yes, I can understand how Monica felt, and I'm sorry."

She listened for a moment while the voice at the other end rose on an interrogatory note. "No," said Alys, smoothly, "I kept Elinor at home today, she has such a sore throat. That cold she had last week . . ."

How easily women lie, Kemp was thinking. They do it all the time, tell the little white untruths that keep lives smooth-running, evading unwelcome engagements, dealing with tradesmen, placating dissatisfied teachers, often having to use lies to protect their children from harsh realities, skilfully avoiding trouble on behalf of their children.

But men do it, too, reason told him. In their jobs (and Kemp knew his own profession no exception) and socially, everyone used those little falsehoods that hurt nobody.

Listening to her, he had to admit that Alys de Lisle was good at it, perhaps having that perfect beauty helped.

When she finally put the phone down she came back to her chair and put her head in her hands. Her voice was muffled: "It doesn't make it any easier that I don't really like Estelle Hodge very much. But I did what you asked."

Kemp waited. He recognised that part of her was not even present in this beautiful crystal room, but out there where she gazed across the neat lawns and shrubberies, over the ploughed field beyond, until the view was darkened by the shadow of the woods.

"They quarrelled, Elinor and Monica, soon after they got to the youth club on Saturday evening. They were supposed to have a table-tennis match but Elinor told Monica to find herself another partner. Monica was upset. She says Elinor went off with that older crowd."

"Would they be from the school?"

"Estelle doesn't think so. Monica says Elinor's always hanging around with them but of course *she* wouldn't. But that's according to Monica's mum. Somehow I don't think any of the older boys would want Monica around . . ." She looked up suddenly, aghast. "What am I saying?"

Kemp smiled. "You're being honest, Alys. Anyway, Monica's mum can't hear you."

She gave the ghost of a smile in return.

Seven

Franklyn Davey suffered from curiosity; he used the verb advisedly when he thought about it but he had no doubt it had brought him to where he was now.

At school this curiosity had been misdiagnosed as an addiction to scholarship, so eager had the young Frank been for learning. Because his father was already in the law, and because Frank didn't have a rebellious bone in his body, he slipped quite naturally into that profession. His curiosity made him so anxious to find out about things that he whizzed through university and law college on a kind of roller-coaster to discover what happened next in common law, tort, real estate and revenue . . . When it came to equity, however, he came to a dead end. Although fired by enthusiasm at the beginning – there were so many imponderables, so many loosely tied ends that needed sorting – in the end he found nothing for his curiosity to feed on. Then he took stock and reviewed his position.

"The trouble with you, Frank," said his girlfriend who had stuck by him despite his uncertainties, "is that so far you've only been curious about deadly dull subjects when I think your real interest is in people."

"You mean I'm a people person rather than a things person?"

They both spoke the same language; Dinah was studying psychology, as well as the social sciences.

"You've been immured too long in the backwater of the law courts – wills and trusts and Chancery buffs. Time you came out into the real world."

So Frank had applied to return to the firm where he had

served his articles, and Lennox Kemp, now head of that firm, was pleased to accept him, recognising in Frank something of the same curiosity which had fuelled his own career, not only in the law but out of it as a private investigator. It was a compelling inquisitiveness about people, the way they behave, the way they react to circumstance, how their outward appearance responds to stimuli, in short what makes them tick. Sometimes Kemp thought of himself – and not in any self-congratulatory way – as a kind of spy as he watched his clients' little movements, the casual gestures, the body language which could give away so much, the difference between truth and lies.

Frank Davey was only at the start of his apprenticeship. In fact he hardly knew what was bothering him except that he had been stung with curiosity about Lillian Egerton, and the itch remained.

Yesterday's interview with her, which should have been the last unless she got into trouble again, had only increased his confusion about her. It was beginning to interfere with his other work which, when he put his mind to it, he could always carry out with speed and efficiency, particularly if he wanted to have an hour or two left over – like now.

"Those contracts of employment we did for Bernes," he remarked casually to Joan, "have they ever been updated?"

"Nobody's asked us to. Why?"

"Changes in the legislation," he said, loftily, "minimum wages, health and safety regulations, and all that . . ."

"Shouldn't we wait till we're asked?"

"It's part of the service we give. We're supposed to be the ones that keep up with the law. That's why we keep getting these pages on Statutory Instruments that the office juniors hate having to stick into those nasty little books with the brass rods in them."

"And Bernes are the ones that probably get all they need to keep up with the times from whatever government department issues them. Oh, all right, I'll get the file out for you. Do you want me to make an appointment with Mr Bexby?"

"No, I'll see to that."

It helped that he'd had a drink occasionally with Alex Bexby in the past so that when he rang Bernes and spoke to him it was very much in the way of a friendly chat.

"That's very good of you, Frank. I can't leave the factory this morning but if you really don't mind coming here we could go over these contracts together. I had been thinking along these same lines myself – there seems to be a new government directive every time you turn your back for a moment."

Suiting a firm which made lenses, most of Bernes seemed to be constructed of glass so that even in the offices there were clear views of the shop-floors and the benches where white-coated figures bent over the tiny fragments of manufacture. It all looked spotlessly clean, and the atmosphere pleasant.

"Would you like to see round?" Alex asked him when they had finished their scrutiny of the various draft documents Frank had brought. He had stretched the necessity for his visit as far as plausibility would take it, and jumped at the opportunity to extend it further.

He was listening with half an ear to Bexby's description of a particularly novel scientific process when he saw Lillian Egerton, and in the same moment she looked his way.

She gave not the slightest flicker of recognition. She was seated at a large desk surrounded by boxes, and had looked up, presumably at the sound of voices.

"Hello, Miss Egerton," said Franklyn. "Glad to see you back at work." It was an idiotic thing to say but the girl did bring out the idiot in him.

"Of course, you two have met." Bexby observed before beginning a short discussion with her about some urgent order to which she responded in a low, flat voice dutifully scattered with a lot of "Yes, Mr Bexby"s, "No, Mr Bexby"s.

While this was going on, and obviously no business of his, Frank moved away to a bench where a group of girls were chattering happily together as if oblivious to the delicate operations being performed by their fingers. They were all, more or less, pretty and as they saw Frank watching them they broke into giggles, and smiled at him.

Lillian Egerton didn't seem to be any part of this group and Frank remembered that he'd been told she was a supervisor – perhaps that prohibited too much camaraderie. But that shouldn't account for the fact that her appearance was so different; whereas they wore their caps and overalls with some individual style, her hat was squashed low on her forehead to the ugliest effect, and her coat drooped on her shoulders as if much too large for her skinny frame.

Yet as they moved away Alex Bexby remarked, when she was just out of earshot: "Best worker I've got, that Lillian Egerton."

As Frank was about to follow his host out of the door he turned for a last look round, and he caught her eye. She winked at him, a slow, deliberate closing of one eye. She had taken off her glasses so he should have the full force of it. It was outrageous, but it had happened; she had given him the eye.

He tripped over the step and was helped up by Mr Bexby who was still singing her praises. "I'm really glad you got her out of that mess with the police," he was saying, earnestly. "I can't think why they keep on harassing her. For that's what I call it – police harassment."

Frank forbore to mention that it was none of his doing that the charges had been dropped; he was much too curious about the part played by the police.

"Why do you think they do it?" he said, casually.

"Well, I think she had a bit of trouble a while back with one of the sergeants. Hopkirk, I think his name is, he's in CID. Do you know him, Mr Davey?"

"Not well," Frank replied, cautiously. Some years ago when both of them were new to the town he and Harry Hopkirk used to have a few beers from time to time, brought together by their bachelor status, and the fact that they were studying for examinations, Frank his law finals, Harry for an external London University LLB which he hoped would help his promotion.

"Sergeant Hopkirk has been promoted to inspector recently," he told Bexby. "He's worked hard for it. I think it's what's called being a career policeman."

"Nothing wrong with that." Alex Bexby was a great believer in hard work and promotion; his own career had been based on it. "Maybe now he'll quit pestering our Lillian."

"Was that what he was doing? Is that what she told you?"

"Oh, no . . . Lillian's never said, and she's not the kind of girl you can talk to about something like this . . . No, it was the other girls who told me. Apparently . . ." Although they were now back in his office the personnel manager lowered his voice. Perhaps it was the effect of living in a glass cell open to all eyes. "Apparently, Hopkirk took a shine to Lillian about a year ago and kept asking her out but she wasn't having any . . . They'd have made a pretty odd pair . . ." Bexby paused as if contemplating just such an unlikely union. "He's a right ugly-looking bloke and she was like a gawky schoolgirl then . . . not an ounce of flesh on her bones . . . Late maturity, don't they call it? Anyway, one of the girls says he gave Lillian a hard time, following her about, watching her every move, even spying on her house."

Franklyn had been fascinated by Alex Bexby's role as personnel manager, in charge, as it were, of the hopes and fears of a galaxy of girls, and saw that it could only function in an atmosphere of gossip and what he had learned to avoid as hearsay. Nevertheless, he was hooked.

"I understand that Miss Egerton's house is in fact opposite to that of Inspector Hopkirk's?"

Bexby nodded, sagely. "Ah, but you see he only got that house when he got married a few months ago. Married quarters for the local police, that's how those properties were designated."

Frank thought for a moment.

"Do you think this harassment, as you call it, has increased against Miss Egerton since the inspector moved in opposite?"

"It's turned nasty, if you want my opinion. And I think, between ourselves, Mr Davey, it's to do with him not wanting his new wife to know anything about him pestering Miss Egerton. I think he wants to run our Lillian out of town in case she says anything . . ."

This piece of cowboy rhetoric suggested that Alex Bexby

had a romantic side to his nature, perhaps that was why he seemed a popular figure among the staff at Bernes. Certainly Frank found him more likeable.

"You don't think that's exaggerating things?" he suggested, on a note of caution.

Bexby shook his head. "I had it from Howard Bradley, and he's no fool. He went round to Lillian Egerton's one night to interview some prospective tenants of hers – she's quite right to be careful who she lets rooms to, there's some bad types on that estate – and while Howard's there he happens to look out of the window. Would you believe it, that Hopkirk was in his front garden opposite, standing stock-still and staring up at her house. Gave Howard quite a start, it did, and you can imagine the effect it had on Lillian. She told Howard that the sergeant's behaviour was beginning to affect her nerves. Well, I had to step in, Mr Davey – when the health of any of our employees is at stake we at Bernes take it seriously. I made sure that Lillian saw Dr Parfitt."

"That's the same Dr Parfitt who's at the health centre in town?"

"That's the man. He's also on our books as company doctor. He's an excellent man, very reliable. Well, he found straight away that Lillian was anaemic and started treatment for it, also gave her something for her nerves. Here at Bernes we know how to look after our employees. It's a great firm to work for."

"I mustn't keep you from your duties any longer." Frank packed up the draft documents, and left this well-run, hygienic and benevolent institution with a promise to Alex Bexby that, yes, they'd meet for a drink sometime.

Back in his office he pushed Lillian Egerton from his mind, interviewed several clients, drafted a couple of leases and exchanged banter with Joan when she brought him his post to sign. He thought he could call it a day when Mike Cantley burst into his room.

"Frank, can you do me a favour?"

"Not that man's thumb again. I couldn't stand another look—"

"Nothing to do with him – thanks all the same. The thing is that I've got to catch the five ten to London but something's cropped up."

"Don't tell me," said Frank, warily, "you're on the horns of the lawyer's dilemma – trying to be in two places at the same time."

"You're right. It's the matter of the policemen's ball . . ."

"It's the what?" Frank subsided in laughter.

"Its not funny." said Mike, "Our local bobbies, high and low, hold this event every year in February at the Castle Hotel and it's this coming Saturday, but some yokel at the station forgot to put in their application for an extended licence at the proper time and place."

"The policemen's ball." Frank chortled. "Isn't that something out of Flann O'Brien? All right, all right, I get what has happened. They're all on orange juice while they have to dance with each other's wives. Talk about a bleak midwinter."

"Shut up and listen . . . I'm in the magistrates' court tomorrow morning to apply for the licence on their behalf but the idiots haven't even signed the form. Needs a senior officer's signature and it seems that Chief Superintendent Upshire has got them all out on some panic mission. That's left only one at the station, and he's CID, an Inspector Hopkirk. I've just been on the blower to him and he's going to be there for the next two hours. What I want you to do, Frank . . ."

Franklyn was already on his feet. "Is to go round to the station and extract a signature to this precious form which you are about to hand over to me. And I do so with the greatest pleasure. But . . ." he said as he took the slip of paper from Mike's hand, "you owe me one, and don't you forget it."

"Anything, Frank. Thanks a lot. I'm off. Sorry to land you with this. Really I'm most grateful."

And I am too, thought Frank as he tidied up his office, took his coat from its peg, and set off for the police station. Fate could not have played more neatly into his hands.

Eight

For the first time in his life Harry Hopkirk was a reasonably happy man. He had clawed his way upwards to his new rank sooner than could have been expected (there happened to be a dearth of similarly experienced officers at the time) and he had acquired a suitable wife. This was quite an accomplishment since Harry was ill-favoured in looks and although he was used to his rather ugly face other people weren't and girls seemed to shy away from it, never staying long enough to get acquainted with him.

He met Amy Pritchard when he was doing a stint with the Met after he had got his law degree and was hoping for a suitable appointment as a result. Amy was a WPC who had joined with one aim, to become the wife of a policeman – preferably one with prospects. Because Harry Hopkirk had done a lot of studying he got the name for being an intellectual, which was not true; Harry was simply a plodder with purpose.

Amy and he suited one another admirably, after a short courtship they got married, and Amy left the force to become what she had always wanted to be, a proper housewife. Harry returned to Newtown as a married man entitled to police housing on the Thornton Estate. Then promotion had come. Inspector West was retiring early because of ill-health, and Hopkirk was about to step into his shoes.

So Harry was reasonably happy this Tuesday evening, although he didn't look it. But then his was not a face to show the lighter spirits. His ears were large, his nose was long, and his skull was narrow. His other features had to fit into this framework as best they could, so the round black eyes and pursed mouth couldn't help but look squashed.

There were only two irritations bothering him, one major and the other minor. The major one, the girl called Lillian Egerton, he pushed to the back of his mind for the present. The other, well that was being swiftly dealt with now as he signed the form given to him by Franklyn Davey, who took it up and stowed it safely away in his brief-case.

"Thank you, Inspector Hopkirk," said Frank, "Mr Cantley will put it to the justices in the morning. Will you be there to give it the nod?"

"I'll have to be, won't I? I seem to be the only responsible officer in the station." It was an irksome duty he'd had thrust upon him, and the only satisfaction he'd got out of it was the bawling-out he'd been able to give the young constable, the miscreant who'd forgotten to check the dates for the application in the first place.

"Licensing laws are a stupid waste of court time," remarked Frank, then added, quickly: "And yours too of course. They're relics of the past and should be abolished."

On any other occasion Hopkirk would have disagreed with anything a lawyer threw at him – he was not overly fond of members of the profession – but in the circumstances he felt it was better to go along with the opinion since Franklyn Davey had, after all, saved the bacon of the local force by his prompt action in coming to the station.

"We could well do without the paperwork," he said. "We're just not manned for it."

Davey commiserated further. "I can see that . . . Where's everyone today?"

Hopkirk responded to the note of sympathy. He had resented the fact that his new ranking did not seem to have been properly appreciated by his superiors. Of course Inspector West hadn't actually gone yet, and it was well known that he and John Upshire had been buddies from way back. Still, they might have let him in on whatever had been making a stir at the station since yesterday morning. The two senior men, Upshire and West, had gone into a huddle with the head of the uniformed branch and they had all left together without a word to Hopkirk who was itching to know what it was all about. He presumed only the desk sergeant knew their destination but he would not stoop to asking Cobbins whom he had always regarded as one degree above a village idiot.

"There's a bit of a panic on," he confided now to Frank Davey, as if he knew what it was about but could not of course divulge it to an outsider. So that the young solicitor would not question him further on the subject, Harry abruptly changed the subject.

He remarked in his friendliest tone: "We didn't do badly at those exams, did we?" referring to some three or four years ago when they had found a bond in their studying. "What made you come back to Gillorns?"

"They made me an offer I couldn't refuse." Frank grinned. He'd been trying hard to get the conversation on to a comradely footing, maybe he had succeeded. "And you've come back too, Harry. Congratulations on your promotion, by the way. And I hear you've got married?"

Harry had never made many friends either in the force or outside it; those who might have been mates were somehow cut off by his determination to achieve higher rank than they might have aspired to, while the more studious had not found him as intelligent as he thought he was.

He used to get on well with young Davey – as he thought of him, giving full weight to the odd seven years between them – and he had sometimes felt that had it not been for the constraints of their separate professions they might have become friends. He had never considered the possibility that Franklyn Davey, kind-hearted to a fault, particularly towards loners like Hopkirk, might not have had in mind anything beyond a casual acquaintanceship.

At this moment, however, it was suiting the young lawyer to be on congenial terms with Harry Hopkirk. After all, it was the reason he was here – he could quite easily have sent Joan to get the precious bit of paper – and why he was sitting in this dusty back room at the station listening to Hopkirk's eulogy on the joys of matrimony.

"You should try it," Harry finished, predictably, with as near a smile as his features would allow. "At any rate, come over one night for supper with Amy and me."

"That's kind of you. Did you manage to get married quarters?"

"Yes, we're at number 21, Marshall Avenue, you've probably heard of it, it's on the Thornton Estate." A shadow fell across his brow, and he lowered his voice. "It's not ideal, of course, far from it. We'd like a place of our own and now my salary's gone up we'll be able to afford it, but unfortunately not for a while yet. Amy doesn't believe in wives that work, so we've got some saving to do before we can think of buying our own house."

Frank suddenly clapped his hands together. "I knew that address was familiar," he exclaimed, "I knew I'd heard it before . . . Marshall Avenue, number 21 you say – why that must be close to where that girl lives . . . What's her name? Egerton, that's it . . . Lillian Egerton."

Hopkirk drew in his lips so that his mouth became smaller than ever, and the words had to squeeze themselves out.

"She's right opposite us. And she's trouble, that girl, not just to Amy and me but to the whole estate. She, and that gang of hers . . ."

"What personally has she done to you, Harry?" Frank chose his words with care.

Hopkirk made a hissing sound through his teeth and Frank had to lean forward to catch what he was saying.

"She sprays things on our garden walls, and once even on to our back door. Amy very nearly caught her that time but she's so fast, that girl. Then she's out in her garden watching Amy cleaning it off, and she's laughing. That's the measure of her evil, Frank, she's laughing . . ."

"I say, what a rotten thing to do. Are you sure it's the same girl, this Lillian Egerton, the one who came to me over that summons?"

"Of course it's her . . . She and that gang of hers, they're a curse on the estate. You know, Frank, there's people who've seen her doing these things but will they come forward to give evidence? Will they heck. Or like that doctor withdrawing his statement at the last minute . . ."

"I did wonder about that." Frank made a gesture with his hand. "It's all right to talk about it, Harry. She's not my client any more. And I couldn't help being curious about this Dr Parfitt."

"Oh, there's nothing wrong with Dr Parfitt. I doubt if it was his fault he had to back off as a witness."

"But surely he was just that – a witness. I've read his statement. He said he saw her throw a brick then climb in at the surgery window. Surely that was breaking and entering *per se*?"

Hopkirk breathed hard down his sharp little nose making a whizzing sound like a kettle on the boil. "Yes, he saw her and he chased her off and he made that statement, but later when he'd talked the whole thing over with his senior partners they decided against prosecution. Didn't want their precious surgery mentioned in court as a scene of crime. And that was after all the trouble my lot had gone to that night, getting her fingerprints all over the place." He let out a snort of exasperation. "I reckon it was because the perp was a patient of theirs and when medicos come to a decision they tend to stick together – just like you lawyers."

Frank ignored the jibe. "But I thought Miss Egerton was Dr Parfitt's patient?"

"Is that what she told you? Truth is she's been going to that surgery for years. Dr Sutherland had her, and then that lady doctor, now it's the new boy's turn. Dr Parfitt's a New Zealander, only been in the practice these last six months. I think he's a good doctor, so does Amy. He was a tad sheepish when he came down to the station to withdraw his evidence. Mumbled something about it not being good for the practice for him to stand up in court against one of their patients – and a young girl at that. Maybe she needed help, all that sort of rubbish, it might be psychological." Hopkirk stopped, and steamed quietly for a moment. "Wasn't much we could do about it so we had to drop the case. But I'll get that young hooligan yet. With budding criminals like her there's always a next time, and I'm watching her like a hawk."

Franklyn waited for a moment to let him simmer down for there was real venom in Hopkirk's voice; perhaps it was psychological with him too.

"This gang you talk about. Have any of them been charged?"

Hopkirk shook his head. "Their families live on the estate and everybody clams up. We can dole out cautions by the score but they just snigger. They're just a bunch of young tearaways, unemployed and probably unemployable but it's her that winds them up."

Frank could hardly believe it of the mousey creature so mealy mouthed with Mr Bexby until he remembered that wink. And the first time he'd met Lillian Egerton he'd felt she was capable of anything. She seemed to fit into other people's categories but she didn't into any of his.

He wondered what she was doing at this moment, and surreptitiously glanced at his watch: five thirty, she would be on her way home – to put her feet up? Cook herself a little supper and retire with a good book? Or get into her smart gear, paint her nails and make for the pubs? He really had no idea, and by this time he wasn't learning much from Inspector Hopkirk who was off on a frolic of his own – the Dick Turpins, as they called themselves. No, he didn't know how they came by the name but he wouldn't be surprised if it wasn't she who suggested it. They had a place in the woods, he went on to tell Franklyn gloomily, where they hung out and plotted things. "They go there to smoke dope," he said, darkly. Indeed the very mention of the word seemed to depress him further. "And if there's harder stuff down from London that'll be on the menu, too."

"Where's this place in the woods, then?" Frank asked, although he had a suspicion by now that the new inspector was unhealthily obsessed. He'd have to have a word with Dinah, his girlfriend, on the subject; after all she was a student of psychology.

Hopkirk snorted. There were times when his nose seemed to speak for him. "Dick Turpin's Cave – it's just a hollow in a bank deep in the woods, away from the roads. Locals say it was where Turpin lay in wait for the London stagecoach. For years it got used as a dump – you know the kind of thing, old mattresses, shopping trolleys, household rubbish – then the council decided to clear it up and got youngsters to volunteer for the job . . . I must say," and he said it grudgingly, "they didn't do a bad job of it. Then the youngsters themselves sort of took it over as theirs."

"Perhaps they had a point . . ." Frank couldn't help murmuring, but Hopkirk was back on his hobby-horse.

"I'd clear that gang of troublemakers out of it," he said, savagely. "A den of thieves, that's all it is now, with that girl in control. The Dick Turpins, indeed. What was he but a common criminal when all's said and done?"

There seemed no answer to that, so Franklyn decided it was time he went home.

Nine

D arren Roding was one of the keenest members of the gang because he was new to it. He'd only been in Newtown a couple of months when his mum got a house on the estate after the divorce, and he swore he'd have been bored out of his skull if he hadn't found the Turpins. He'd hated leaving Hackney where all his school pals still lived and had despaired of finding new mates out here in the sticks. In fact it was the Turpins who found him, and he was thrilled when he passed his initiation test and joined. It had been dead easy. When he told them he had a Sunday job at the supermarket where his mother worked all they said was: "Nick a few fags." Which he did. He said he'd not do it again, once it was on a regular basis he'd be found out for sure, no one knew the checking system better than he did. Anyway, he wasn't asked to do it again; the gang, too, had its rules.

This Tuesday night his mum was on late shift and Darren was at a loose end, but he had a plan. There was no word of a get-together of the Turpins till the weekend, and that was usually at Lily's place, but Darren had heard the gang talking about a hideaway they had in Emberton Woods. He'd never been asked to go there; they said they didn't use it much in the winter but Darren knew that that wasn't strictly true, he'd heard they had it all rigged up nice and cosy with a bit of carpet and seats. He reckoned they stashed things out there, stuff that was too risky even for Lily's place . . .

He decided to go and have a look at this den, Dick Turpin's Cave as Lily called it, as if she knew all about it. He knew roughly where it was in the woods so he set off on his bike. But there had been a frost a few nights ago and then a quick thaw so the forest floor was slippery with its covering of last autumn's leaves, and the ground too soft for cycling. He left his bike under some bushes, putting on a chain and padlock just in case, and set off on foot.

Several times he slipped and fell as he clambered over the long ridges that led deep into the trees. They were banks or earthworks running parallel to each other as if maybe they'd been some sort of defence system in the olden days. In between the banks there were pits and hollows, and down in the last one was the cave. By this time there wasn't even a glow from the sky and down in the hollow it was black dark so Darren switched on his torch as he slithered down the bank, grabbing at low-lying branches to keep his balance. Then he saw the entrance, a round hole just a shade darker than its surroundings.

He was jubilant. Gotcha! he told the trees. Not bad, eh, for a city boy, as they'd called him.

He went closer, sliding on the wet leaves. Damn. Someone was already there. His torchlight flickered on a pair of legs sticking out from the entrance, blocking the way into the cave which was in fact no more than an overhang of the bank held by a tangle of low bushes and old roots. He pushed aside a low branch and shone his torch further in. He was about to call out something, then he saw her face. He didn't know her name but he'd seen her once or twice with Lily.

She seemed to be asleep . . . Or doped to the eyeballs, he thought. He bent over to get a closer look and touched her leg. The shock sent him reeling back, the toe of one of his trainers caught on a tree root and he fell full length across her body.

He screamed. At least he must have screamed, he thought afterwards, but he only heard silence and the rasp of his own breathing. It was the terrible coldness that got to him . . . The coldness of the flesh through her clothing and the coldness of reality. As he scrambled to his feet his stomach heaved and he was sick.

Panic followed. His hands were sticky with mud where they'd dug into the earth. He hoped it was only mud.

There was only one thing to do and that was get away from

this place fast. He climbed up the bank on all fours in a frenzy of haste, wiping the stuff from his hands by grasping at twigs and bunches of dead leaves. By the time he had reached the spot where he'd left his bike he scarcely had breath left, but sank down panting. There wasn't a sound except for the hum of traffic on the nearest road through the wood.

Get away from it, get away from it . . . That had been his first instinct. Now, what? He should, he knew, go for help but what kind of help? If he stopped a passing motorist he'd have to go back to show him the place. That was out of the question; Darren vowed he was never going to go back there. He should tell the police but how could he do that without having to go with them? He could find a phone box and make an anonymous call but the only telephone box he knew of was by the Drill Hall on the other side of the woods. Besides, what could he say? There's a girl . . . Darren stopped. He knew there was no way he could tell the police, they would trace him, they would find him, and then . . . Gradually a scenario more fearful than what he'd already been through put itself together in his frantic mind.

Having something to do – his dirty fingers fumbling with the padlock – cooled him down and started up his thinking.

The girl had overdosed, OD they called it in American cop dramas, she'd gone there to smoke dope or, more likely, to inject and she'd got a bad packet. Which meant that the stuff was still there in the cave like he'd worked it out for himself, and anybody going there now would be bound to find it, and they'd think that's why he'd gone there.

He tried out the simple truth but found it was neither simple nor believable. *Just a hunch, sonny, you went there on a hunch? On a dark winter night you went out there just to have a look, not even knowing where the place was? And you found it, surprise, surprise . . . You were out there for the drugs, son, weren't you, like she was.*

Darren had heard a lot about police interrogation from his mates back in Hackney; stitch you up, that's what they do. If you're just under twenty, you've left school with fuck-all, you're unemployed and you've had at least one run-in for possession, then you're a dead duck. Darren was right there in the category, every policeman's dream perp. No, the truth wouldn't hold, so forget the police.

By this time Darren was pedalling fast on a minor woodland road. Another blot on the screen of truth was the effect it would have on the gang. Well, he'd be kicked out of it, for starters. Spying on their secret hideaway, hoping to score for himself and then blurting it all out to the cops. Betrayal was the dirtiest word.

Going downhill now towards the lights of Newtown, Darren spared a thought for his mum. He hadn't been told much about the divorce, and he hadn't asked. He knew his dad had once been big on the drug scene and their lifestyle had reflected its glory, but something had gone wrong. Darren had been sent to live with his grandma two streets away until the storm blew over, but even when the wind died down there were no happy landings. All Darren knew, or was allowed to know, was that his dad was in jail, there'd been a divorce and his mum had a new life, starting right now in the place for which it was named, Newtown. The only bit of the past that stuck was that every time his mum heard, saw, or read about drugs she had the screaming abdabs, and when Darren got done for possession of the minutest quantity it was then that she finally blew her top and left her birthplace for pastures new. Thinking now of his mother Darren realised the sheer impossibility of telling the truth.

But there was one person who could help him, someone who already knew about the place; she would know what to do, she would take this frightful burden of knowledge from his shoulders and tell him what to do next.

Free-wheeling now, he was making a beeline for 24 Marshall Avenue.

There was a light on, and faint music playing. Thank God, she's home. But it wasn't Lily who answered the door. Instead it was an older woman in a drab jumper and skirt, wearing specs. Must be her sister, thought Darren, he'd heard there was a sister.

"Is Lily . . ." he stammered, "is Lillian in?"

She pushed her glasses down her nose and stared at him.

"Is that you, Darren Roding? You look a right mess. Better come in before the neighbours see you."

She pulled him through into the hall, and shut the door smartly.

"In here," she said, taking him by the shoulders and pushing him towards the big sitting-room, the one where they held their meetings, beanbags all over the floor, beer cans piled high, a blazing fire and fags and smack on offer. It didn't look the same, apart from the fire, the rest of it too clean and tidy.

She brought him to the centre of the room. "Don't sit down," she said, sharply, "I don't want to have to wash the covers. What's going on?"

The relief was like letting go on a long-held piss. Once started, Darren couldn't stop. He didn't care whether it was Lillian herself or her sister, just that someone was listening. The words seemed to come up from his stomach and out of his lips like the vomit he'd left on the body. He was so engrossed in his story that he hardly noticed that she had sat down with a thump when he described the girl.

He ended by telling how he'd cycled down from the woods, and then spurted out his thoughts and fears, how terrified he was that he might be linked to this dead girl when really it had nothing to do with him. Please, would she tell him what he should do now?

Even when she had sunk down on to the sofa her eyes had never left him. They continued to hold him until, after it seemed that minutes rather than seconds had passed while she thought things through, she finally spoke.

"Darren, I want you to do exactly what I tell you, and ask no questions. We're going to have to sort things out, you and I, but I might have to be away for an hour or so. You're going to stay here in this house, and get yourself tidied up. Take off those dirty clothes and stick them in the washing machine. Do you know how to work one?" Darren nodded. "It's in the kitchen. And there's a shower in the bathroom, get yourself clean right down to your fingernails. You hearing me, Darren?" Again he nodded. "There's some sports clobber in one of the bedrooms, get yourself into it till your clothes dry. Sit in here and put on a video – you know where they are." She got to her feet. "But remember it's in your own home you've been all evening. You said your mum was working, when does she get back?"

"Not till after ten."

"Good, you'll have got your clothes dry and be out of here by then."

She hustled him out, and into the bathroom. He'd his kit off and was about to step into the shower when he heard the motor bike start up. He raised a corner of the blind. By the streetlight between the houses he could make out the figure in black gear.

Good. She'd told her sister. Lily was away to check up on things, Lily would take care of everything.

His stuff was dry enough to take home by the time the nine o'clock news had finished.

Lennox and Mary Kemp had been watching the nine o'clock news. At the end there was a brief, rather dull, statement to the effect that a détente had been reached at the meeting of the International Monetary Fund in Toronto, and the conference had finished on an optimistic note.

Mary raised an enquiring eyebrow at her husband.

"I think the time difference is about five hours behind us," he said. "Of course there'll be the usual junketings before the delegates can leave, but—"

"So George should be back tomorrow? Does Alys usually meet him?"

"She says, never . . . When he's been away for a few days like this time the one thing he wants is to get home to Newtown as quickly as possible."

Mary screwed up her eyes; she never cried for herself but now the thought of Alys up there in the house called Fairlawn brought stinging tears. "And there's nothing we can say or do," she said.

Kemp sighed. "Everything that could be done has been done despite the blanket of silence. Enquiries have been discreet but they've been thorough." He'd told her of his own dispiriting day, how his diplomatic visit to Thornton Comprehensive had told him a lot about Dougal Hunter, the headmaster, and his wife Catriona, something of staff-room tensions, a little about education in the nineties but absolutely nothing to explain the disappearance of Elinor de Lisle. Questions at the youth club – on the pretext that its trustees were concerned about new Health and Safety regulations – only confirmed that there had been a blazing row between members of the girls' table tennis team on Saturday night because one player was missing, and another showed unsportsmanlike temper . . . Monica in a tantrum was apparently something to be remembered.

It had been when he was among these young people that Kemp had felt closest to Elinor – it was in that youth club where it had all started, of that he felt sure. Without alerting them to the seriousness of his enquiries he had casually talked of the concert at the Drill Hall. Yes, it had been a greater attraction that night than games at the club, but when he tried to probe deeper they shied away, perhaps becoming suspicious that he was a spy for their parents. He would have to go back, of course, if . . .

He didn't want to face that thought but Mary said it for him: "When will John Upshire up the ante into a full-scale search?"

Kemp looked at his watch. "He'll have the dog-handlers out in Emberton Woods by now. He had to wait . . . But a preliminary search has already been made, his men have been carrying it out since Sunday. He can do that kind of thing without too much notice being taken but to bring in the dogs, well that would have the media out for a story."

"And it still might be a story." Mary was thinking of that stolid, dark stand of trees guarding the ancient woods and its secrets. "If . . ." she went on, then stopped as the telephone rang.

She followed Lennox into the hall, fear clutching her heart. She felt a flicker in her womb, the merest tremor against her skin, but a kick all the same. For a second the realisation of what it was drove all other thoughts away.

Then she was aware that Lennox wasn't saying anything,

that he'd been a long time on the phone, only listening. And he had turned his back to her.

She knew why. So that she couldn't see his face.

Finally, she heard him say: "That will be taken care of, John. I'll go myself to meet George de Lisle when he comes off that plane. It shouldn't be up to your people, and Alys is in no fit state."

He put the phone down, turned and took his wife in his arms.

"They've found her body." The words were breathed into the flesh of her neck. She wished they'd never been said.

Ten

Franklyn Davey had found Gillorns to have a relaxed attitude to work when he was there as an articled clerk. Even before flexible hours became an option, the firm had had leanings towards letting the staff regularise their own hours so far as possible. Finding that the custom still prevailed was one of the reasons which had drawn him back to the Newtown office. He could, and did, work very long hours when necessary and took time off when he was up to date, with nothing on his files that couldn't wait. This particular week he had informed the partners in plenty of time that he would like to take a few days of holiday and as he had no court cases coming up until the following week, there was a lull in his matrimonials, and conveyancing was merely ticking over, it had been agreed that he'd be away till Monday.

He came in on Wednesday morning to check his mail and leave any further instructions with Joan. "You going to the sun?" she asked, rather enviously.

"Not at all. I'm going over to Dublin. I'm being vetted."

"For a horse show? You'll never pass."

"I'm going to meet Dinah's parents. They're going to give me a going-over."

Joan burst out laughing. She knew something of Frank's private life which was whiter than white and totally uninteresting.

"And about time too," she said. "You and Dinah have been together longer than Mutt and Jeff. You ought to know your minds by now."

"Marriage is a serious business," he told her, primly. She threw the Law Diary at him and he ducked, retrieved it from

69

the floor and handed it back. "Don't forget to water my plants, Joan. I'm not worried about my clients but if you let my ferns dry out I'll skin you."

"Yes, sir." Joan saluted him. "Have a good time," she said, "and lay off the Guinness. Perhaps it isn't all that good for you."

Frank would have liked to have had a word with Lennox Kemp before he left but there simply wasn't time; he had to meet Dinah at the airport. Anyway, the senior partner wasn't in his office, and Mike Cantley didn't know where he was, so Frank decided to leave it at that.

As he left the building, however, he had the oddest feeling that he had missed something, as if he had brushed closely against something and not noticed it. Something important . . .

He liked to keep his thoughts in orderly bundles, though not necessarily tied up with pink tape. He worried about loose threads that wouldn't fit, and this one teased him all the way to City Airport. He had plenty of time to think about it because he was early – Frank was always early – and would have to wait for Dinah, who was generally late.

When she did arrive she watched him for a moment, and smiled. There he was sitting so neatly, a folded morning paper in his lap, gazing away into the middle distance not yet seeing her. He always looks just right, she thought, it was the word that suited him. Her mother was going to eat him.

Dinah Prescott had kept out of touch with her parents for all the years she'd been in London, not from any animosity towards them, rather the opposite. She was now a serious mature student, twenty-six years old, who had already held down some pretty responsible jobs before deciding on a change of direction, and further study. When she was young she harboured thoughts of bringing home to Dublin some utterly disreputable character as a possible life partner, someone so unseemly her parents would have to object. A crook might do, a drug addict might be better and one of the Sex Pistols would have been ideal but none had been available. It was no use just thinking coloured, her parents were all for the multi-racial society, nor would outlandish politics be a bar, they would have accepted an anarchist, a Maoist or an unfrocked priest if he would make their darling daughter happy. For Dr and Mrs Prescott were so laid-back liberal they were unshockable, which became a burden on Dinah as she grew up. All her friends at school and, later, at college had terrible rows with their parents over their choice of mates, and when it came to choosing partners or even husbands there were traumatic events, terrible things were said on the lines of: "Never darken our doors again" or "You'll bring your mother's grey hair in sorrow to the grave . . ."

Poor Dinah was no match for these tales. She was never attracted to the kind of men her parents should have objected to. She only liked nice men, and there couldn't be anyone nicer than Franklyn Davey.

He turned and saw her, and grinned. She kissed him on the back of his ear.

Halfway across the Irish Sea, she said to him: "I suppose you left all your work tidy and shipshape back at Gillorns?"

"I think so. Although I have an impression that I forgot something, but I can't remember what it is."

"It's unlike you to forget anything to do with work, Frank, so it can't be that important. Outside of the office, well, that's different. Did you pack that blue shirt I said I liked?"

"Er . . . I'm not sure."

"There, you see. What's it to do with anyway, this forgotten thing you've half remembered?"

Frank had managed to tuck the loose thread into one bundle. "It must be in connection with the Egerton girl. Maybe it's just the feeling I have that it's unfinished business."

"And you don't like unfinished business, it doesn't stack away neatly into the folds of your memory until it's wrapped up."

She really does understand me, thought Frank, gazing at her fondly. Fondly could also mean foolishly but he didn't care.

"You've got me taped, Dinah darling."

"Yes," she said. "Now about this Miss Lillian Egerton, you've told me something of her, do you want to unravel her a bit more?"

71

"It's these conflicting stories. With most people you're prepared for different points of view. Take a matrimonial: one sees an outraged husband, the other side sees a bully, his mates say he's a great chap, her friends say he's a bastard. All that's perfectly normal."

"Dear me," said Dinah. "I don't think I should let you loose on my parents."

"What?" Frank turned in his seat to look squarely at her. "You're being funny," he accused.

"Never mind that. How does this attitude problem affect your Lily of the Valley?" From the moment Franklyn had spoken to her about this Egerton girl, Dinah had had her suspicions. When he had described her hair, her clothes, her eyes it showed he was a good observer, truly a people person. But that could go too far. Naturally as she had been his first client he would have taken more than a passing interest in her, but Dinah now wondered if the interest had been purely professional. Would he always be able to separate the two, the legal involvement and the personal interest?

Perhaps he was too nice, too decent for the general practice of law where he was laid open to the tricks and travesties of humankind, and might have been safer still walking the purer paths of Chancery where you might go for days and not see another person. But then, thought Dinah, even there some red-haired floozie of a typist might still pop out of a cupboard and grab him. She sighed. She had reached this conclusion about Franklyn Davey before; the only way to save him was to grab him herself.

He was at the moment busily unwrapping a mint humbug with the same concentration he would bring to drafting a sticky clause in a contract. He was considering his answer to her question of a while back. He had found that travelling by air gave one pause for thought.

"It's not just the diversity of other people's views of her, Harry Hopkirk's, for example, or Alex's that bothers me. It's also the effect she has on me."

Dinah noticed that he used the present tense, even though the girl was no longer his client. So this was ongoing, and becoming obsessional; she would have to be firm and nip it in the bud.

"It seems to me," she said, "that she's being manipulative. She tries to be whatever other people want her to be, or rather how she wants them to think of her." Dinah felt she was wobbling a bit; she could write an essay on the subject but found it a bit difficult to get the words right without a textbook on hand. "It's a tendency among young girls of your Lillian's age, they do want to be noticed, to be different from their peer group."

Frank shook his head. "But I saw her change. Her whole identity seemed to alter in the space of a few minutes. One reason I told you about her, Di, was that I did wonder if there would be a psychological basis for her odd behaviour – and that's your line of study."

Dinah eyed him severely. "How did you figure that one out?"

"Isn't it possible for people to be possessed at different times by different personalities? Isn't there something called multiple personality?"

Dinah was trying hard to restrain rising anger.

"Hold on, Franklyn. You're a lawyer, remember, not a psychologist, and I can tell you right now that that whole myth of multiple personality has been shown up to be exactly that – a myth."

But Frank, once he got an idea in his head, was dogged. "Wasn't there a film about a woman with a lot of different personalities?"

Dinah exploded. "Oh, of course, everybody remembers the film, the little girl and the bucketful of snakes. But analytical psychology has moved on since then even if Hollywood hasn't. Cases of multiple personality have been declining for years since things like schizophrenia have been found to be a chemical imbalance. No, Frank, take it from me, your Miss Egerton is just a teenager who wants to draw attention to herself and away from the offences she commits."

There was no time for Frank to answer. They fastened their

seatbelts as the captain informed them that they were about to land in Dublin.

"And about time too," remarked the man on the other side of Frank, "if we'd gone on any longer we'd have been in New York, and I haven't the ticket for it."

Frank knew he'd arrived in Ireland.

By the time Franklyn Davey and his Dinah had arrived in Dublin, Lennox Kemp was back in his office in Newtown. He felt tired, and drained of emotion. Sleep the night before had been impossible after the news given to him by John Upshire. They had both gone to the house of the de Lisles and told Alys. She had remained dry-eyed until assured that Lennox himself would meet George and tell him. This seemed to give her such enormous relief that her tears flowed like a pent-up stream. She would wait, she then told them stolidly, for George to come home – just as long as he knew before he returned.

So early next morning Kemp drove to Heathrow and was there long before the plane from Toronto was due. He wanted time to think, but thinking didn't really help. He went over and over in his mind how the thing was to be said. For all that this was the age of rapid electronic communication when words could flash in seconds over continents and oceans, there was still only the one way to tell such tidings as he had, and that was face to face. No wonder the immediate reaction had so often been: shoot the messenger.

Arrangements had been made. He sat in a comfortable chair in a private lounge. As soon as the delegation stepped off the place George de Lisle would be gently drawn aside and taken to that lounge. The senior civil servants who travelled with him would be quietly informed that the banker had personal business to see to at his home – perhaps an aide could be found to look after the official papers, etc., for the time being?

So George came into the room unencumbered, and shook Kemp's hand warmly, but warily. "What on earth brings you here, Lennox? Though I'm glad to see you." Friendly and composed, yet his voice shook a little; he had already guessed that something was wrong. "Is it Alys?" he asked. "Come on, man, tell me."

"No, George, it's not Alys." No room for hedging, this news must be given fast. "I'm afraid it's Elinor. She's dead."

George sat down. "Elinor? I can't believe it. She was fine when I left on Saturday. When was she taken ill? Or was there an accident?"

Again, no kindly screening of the facts. "I'm afraid that Elinor has been found murdered, George."

Coffee was brought for them by an airport official. Did they want breakfast? No, they did not.

Kemp told all that he knew, leaving out the bit about the drugs found by the police at the back of Dick Turpin's Cave. Superintendent Upshire had been adamant on the point. "We're keeping it from the press," he said.

George had his head in his hands while he listened. He raised it now.

"You say there was no sexual assault?"

Kemp shook his head. "It can only be confirmed by the post-mortem but the police surgeon who attended the scene found no such interference, and Elinor was fully clothed." These were but small crumbs of comfort, but they did matter to the stricken father. For the moment Kemp forgot that the girl had not been George's own daughter. When he was at the police station late last night talking to John Upshire and his officers, one of the inspectors had remarked: "Well, at least here we don't have a stepfather as chief suspect . . . Funny how often he's the perp."

Kemp had wondered at the time just how many of the men who heard the comment were into second marriages with children not their own. In the old fairy tales it was the wicked stepmother who was always to blame.

George's new concern was for Alys. Kemp assured him, as best he could, that she was all right, banal words but all he could raise. "She's gone through a bad time," he warned. "She didn't want you to know until the conference was over but I can assure you everything was done that could be done as soon as we were told Elinor was missing." He would like to have added that an earlier full-scale search would have made no difference, but, apart from a conjecture by the police doctor that the girl was dead before Sunday morning, he was not sure enough of the facts.

Dr Mumford could only certify the death itself, and the likely cause – strangulation by a ligature round the neck – and not the timing of it, that would be for the pathologist to determine. Dr Mumford was apt to throw his opinion about, and John Upshire for one would have liked to believe him on this occasion – if only to reassure Alys de Lisle that procrastination had not added to the tragedy.

"Do you want me to drive you to Newtown?" Kemp asked when they had swallowed their coffee without tasting it.

"They've laid on a car," said George, heavily. "Thanks all the same. Anyway, isn't it time you were back in your office?"

In many ways Kemp was relieved. What were they to talk about, two men in a car with nothing to say? Already the murder investigation had begun; until at least the first stages had been carried out there was no point in speculation. Once the media got hold of it there would be speculation enough – a grim prospect indeed.

Eleven

Dinah's parents didn't live in Dublin – she had never said they did, Franklyn had only assumed it and he should have known better than to assume without evidence. Dinah had arranged for a hire car by which they progressed by surprisingly wide roads and pastures green, strictly observing Eire's sensible speed limit – it came with the territory – and stopping for nourishment on the way, until they reached somewhere called The Dingle, which Franklyn got confused with Dingley Dell. By this time it was dusk and he was seeing everything through a delightful Irish mist composed of three parts Guinness to one part weather. Dinah had stopped the car at the gate of a modish new bungalow tacked on, as was the way of the country, to an ivied ruin of a larger establishment.

"We're here," she said, "and you're either Daniel entering the lions' den or you're a wolf for the slaughter."

That had been Wednesday evening, it was now Sunday night, and they were at City Airport and nearly home. In a moment Dinah would take the tube to her flat, and he would haul his car out of the long-stay car-park and drive to Newtown. The four previous days had passed in a dream from which he was only now emerging. He had had to sober up on the journey back. He reckoned that getting engaged was supposed to be a sobering experience (though not necessarily so in Ireland) and called for reserves of earnest reflection on what had happened in the run-up to the final event.

Not that Franklyn Davey was displeased to find himself in the engaged state, he was in fact over the moon, it was just that it seemed to have happened without his knowledge. Everything about the visit to the land they called The Dingle had been pleasurable: the walks through squally showers on shingly beaches, the trips to rocky outcrops known as local beauty spots or tourist attractions which couldn't even be glimpsed because of driving rain, the calls on innumerable friends or relations of Dinah's who held out food and drink all hours of the day or night in houses where fires smoked and draughts were not excluded. Or the houses were so up to date they were furnished in minimal style so that you had to sit on the floor to get near the stove.

Dinah's father was in general practice, a great doctor, they all said, and known throughout the district for the decent man he was. To Frank he seemed so laid back that if he went any further he'd have disappeared under the carpet. He and Frank got along famously, and, as Dinah had predicted, her mother could have eaten him, collar, tie, blue shirt and all . . .

All this Irishness of the last four days was still with him on his return. The Sunday papers were on the mat, he picked them up but didn't read them. After a bite to eat he went to bed, had a long, lovely bout of pillow talk, at a distance, with Dinah, then he went off into sound sleep.

Something of the haze of euphoria remained with him even as he entered Gillorns on the Monday morning. He actually caught his foot on the rug outside his office door, and stumbled. It brought him partly back to normality and he hoped it hadn't been an omen.

He was not reassured by Joan who had noticed his slip and only half commiserated when she brought in his mail.

"Don't bring your Irish troubles here," she said, "we've enough of our own."

For once her banter lacked conviction. Frank looked at her sharply. "What's wrong then, Joan? Nothing personal, I hope."

She stared at him soberly for a moment. "Where on earth have you been?" she asked.

"Only the far west of Ireland. Why?"

"Don't they have newspapers, television and all that?"

"They probably do, it's just that I never saw any . . . Come on, what's up?"

"You really haven't heard . . ." Joan sat down. "Then I'd better tell you. No, what's happened doesn't affect me personally nor the firm, I suppose. But the de Lisles are such friends of Mr Kemp's . . . There's been a murder in Newtown, Franklyn. The de Lisles' daughter, Elinor, she was found strangled in Emberton Woods last Tuesday night. Of course the news didn't break until lunchtime on Wednesday – by that time you were probably in the air."

"Have they any idea who did it?"

"Oh, everyone has ideas. The papers are full of them, and local gossip is full of speculation. Mr Kemp has had a word with us all. I think he was really explaining to the other partners and the staff that he might be out of the office a lot these days. I know Mr Belchamber and Mr Cantley are taking over some of his work. I think Mr Kemp and his wife are trying to support Mrs de Lisle as best they can. She's in a bad way." Joan stopped as if looking at the banality of her words but unable to improve on them.

"I don't know the de Lisles," said Frank. "Wasn't he a bank manager here who went on to higher things in the City? I can just imagine . . . No, I don't think I can, to be honest."

"Neither can I," said Joan, brushing away a slight feeling of guilt at the excitement of being the first person to bring the news. She proceeded to tell Franklyn all she knew about the murder of the schoolgirl, most of it gleaned from the media, although there were one or two extra tidbits going the rounds of the office because the firm, through their senior partner, were closer to the de Lisle family.

"It's affected the whole town," she finished, "and certainly kept people out of those awful woods." Joan and her husband were both incomers from further up the county, and lived on the other side of the town from Emberton. "I could never see why people went there anyway. It's not a real forest, just a rubbish dump really."

Franklyn didn't share her view; he rather liked the woods, and in the early days of his courting of Dinah, when neither of them had a place of their own, they had taken advantage of summer evenings under the trees.

"I don't know," he said, "they're about the only bit of countryside the developers left the town. The Green Belt, as they called it, was a bit of a joke and look how they've eaten into it! But if they start pulling down trees people will complain – it's not something they can hide. Could you find out if Mr Kemp is in, Joan? I'd like to offer my support if there's any of his work I could take over."

Joan got up. "I'll give you a buzz. You haven't a lot of appointments for today."

"Just as well. I've got all those building contracts to draft for Horrocks." He was quiet for a moment. "I know it's always said that life must go on, but I can't help thinking about that poor girl. And the parents. If you could find me a local paper."

"Last week's *Newtown Gazette*'s in the office. I'll let you have a copy. They say that the scene of the crime was swarming with reporters by the weekend, not to mention the police."

"Scene of crime – what a horrible expression! I wonder how many years it takes to eradicate the slur on some beauty spot or other."

"This was no beauty spot, I can tell you," said Joan, robustly, "just a dirty old den they say Dick Turpin used, as if it ought to have had a place in history. Well, it has now." She threw the last remark over her shoulder as she went out of the door.

Franklyn sat back and thought about it. Where had he heard of the place? It was quite recently, and in this very office. That was it, Dick Turpin's Cave. Lillian Egerton had told him about it.

Joan rang him through. "Mr Kemp's in his office, and he'd like to see you, Frank."

"Glad to see you back, Frank." Lennox Kemp had always called him Frank, never Franklyn. If asked he would have said that when the young man had come to the firm straight from university he had had the open countenance to fit the name, and a certain candour which would stick.

"How was the Irish holiday?"

"I got engaged."

Kemp didn't laugh as others in the office had done; indeed he seemed pleased.

"To your Dinah, I hope?"

Frank nodded but felt enough time had been expended on himself. "I'm terribly sorry about what's happened while I was away. I've only just been told."

"Well, I'd better fill you in . . ." By now Kemp was weary and frustrated. The story of Elinor de Lisle's death had been told again and again in the media as well as being thoroughly chewed over in the shops and pubs of Newtown. The police were about to make an arrest, the police were baffled; because of a London connection the Met were being called in, because it was a local matter the Newtown force were going it alone. All was speculation, nothing was certain except the grim facts of the actual murder.

"The only comfort for the de Lisles is that Elinor wasn't sexually assaulted in any way, and that an earlier search would not have prevented the killing." Even as Kemp was speaking he was seeing Alys's face; she was not to be comforted, she wept for her daughter, she wept for herself, she was guilty she repeated over and over again, nothing would take away the blame that was hers.

"The body was moved, you see," Kemp told Frank. "The pathologist is sure of that. She was not killed where she was found, and the post-mortem seems to show she died on the Saturday night she went missing."

"I guess you might have to be out of the office more than usual, Mr Kemp. Can I take over some of your work?"

"That's why I wanted to see you. I've already had a word with Michael and Perry that I might get tied up with this case more than I should like to. George de Lisle has asked me to do some rooting about. It's not that he doesn't trust the police—"

"But he knows your reputation," Frank suggested with a smile.

Kemp shook his head. "At this moment, Frank, I'd rather I didn't have it. This one's too close to home."

"You can count on me. I could take on some of your appointments."

"I'd be glad if you would. I'm due to talk to the headmaster

81

of Thornton Comprehensive later this morning and I've got a couple of clients coming in."

"I can take both of them," said Frank, briskly, "I've got spare time."

"You're not supposed to say that in any office," said Kemp, "but your honesty does you credit. Anyway, the first is easy enough. Mr Horrocks, our builder friend, I think you're already working on his leases. He's in a spot of bother with the planners. Actually, he's in the wrong but just be very tactful in telling him so. He must know by now that he can't win when he's up against the Newtown Planning Department – they're the Lord's Anointed around here."

"I think I can handle Mr Horrocks. I've already recognised his problem."

"The other is a Mrs Roding, a Mrs Margaret Roding. I've no idea what it's about." As he spoke Kemp was wondering why the name was strange and yet familiar. He had a good memory and if he'd had more time he'd have worked it out for himself. On an impulse he buzzed his secretary: "Audrey? That Mrs Roding who made the appointment for this morning, did she give you an address?" He waited a moment. "Runneymede Crescent? Thanks."

He remembered. A council house, about ten years ago. It was after a funeral, and a little woman sitting hunched among other women . . . It began to come back to him. But how much was relevant?

"Margaret Roding?" Frank was querying the name. "That's a village in Essex."

"I know, but it's also the name of my client. I came across her once before. It was an old case of mine, before your time. If it's the same Margaret Roding, be nice to her. She had a hard life, and lost a son in unpleasant circumstances. She probably just wants to make her will, she must be getting on a bit. She was left an annuity, I remember, perhaps she wants some advice about it. Anyway, Frank, I'd be obliged if you would see these two appointments. Audrey will let you have the files, though in Mrs Roding's case it may well be a simple matter of Legal Aid advice." He looked at his watch. "Damn, if I don't get a move on I'll be late for school. It wouldn't be the first time." He grinned at Franklyn, grabbed his briefcase off the desk and made for the door.

Twelve

Lennox Kemp was unsure of his welcome at the comprehensive school. He had been to see the headmaster on the
Monday after Elinor's disappearance, but that visit had been,
as it were, under false pretences. Alys de Lisle had been so
anxious for any scrap of information and Kemp had considered
the school a likely source, even if he was barred from giving
the real reason for his interest. He had argued with both the de
Lisle women that it might be wise to take the headmaster into
their confidence but again the risk that the awful news might
reach George outweighed for them all other considerations.

So Kemp had gone into the arena with neither weapon nor
armour, and been promptly bitten in half by Mr Dougal Hunter
who was a formidable fellow not only to his pupils. He had
observed caustically that Mr Kemp was not a parent, and the
fact that he was a solicitor cut no ice with him, rather the
opposite – he'd had trouble with solicitors before.

Kemp said that he had been delegated by George de Lisle
to enquire as to the school's interest in the event at the Drill
Hall because Elinor had been forbidden by him to attend it, but
that if there had been a group going, sanctioned by the school,
then her act of disobedience might be mitigated. Even as Kemp
had spun the tale as adroitly as he knew how he could feel it
was a non-runner with the head who must have heard more
lame excuses than a stipendiary magistrate. However, Dougal
Hunter did seem unnecessarily prickly on the whole subject
of the Drill Hall concert, and strongly denied that the school
had any part in the distribution of tickets or sponsorship of
the event. Mr Hunter had the music master in, a timid little
man (with a headmaster like Hunter, it would be difficult to

be other than timid) who said he'd left it entirely to the boys' jazz club to liaise with the people from London who hired the Drill Hall.

Mr Dougal Hunter had finished Kemp off by bringing up reinforcements in the shape – and a splendid shape she was too – of Mrs Elspeth Hunter who was not only a senior mistress but the headmaster's wife, who told him to go back and tell Mr and Mrs de Lisle that they would shortly be receiving a letter from the school in connection with their daughter. Kemp had stuck to his guns at this point and stubbornly held on, as he could do when he liked, by asking for details. Apparently it had been noticed by her teachers in the last six months that Elinor's standards were slipping, she was careless in her work and disrespectful in her behaviour. Elspeth Hunter softened sufficiently to say they were genuinely worried about the girl who, when she first came to the school from the private establishment she'd attended, had seemed an ideal pupil.

Of course none of this was ever passed on to either Alys or George. As Kemp thought of it now he was overwhelmed by a sense of utter desolation. Death removes all human attributes, the good with the bad. Reminded of that letter which would never be sent he felt the pain of a loss which wasn't his but stung as sharply as if it had been . . .

What did it matter now, those lost lessons, the lip she gave her teachers, she was thirteen for God's sake. He was swept by anger. She'd every right to live, be as cheeky as she liked, plague her parents, shock her grandmother.

Emotion will get you nowhere, he told himself, what you need are facts.

Dougal Hunter was no less fearsome today than he had been previously, but at least this time his anger was deflected so that all Kemp came in for was a scatter of gun pellets. The headmaster was bent on defending his school to the last ditch – where some of the right-wing press were hinting it belonged: "School-sponsored rave after which pupil died." "Was Ecstasy on the programme at the school jazz event?" These were the kind of headlines he could either ignore or dispute.

"We've decided to ignore them on the advice of our law-yers," said Elspeth Hunter who was sitting in on the meeting. "And Dougal is coming round to the idea, aren't you, dear?"

Dougal was coming round to the idea slowly rather like a bull in the arena when he knows the odds are against him. "You're well advised," Kemp put in, quickly, speaking both tactfully and truthfully, "they're only speculating, like everyone else."

"Hmm." Dougal didn't seem convinced. "Anyway, what are you here for, Mr Kemp? Surely we've told you all we know."

Kemp knew that Chief Superintendent Upshire had been both careful and thorough in his investigation at the school. People had been interviewed, and a picture of Elinor's school days and, more particularly, her school chums, had been sensitively built up. All the same there were still things that Kemp wanted to know for himself. He turned to Elspeth.

"There was a boy, Ronnie Sears, who was a friend of Elinor's. Do you think I might talk to him? And your music master, Mr Higgins, would you mind if I had another word with him?"

Elspeth glanced at her husband. "I don't see why everyone blames Geoff Higgins," Dougal burst out. "That jazz club wasn't even his idea in the first place. The boys got it up themselves in the last two terms. All Geoff Higgins was trying to do was teach the syllabus. I won't have him blamed for what happened."

"It's all right, Dougal, nobody's blaming Geoff."

"Oh, yes, they are. They're out to blame all of us, and the whole comprehensive system. Haven't you ever noticed that all these journalists from the posh papers went to private schools, aye and to Eton and Oxford." The headmaster wasn't to be thwarted of an opportunity for a display of wrath, righteous or otherwise. Elspeth seemed used to it, perhaps it had run through their married life like an underground stream. She just smiled at Kemp, as if to say this behaviour in the child is perfectly normal . . .

Dougal Hunter seemed surprised to find Kemp still there.

"Of course there's no reason why you can't talk to Mr Higgins, and any of the boys you want to. The police have already been through this place with a tooth-comb. I don't know what they expected to find – subversive material, I suppose." He calmed down as suddenly as he flared up, and showed himself as a fair man, perhaps even an astute one. "I'm just sorry that the last time you came here, Mr Kemp, you didn't take me into your confidence. You did not tell me that one of my pupils had disappeared."

"I'm sorry for that, too." Kemp meant what he said. "I was on an impossible errand but I couldn't betray Mrs de Lisle's trust."

"Poor woman." There was genuine feeling in Elspeth Hunter's voice. "She is not the strongest . . ." – for a moment Kemp thought she was about to say "character" – " . . . in health. I quite understand how she felt with her husband away. I remember when they brought Elinor to the school the first time. I did tell Mrs de Lisle that her daughter might find it rather different from St Olive's – that's the private school she had been in."

"And did she? Find it different, I mean."

Elspeth looked at her husband for a reply. "On the contrary, Elinor settled in very quickly, and I think it's fair to say that in her first years at Thornton she was a considerable success."

Elspeth took up the tale. "Her teachers were very pleased with her, she had great abilities. And of course she was very popular. It was only in the last six months there was a falling-off. She got into the wrong set."

The headmaster's buzzer went off, and he answered it. "Mr Higgins is free if you'd like to go round to the music room. And that boy Ronald Sears is there so you can kill two birds with one . . . er . . ." The words seemed to stick in his throat, so he gave a great "hurumph" instead of finishing the sentence, and he ushered Kemp to the door, not exactly pushing him out but certainly glad to be rid of him.

Geoff Higgins might look like a mouse for he had all the proper characteristics, neat pointed ears, crushed-up features and a small quivering pink nose, but he was a mouse rampant

– he squeaked on a high note when out of range of the headmaster.

Yes, he had known Elinor de Lisle well for she had come to him originally as a keen flute player from her private primary school, and yes, he had hopes for her. Intelligent, yes, gifted probably not – at least musically – well spoken and fairly biddable. But all that changed as she made her way up the school. She had effectively dropped out of music, refused to play in the school orchestra and had become, in Mr Higgins' words, an ordinary, run-of-the-mill teenager.

He shrugged off Kemp's persistent questioning. "How do I know?" he asked. "They take up one thing, then another, they have no concentration, they flip from subject to subject like moths. How do I know what takes their fancy? One minute it's music, the next it's drama, or they want to save the whales."

"Did you like her?" Kemp found it necessary to be direct with this will-o'-the-wisp.

"Not particularly," said Geoff Higgins. "I'm not sure I like any of them. Do you have to like people before you take them on as clients?"

Kemp had to admit this could hardly be a criteria for running a successful legal practice. He was finding the music master a fidgety person, not easy to pin down. He seemed to have a chip on his shoulder but it wasn't easy to find out why because it might not have been relevant to the killing of Elinor de Lisle.

"This school orchestra?" he asked, "was that the same as the jazz club?"

Mr Higgins turned on him, hissing, more snake than mouse. "Of course not. These youngsters, you give them a bit of a start – what's in the music syllabus – and they take off on their own in an utterly new direction."

"All rock-and-roll rather than the classics, is that what you mean?"

Geoff Higgins maintained a schoolmasterly silence which was enough for Kemp to realise that, musically speaking, he'd no idea what he was talking about, so he changed the subject. "This event at the Drill Hall, I understand that the school jazz club managed to get a foot in the door?"

"Nothing to do with me. They were out on their own, Mr Kemp. That's what I told the police, and it's the truth. They asked me about tickets, what would I have to do with tickets for a show like that? They went on about it as if it was the last night of the Proms."

"Perhaps you would give me the names of the boys who were in this group who played at the Drill Hall that night?"

"Well, one of them is waiting now. Ronald Sears. You said you wanted to see him. Doubt if he can tell you much."

Let me be the judge of that, said Kemp to himself as Geoff Higgins opened the door. Why is it I don't seem to be popular with teachers today? The thought came as he heard the door slammed shut behind him.

A tall youth got up from where he was sitting on a bench in the corridor. "Mr Kemp? Mr Hunter said you wanted to see me."

"Yes, I do. Is there anywhere without ears?"

Ron Sears grinned. "The playground's the most private," he said, "though everyone looks out the windows at you."

"The playground it is, then."

They sat at the side of the netball pitch, facing the serried ranks of glass where shadows passed, and sometimes heads poked out.

"Was Elinor a friend of yours, Ron?"

"Sort of."

"One of your group?"

"You mean the band? No, she was never in that."

"Did she have a ticket for the event at the Drill Hall?"

Ron shrugged. "I don't know. I've told the police all this."

"I'm asking you. I'm not the police. I work for Elinor's parents and all they want to know is whether she went there that night."

Ron hesitated. "Yes, she got a ticket. I gave her one because she asked. She used to be a friend of mine, then for some reason she went off me."

"Any idea why?"

"I guess there was someone else. But it wasn't in the school, or I'd have known."

"She was a bit young to go with someone outside of school, Ron. Are you sure she found someone else?"

Ronald Sears stared up at the school buildings. "I don't think it was another bloke. You don't understand. Nobody does. Elinor was old for her age, if you see what I mean. She wasn't looking for dates, she said she wasn't interested in boys. And I believed her. She wanted something, I dunno. Something exciting. She tried the music thing, and the gym and all that . . . Trouble was, Elinor was good at whatever she tried, then she'd get fed up, and want something new. Know what I mean?"

Kemp did know what he meant; it was the best insight he'd been given into the dead girl's character.

"You said Elinor got a ticket, but did she go to the concert?"

"I dunno. I was pretty busy getting the gig going and all that, but I never saw her. And I would have, I think, if she'd been there."

"If she didn't go out with boys from the school, then who did she go around with? Monica Hodge?"

"You gotta be joking. Monica Hodge is a slug. Elinor couldn't shake her off. Nah, when Elinor wanted company it was out of school."

"Come on, Ron, you must have some idea."

"I never told the police. None of their business. But I was worried, like, about Ellie. You won't tell her parents, will you?"

"Ron. All I want to do is find her killer. And it's up to me to decide what to tell her parents. You must let me decide what is good for them to know and what is not."

Ronald Sears was quiet for so long that Kemp thought he'd lost him. Then he said: "There was this gang from lower down the estate. Some of them are school-leavers who haven't got jobs, some of them are from up-country, or even London. They're older than us, some of them even have motor bikes . . ." Ron brooded on that for a minute as if wondering whether he'd be tempted by such a vehicle. "Well, Elinor told me they'd asked her to be one of their gang."

"Surely not. She was only thirteen."

Ron shrugged. "Maybe she was boasting a bit. But I could see the idea appealed to her."

Kemp raised his eyebrows. "Sounds a long way from playing the flute in the school orchestra."

"Did old Higgins tell you about that? Bet he didn't tell you the whole story."

"He said Elinor had rather gone off the idea of being a flautist."

Ron gave a hoot of laughter. "You bet she did when he put a hand on her bottom. She slapped his face. Everybody fell about laughing. All the girls knew about Higgins' little antics but nobody before Elinor had had the balls to biff him one." Ronald grinned at the memory. "He was in trouble at the last school he taught in but he got away with it."

"Did you tell all this to the police?"

"'Course not. None of their business. It's just that one of the boys was at school in Durham before coming to Newtown, and he'd seen the item in the paper up there about Mr Higgins. He reckoned Higgins was lucky, the girl withdrew the charges and the whole thing was dropped. I bet old Higgins thought Elinor was going to tell on him but that wasn't her way. She told me she'd keep it up her sleeve for later."

Kemp drove out of Thornton Comprehensive with a higher opinion of its headmaster than when he'd arrived; not just the misdemeanours of pupils to contend with but latent peculiarities in the staff also . . .

Thirteen

Franklyn Davey felt that he had handled Mr Horrocks rather well. He had spoken to him courteously but firmly; rather than lay down the law he had merely spread it out smoothly before the builder so that he must have realised that he hadn't a snowball's hope in hell of putting up twenty-four semi-detached bungalows when planning consent had only been given for twenty. Mr Horrocks had expressed his thanks on leaving, and at no time had he hinted that he knew Davey had been brought on as a substitute for Kemp.

Mrs Roding, however, could not get over the fact that she was being fobbed off with a lesser mortal than Lennox Kemp. She kept looking round as if to see him lurking in a corner. "But it was Mr Kemp I wanted to see," she'd said, on entering. "I don't know whether I could speak my mind to anyone else. I'm not used to it, see, not coming regularly into lawyers' offices."

Frank assured her of his own ability to listen, and that he had Mr Kemp's full confidence to hear whatever she had to say, but it was still not enough.

"He was good to me that time before. He was the only one that understood. All them hoity-toity folks they never come to the funeral, did they? But he came, I remember him coming."

As Frank had no idea what she was talking about, although Kemp had murmured something about it being an old case, he decided not to hurry the woman, let her brood on the past for a minute while he got out a fresh note pad.

"Now what can I help you with, Mrs Roding?" he asked eventually, when her rather watery eyes had stopped searching the room and settled on his.

"It's police harassment I want to know about."

It seemed a strange topic to engage the attention of such a woman as Margaret Roding. She was in her late fifties, respectable-looking and nicely dressed. "Surely you've not been troubled . . ." Frank began, and was met by a withering look.

"Of course it's not me. What do you take me for? It's my grandson, our Darren, they keep on bothering. It's got that me and his mother, well we've hardly had a wink of sleep these last few nights. They're coming to our doors in twos and threes, asking questions of Darren, then taking him down to the police station for more questions. Sometimes he's never got time to finish his dinner. And he never knew that girl, never laid eyes on her. He's told them that over and over but they still keep on at him. What I want to know is how far does it have to go before it's harassment?"

Franklyn wasn't going to grasp that particular nettle until he had a few facts to go on.

"Because the murder is local the police will have to question a lot of people, Mrs Roding. It can't be helped even if it does seem intrusive. How old is Darren?"

"Sixteen. He's left school but couldn't get a job, not right away, but Megan, that's his mother, she's on the check-outs at Tesco so he gets a bit of shelf-stacking at weekends."

"And they used to live with you at . . ." – he looked down at his notes – " . . . 32 Runneymede Crescent. Is that part of the Thornton Estate?"

She nodded. "I was on my own, see, so when she gets the divorce from Ted, well Megan wanted to get out of Hackney and I don't blame her, so I said she and Darren could live with me till they got a place of their own. I don't regret it. She's a good worker, Megan, and I couldn't want for a better daughter-in-law."

"What about Darren's father?"

Mrs Roding drew herself up. "You don't want to know about him. You just ask Mr Kemp about Ted Roding. Though he's my own son I don't mind telling you that he's a wrong 'un. Same's his dad was . . ." The lines on Margaret Roding's face

93

deepened, and she seemed a lot older. "My husband, Ted's father, he was what they call a recidivist." She brought the word out straight as she must have heard it dozens of times from police, probation officers and social workers. "He died in Pentonville."

Frank was sorting out the good from the bad; Ted Roding was a criminal, as his father had been, but Margaret Roding and her daughter-in-law, Megan, were on the side of the angels. Where did that leave Darren Roding?

The Newtown police would almost certainly be conversant with the background to the Roding family both here and in London, and possibly felt that that was reason enough to pay attention to Mrs Roding's grandson. But this wasn't some petty crime, this was murder, they must have something more.

"I think it would be better if I saw Darren myself. Of course I shall look very carefully at the behaviour of the local constabulary. Perhaps you could give me some idea of the amount of time they have spent in questioning your grandson? If, as you say, he didn't even know the girl—"

"That's what he's said, over and over," Margaret Roding interrupted, "and I believe him. Why, he was never even at that school where she was, he was at school in London."

"Has he made friends since he came here? Do you know who he tends to go around with?"

"I dunno really. He's not likely to talk to his grandma about his mates, is he? But I know he's had Jeff Coyne and Kevin Williams to the house, though they're a bit older than him. They've got no work neither, so they hang around the streets. I don't like that kind of thing for Darren but the youth club it don't open all day – can't get the staff, so there's nowheres for them to go."

Frank noted the names, and learned they lived the other side of the estate, in Marshall Avenue. Curiosity made him ask: "Does Darren know a girl called Lillian Egerton?"

Mrs Roding made a face. "Our Darren's not one for the girls, Mr Davey, and I've never heard mention of her. Darren's still at the stage he prefers going out with his mates, rather than bother with girlfriends. That's why I think it's all wrong the police keeping on at him – they're not doing it with any of his pals. His mother asked both Jeff and Kevin if the police had been round to their houses, but no, it's only Darren."

"Then I'd better see him as soon as possible," said Frank, briskly. "Can he come into the office here this afternoon?"

Margaret Roding brightened up. At least something was being done.

"I'll make sure he comes in," she said, as she went to the door.

"Just give my secretary a call about the time, Mrs Roding."

"I'll do that." Then she turned, hesitantly, "You don't think Mr Kemp might be in by then? It's not that you haven't been helpful, listening to me the way you have, but . . . Mr Kemp, he were the only one that could handle our Ted back then, treated him like a human being, he did, like as he'd never been in prison. Reckon he was the only man Ted had any respect for."

It was well known in the office of Gillorns that Lennox Kemp at one time had had a soft spot for those on the borderland of crime, the petty crooks and casual thieves who just couldn't help it, slipping back time and time again into prison life until they knew it better than the streets. He'd spoken of them as a sad lot, lacking the brains to get on and the resources to fuel their little ambitions. Ted Roding sounded like one of them.

Thinking in this way, Franklyn wondered if he should get Mr Kemp to interview Darren. He was becoming conscious of his own lack of experience in dealing with what Dinah would call "real people" instead of just names on title deeds or trust documents. He found he was overlooking things which might be important. For instance, when Mr Kemp was talking about the murder, why had Frank forgotten to tell him about that odd remark of the Egerton girl? She had asked him about tracing a missing person – and that was the Monday morning after the girl had disappeared, but no one was supposed to know it then.

Lennox Kemp had had to talk his wife Mary into going to stay with Alys.

"But I hardly know her," she protested when told it was Alys's wish. "Why me? She and George must have lots of friends. What about those people she plays bridge with, the Finlays?"

"Apparently she simply can't face anyone they know. She can't bear sympathy."

"Does she think I'm without it?" Mary smiled. "Or is it because I have nursing experience?"

"I don't think it's as simple as that."

Kemp sighed. It had all been explained clearly enough by George de Lisle, but even then it hadn't made sense.

It was imperative that George went up to London for a couple of days; there was urgent business arising from the Toronto Conference which only he could attend to properly. And there was Evelyn . . .

"I have to take her home, Lennox," he said, "She has her routines, well, people of her age do, don't they? She's already been away longer than she intended, and she says she must go to her hairdresser and her chiropodist, get her laundry done, see her housekeeper. I know, I know, in the middle of our tragedy such things seem trivial but they're what keeps my mother from falling apart. And there's nothing she can do here in Newtown, she knows that. I shall take her up to Chelsea and stay with her while I attend to these finance matters that are pressing. It's not fair on my colleagues that I am away so long. Alys understands." When he spoke of his wife, George's voice faltered.

Kemp understood. Alys was in a very bad way, seeing nobody, spending much of her time in bed.

"I think she is anxious for Evelyn to leave," George went on, "her being there puts an additional strain on Alys. They have never really got on. You might think that Elinor's death would bring them together."

"It often doesn't work that way," said Kemp. Inadequately, he felt.

"I can't leave Alys alone in that house, and she won't go and stay with friends, although many have asked her. She says she cannot bear their sympathy. Even when our cleaner comes Alys stays in the bedroom with the door closed."

"But she would have Mary?"

"It was her suggestion. Someone she doesn't really know, was what she said. Someone from outside. Of course I was keen on the idea. Otherwise I had been going to ask Dr Parfitt to suggest a nursing agency. We're lucky to have a doctor like Gerald, he's been of enormous help. To get back to Mary, can you persuade her to come?"

So here he was being persuasive. He knew that his wife had just those qualities called for in a situation like this, and he did not simply mean her nursing skill. What Mary would bring to Fairlawn was her own calm presence, someone who would be there but not impinge upon the house. Kemp often wondered how it came about, this gift Mary had to self-efface when in the presence of grief. She would take on people's troubles, be a willing ear if they needed a listener, or a silent help in practical matters where life must go on.

"I'll only talk about Elinor if that's what Alys wants," she was saying now. "Or we'll speak of other things. She's not been alone since Elinor disappeared, and yet who can she say her feelings to? Only George, but he's part of her sorrow."

"I think there's relief that George's mother has gone back to London."

"A formidable woman, Evelyn de Lisle. I liked her, but I can see they'd be of no great comfort to each other. It was like a great gulf between them the night Elinor went missing, now they're oceans apart."

"I believe they hardly spoke that night," said Kemp. "John Upshire sent a WPC up to the house after I'd spoken to him. Just in case there were any telephone calls."

"I'd wondered about that. Did he really think there might have been a kidnapping?"

"Well, it could have been. George is known to be well off, certainly by the standards of folk round here. John wanted to ensure that if there was a call he had someone unobtrusive in the house."

97

Mary smiled. "How did Mrs de Lisle, senior, take the presence of a policewoman in the kitchen?"

"She thought she was the maid and treated her so. But of course no call came."

"Well, I'll get my little case ready and go up to Alys. Poor soul, it's the least I can do. Mrs Chard comes in to do the cleaning tomorrow, Lennox, don't forget. She won't bother you with questions as she does me, though I tell her nothing. That reminds me, she says that Elinor's real father, that Charlie Hawkins who went to Australia – he died there last year."

"So John told me. Of course they'd checked, it would be the natural thing to do."

Again, on the way up to Fairlawn, Mary's mind was full of the woman she was going to. All that beauty, all that grace, they counted for nothing when tragedy struck. All that remained was character and that might well swing with the wind.

Fourteen

It was hardly surprising that Darren Roding didn't turn up to keep any appointment that afternoon. Even Franklyn at his most optimistic had doubted he would; after all, what teenager these days listened to his grandmother?

Darren was in two minds about the Newtown police. The gang despised them, said they weren't a patch on the Met, an opinion which Darren had endorsed but now he wasn't so sure. They'd all jeered at the sergeant they called Hopalong who seemed to have a down on Lily. Of course they all knew why. Before he got married to that London woman cop – who was probably a dyke anyway – the sergeant had had a crush on Lily, so now she had him by the balls which was why none of the gang ever got really challenged. But now Darren was being picked on, and he wasn't sure how long he could keep his nerve under questioning. All he could do was keep his mouth shut like Lily's sister had said. She'd made a good job that night of cleaning him up, she even sponged the mud from his anorak before she'd hung it up. While he had been in the shower at 24 Marshall Avenue he'd heard the roar of a motor bike starting, and he guessed that the sounds had been Lily going off to the den, after he'd told what he'd seen there.

Had she got there before the police? Had she managed to get hold of the drugs which Darren was sure were cached there? There'd been no mention of drugs in the report in the paper about the finding of the body by the search party. Darren reckoned that must have been within two hours of him being there. When he thought of that he was scared but Lillian had told him herself not to worry, nobody would ever know he'd been there. But she wouldn't say anything about whether she had gone there, whether she'd got there before the police. "Best you don't know, Darren," she'd told him, "best you know nothing. Keep your lip buttoned and you'll be all right."

But he wasn't all right. So far as he knew none of the rest of the gang had been questioned. They'd met once since the discovery of the body, not in Lillian's house but just on the common with their bikes so as to make it look casual, like. Lily had been quite fierce. "No one's to say nought, got that?" They'd all nodded. She could be scary sometimes, could Lily.

About three o'clock there was a knock at the door; the police again, always in pairs. This time it was PC Andrews, a bit of a weed, and Sergeant Martin. Would he come down to the station? Fat lot of good it would do refusing to go. Sergeant Martin even helped him on with his anorak. It was a good one, a bright canary yellow, he'd bought it with the money he earned at weekends and he knew it was better than the rest of the gang could afford.

Even Sergeant Martin – who was always trying to look like the guy in LAPD just because he had ginger hair and no expression – liked the anorak: "Nice colour," he remarked as he followed Darren down the path to the car. It was all in full view of the neighbours, of course, but they must be used to it by now, thought Darren sardonically, though he was glad all the same that his mother was at work.

This time at the station it was an older officer who sat at the table beside the recording machine, an Inspector West, he said he was.

They ran through the whole story once again: no, he'd never heard of Elinor de Lisle, nor had he ever seen her. No, he didn't know what they meant by the Turpins, and he didn't belong to any gang. And then there was the Saturday night up at the Drill Hall, yes he'd been there, he'd got a ticket from someone. Was it Jeff Coyne? Could have been, he couldn't remember. Yes he was with Jeff all evening, and Kevin Williams. Did he know Lillian Egerton? Lillian who? He didn't think so. He might have met her with his mates but he wasn't interested in girls.

Then the questions about his bike, how long he'd had it, where'd he go on it? And that brought them round to the Tuesday night. No, he'd not been out, he'd stayed in and watched the telly; he even gave them the names of the programmes as he'd done time and again. Was there anyone in the house with him? No, his mother was on late shift.

"You know your mother has worked hard for you, Darren." This was the older officer talking, while old Hopalong prowled around in the background. "You owe her a good deal." What was he on about? All Darren could do was nod.

"Then why don't you come clean, lad, and tell us where you went on your bike that Tuesday night, say between the hours of seven and nine?"

"I never went out. I was in all evening watching telly."

This was different from the other times of questioning. The officers were more confident, and now they'd put this older geezer on.

Hopalong – Darren realised that he was now an inspector – took a chair and brought it up to the other side of the table. "Now, Darren, I want you to be very careful in what you say. You were seen by two witnesses on that Tuesday evening riding your bike up into Emberton Woods. They recognised you by your yellow jacket, and they know you. So I shall ask you again, did you leave your house that Tuesday evening between the hours of seven and nine?"

Darren squirmed in his seat, but clamped his mouth shut. If he kept quiet they couldn't know anything for certain. He remembered his dad on one of the few occasions when he'd taken him to the swings in Victoria Park, saying to him: "Always stay shtum, son, when the Bill's about."

"We shall be ordering DNA tests, Darren." Inspector West spoke the words softly but they struck terror into Darren's heart. Could they do this? Another piece of advice from his father came into his head: "I want a brief. I want a solicitor," he cried wildly.

Fifteen

Frank might have been disappointed at the non-appearance of Darren Roding that afternoon but he was not to be deprived entirely of representation from Thornton Estate. About three o'clock a worried Joan interrupted his pure cogitation regarding clauses to extricate Mr Horrocks from his building dilemma.

"It's the Egerton girl," said Joan, "she's demanding to see you. I know you've got a free moment, but . . ."

Frank still retained his curiosity about Lillian Egerton, though he was not disposed to show it. He looked at his watch. "I could fit her in," he said, curbing a rising excitement which surprised him.

She was all in black. The black leather jacket barely covered her neat bottom tightly rounded by black leggings, and the knee-high boots with the sharp heels were black too, and shiny. Her hair, shoulder-length but today smooth as silk was black too but streaked with crimson and framed her perky little face like the draped curtains of a music-hall stage. This absurd image momentarily took Frank's breath away. He regained it by standing up, and gesturing at the chair across from his desk.

She took it with a swift economy of movement, pulled it up closer and rested, first her arm then her chin on her uplifted palm. The speed with which she settled herself gave him little chance. By the time he had got out the words "And how may I help you, Miss Egerton?" she was off.

"What's police harassment? You're the lawyer, you tell me. What's the legal definition then for when the fuzz push it too far? Don't give me no Legal Aid forms, Mr Davey, I'll pay whatever's the going rate."

Since the visit of Mrs Roding, and because he thought Mr Kemp might question him about it, Franklyn had looked it up. What he'd found was hardly enlightening. It was in those new areas of law which the textbooks had not yet caught up with; it was a matter of discretion (an easy way out when nobody knew how else to deal with it) or, to put it more bluntly, you played both sides against the middle and said it all depended on the circumstances, and, as lawyers with the police were all supposed to belong to the same jolly band of law and order, that was that.

"Well," she demanded.

"I presume Inspector Hopkirk has been making a nuisance of himself again. Is it his activities you're complaining about?"

"It's the whole bleedin' lot of them. Just because there's been a murder they think they can bust in anywhere and ride the range like the Four Horsemen of the Acop . . . of the Eclipse . . ."

"The Four Horsemen of the what?" Frank relaxed in a great hoot of laughter.

She could not help but catch the infection of his laughter, but all she allowed herself was a faint grin before gathering speed again.

"Coming into my house at all hours. Handling my stuff. What if I tell 'em to get the hell out? Get a search warrant, Harry Hopkirk says, real nasty, so I let 'em in. When they gets to the bedroom I says to him, just as nasty, 'That's what you always wanted – your smutty hands in my knickers.' You should've seen his face! The young bloke who's with him goes red as a beetroot and slams my underwear drawer shut so fast he catches his finger and swears. I says to him, 'I don't give a monkey's what you take outta there, have a good peek while you're about it.' Then old Hoppy he's poking around in the kitchen, even looking in the washing machine and asking how many times a week do I use it. I tells him to get lost. I'm not going to answer to that pig. What I want to know is how's I put a stop to it? If this ain't harassment I'm Posh Spice. Right?"

Franklyn took refuge in trying to gather a few facts.

"How many times have they come questioning you?"

"Um . . . It was Friday they searched the place, then there's two different ones come Saturday to have a look at my bike, they have a good look round the other vehicles out there which I tell them have nothing to do with me. Then Sunday evening it's Hopkirk again with another sergeant, Martin something who's the smarmy kind. 'Let's sit down and have a little chat,' says he, spreading his bottom in my best armchair. 'Or we can take a statement from you down at the nick' – that's Hopkirk putting his oar in, playing the heavy like this was LA. You know people talk about kids being influenced by violence on the telly – well, I've got news for you, it's the coppers you've got to watch out for, they all think they're so tough."

Franklyn had to break in. "Exactly what questions have they been asking you?"

"Where was I the night of the do at the Drill Hall, did I know this de Lisle chick, where was I on pretty well every night since . . . I know they're going around asking lots of people the same questions. It only shows they know they're up the creek and haven't a clue who killed her. What I says to them is, those are dangerous woods, there's a lot of very funny folk go around in Emberton Woods that could have done her in."

"Well, Lillian, can I ask you the same questions? Where were you on the night of the event at the Drill Hall?"

She gave him the benefit of a wide-eyed green stare.

"I was up in London, wasn't I?"

"So you weren't up at the Hall?"

"Who says I was?"

"I only want the truth, Lily. What were you doing in London?"

"Clubbing, of course. I often go up of a Saturday night. I got a gentleman friend who likes to take me where the music's funky."

"Which club were you at on that particular night?"

"I dunno its name. Off Leicester Square, Coventry Street, I think. We got there about half-ten and left around three, then he drives me home. And, save you asking, no, he didn't stay."

"You wouldn't mind me asking his name?"

"He's Simon Marco, and he's in the music business."

"Was he connected with the event at the Drill Hall?"

"I guess he'd something to do with getting the acts. He owns clubs in the West End, don't he? But the venue and all that's up to the locals, so there weren't no need for him to be there. Anyway, the Drill Hall in Newton is hardly Simon's scene, he's into a lot more sophisticated stuff."

"And you told the police all this?"

"Sure. Seems this Sergeant Martin knows who Simon is so he's quite impressed."

Frank wondered if they'd check out Lillian's story. It sounded terribly like the one with the moonlight and the white Mercedes. She was quick to read his mind.

"Simon drives a Porsche," she said. "Anyway, he says he's off to Amsterdam to sign up a couple of rock bands so Harry Hopkirk'll have to wait, won't he, if he wants to question him." With scarcely a pause or change of tone, she went on: "I wouldn't mind a cup of tea."

He told Joan on the buzzer and while he was doing so his client got up and began walking restlessly up and down.

"Lillian," he said, "when you came into my office last time, you asked me how we begin to search for missing persons. Do you remember?"

"I might have." She had her back to him. "It was just one of those things you sometimes want to know. Why?"

"Did you know Elinor de Lisle?"

She was standing looking out of the window, from which there was in fact no view other than a brick wall. "Why shouldn't I?"

"No reason why not. Did you meet at the youth club?"

"Could have." She came back to her seat as Joan brought in two mugs of tea, milk and sugar. She seized one, sugared it heavily and raised it to her lips. "I needed that," she said as she replaced the mug on the tray. Her voice was softer, and she was being careful with her movements.

It's going to happen, thought Frank, and this time before my very eyes. As he sipped his tea he scrutinised her carefully. She looked tired. The reddish lights in her hair were dimmed like electric lamp bulbs on the blink.

"What you staring at?" she asked him, with only a residual hint of her former belligerence.

"Sorry," he said, automatically. "Did you tell Inspector Hopkirk or any of the other officers that you knew Elinor de Lisle?"

"Course not. No business of theirs. Anyway she must have known hundreds of people in Newtown."

"I'm not asking them, Lily, I'm asking you. How well did you know her? Did you see her often at the youth club or elsewhere?"

"I might have done."

"Why, for heaven's sake, girl, didn't you tell the police?" Franklyn was angry with her, and didn't mind showing it.

"Tell that lot who I'm friends with? Not likely. They've got the dirtiest minds in Newtown, them down there at the station. Oh, yes, I can just hear them: nineteen-year-old going out with a thirteen-year-old schoolgirl, they'd be going on about lezzies in the wink of an eye."

Frank thought about this aspect. There was always something near the truth in Lillian Egerton's remarks and at this moment when he was sure she was tiring, changing, whatever, she was abandoning her other language. He wanted to encourage her, not in the fantasies (which he was certain they were) but in the real world of her mind – if he could get to it.

"Think this through carefully, Lillian. If you don't tell the police that you knew Elinor they'll find it out from somewhere else, and then they'll suspect you of knowing more about her death than other people . . . They'll want to know why you didn't tell them something so important."

"I've told you," she said, sulkily. "I don't trust Sergeant Hopkirk."

"Inspector Hopkirk. Now will you tell me more? How long have you known Elinor, and where did you go together?"

She had no fluency left, her speech had lost its rhythms, and her words came haltingly. Frank was reminded of trying to take a statement from an invalid in a hospital bed, weak after an operation, only just coherent and stumbling after words as if they were wayward signs the mind had to grab in passing. He had the same sensation now as he gentled and probed, watched and listened . . .

She had met Elinor at the youth club about six months ago when they were in the same netball team. Lily had long since given that up, and after a bit so did Elinor, though she told her parents she still played – it served as an excuse when she and Lily went off together. It wasn't difficult to see why they had been drawn to each other; both, in their own way, were beauties, both were "loners" – this was in each case a self-description and meant no more than that they happened at the time to be dissatisfied with the group they were going about with. Although Lily was evasive when talking of the Turpins, she hinted that for Elinor the gang had been a great attraction. The sense of belonging to a set older than her in years, and of a totally different class meant excitement, and a chance to show off her own considerable feats of daring. Lily described Elinor as a proper little go-er, she'd try anything so long as she got applause for it, no, she didn't think it was just showing-off, more like wanting to prove herself over and over again.

It was when Franklyn tried to get down to dates and times that he realised he was losing Lily's attention. She would get up and wander round the room, stare out of the window, and wouldn't look directly at him so that he could hardly make out her muttered answers.

"Did you expect to see Elinor up at the Drill Hall that Saturday night, or at the youth club?"

"I was in London." A flat voice, devoid of expression.

"Were you meeting her on the Sunday, the day after? She didn't turn up. Is that why you asked me about missing persons when you were in here on Monday morning?" It seemed to him a reasonable sequence of events.

"Anybody might ask any lawyer that." It was a poor attempt at her former aggressive style.

He had to broach the subject. It was so obvious what the police had been searching for at her house in view of the stuff found in the cave.

"Lillian, you have to tell the police that Elinor and you were friends but before you do so I must ask you whether you or any of your group ever used drugs?"

She laughed then. But it wasn't her usual high-pitched cackle which rang in the ears yet had genuine merriment behind it. This laugh was bitter.

"So that's what it's all about. I might have guessed. That's all the fuzz is after – someone to pin a drugs charge on. And you, Franklyn Davey, should be ashamed of yourself for taking part in their little game." This was a new Lillian, an angry Lillian, speaking in a level tone but spitting out words to wound.

He watched her in silence for a moment, unsure how to respond. Finally he said, as gently as he could manage, "Come back and sit down, Lily."

She came obediently, did as she was told and looked him straight in the eye. Her mascara was smudged where she had been rubbing at it with a paper tissue.

"You bloody fool," she told him. "Of course we do drugs. What do you take us for, two-year-old toddlers? And, of course, the police know we do drugs but there's never been charges, has there? That's 'cos we're careful, that's what I taught the gang, how to be careful. They've never had the evidence, the pigs, and they're not going to find it in my house, that's for sure." Despite the trace of bravado her voice was feeble now, and this was no longer the creature who had come in so full of righteous indignation.

He had been watching the difference in her but even so he was alarmed by the sudden slump of her shoulders. It was as if her head was about to hit the desk. He put a hand on her arm, but she shook it off.

"Water," she gasped. He ran to the door. When he returned with a tumblerful he watched her drink it, first in small sips and then in great gulps. She put the glass down, and stood up.

"I have to get back to work," she said, heavily. "I never said I'd be taking the whole afternoon off. There's things to do before we close at half-past five."

Given a white overall to hide the black leather and the long, liquorice-stick legs, this was Lillian Egerton, the highly praised worker at Bernes.

"Wait – Miss Egerton – wait . . . I'll phone Mr Bexby. I'll explain."

She trudged to the door, her leaden feet incongruous in the flashy boots. "Don't bother," she said. "I wouldn't want to put you to the trouble."

Frank did phone the personnel manager at Bernes. He explained that he'd had a visit from Miss Egerton and kept her longer than expected. "Thanks for letting me know," said Alex. "We've been worried about our Lillian. I don't think she's very well."

That was enough for Frank. He'd been going to do it anyway; he rang the health centre and asked which of the doctors had a patient named Miss Lillian Egerton. It was Dr John Sutherland, the senior partner, and Frank made an appointment for that evening.

Although Lily had said she got her pills from a Dr Parfitt Frank was glad that she was on Dr Sutherland's list since he knew him from his earlier time in Newtown whereas he gathered that Dr Parfitt was a newcomer to the practice. He would have liked to have met him, however, if only to find out why he'd dropped out as a witness in that first bizarre incident. Perhaps Dr Sutherland could enlighten him on that. Any discussion on Lily's medical condition would of course be circumscribed by professional ethics on both sides so it might take some persuasion on Frank's part for the good doctor to open up. But surely as her legal adviser he had a right to know . . .

It wasn't drugs. Whatever her opinion of him, Frank was not a complete bonehead. Out of his own experience and from observation of Dinah's student friends, many of whom indulged in illegal substances just as he and Dinah drank wine, he could spot those under the influence of their favourite drug, and he was certain that in all the interviews he'd had with Lillian Egerton her erratic behaviour could in no wise be caused by drugs. Her abrupt changes of moods, the more subtle alterations to face and voice, these went beyond any easy explanation.

He was still deep in such speculations when Joan bustled in. "I'm ever so sorry to have to ask you," she said, not in the least sorry since she had taken exception to his long session with Miss Egerton, "but there's a Mrs Hodge and her daughter in the waiting room to see Mr Kemp and he's not back yet, and Mrs Hodge is going berserk."

"And you want me to see her?"

"Just to get her out of my hair."

"OK. Let them all come. I hope it's a simple matter she wants to see a lawyer about – like suing the Queen for libel."

"Oh, no, it's something right up your street, Franklyn. Police harassment. You're the expert."

Frank groaned. "Not another one." A thought suddenly struck him. "Were these Hodges in the waiting room when my last client went out?" He knew the passage to the outside door went through the waiting area. "Were you there at the time?"

"I was," said Joan, stoutly. "I've been pandering to Mrs Hodge for the last half-hour, bribing her with cups of tea to save her climbing the walls in disgust. Yeah, I saw your Miss Egerton go, though, and a right frump she looked. I don't know what you do to her but she leaves here like a rape victim."

"Stop that, Joan. Did Mrs Hodge or her daughter seem to know Miss Egerton?"

"No way. They looked at her like they thought that if she was the kind of low-class client you went in for, then they didn't want to see you. Why? Should they have known her?"

"Police harassment isn't as common as all that, and at the moment it must be connected to the murder."

Joan's eyes opened wider.

"And the Egerton girl's involved?"

"I didn't say that. And don't gossip, Joan – you know it's one of Mr Kemp's rules of the office, and he doesn't have many of those."

Joan acknowledged the mild reproof with a smart boy scout salute, and went off to fetch the Hodges.

After his interview of Lillian Egerton where he'd had to be on his toes and alert to every nuance of her voice and gesture, Frank found Estelle Hodge comparatively easy. She had already expended much of her indignation on the staff of Gillorns for keeping her waiting – and in a public area, too, when she felt she deserved a private room.

"As if my poor daughter hasn't had enough of all this hanging about waiting for someone to take her statement – not once but three times – and then find it's some underling constable who's barely literate."

The poor daughter looked smug but she slid a glance out of the corner of her eye at Frank as if she was not averse to getting attention from any young man, literate or otherwise. She was plump as to body and face, and had her mother's features. She had just turned fourteen, and hoped that she might grow out of both conditions.

Estelle was further appalled by the laxity of Gillorns' inter-office communications system when she learned that Mr Kemp had not informed Frank as to exactly who she was, and the important part that her daughter, Monica, had played in the case of Elinor de Lisle. She soon brought him up to date with that, at the same time giving him her opinions on many subjects, young people nowadays, the horrors of comprehensive education ("we'd never have sent her there if it hadn't been for the de Lisles deciding it was the place for Elinor, and now see where that mistake has led . . .") and the state of the country in general. Without her actually saying so, Frank gathered that Estelle had married beneath her else she would never have been living in Newtown.

When Frank attempted to ask Monica certain questions about her friendship with Elinor – questions which he now knew had more point since Lillian's admission that she too had been close to the dead girl – Mrs Hodge interrupted so many times that he very nearly told her to shut up. Apparently this was one of her objections to the police, a certain WPC Morris had told her to do just that.

Eventually Frank's patience had nearly run out. "You must let Monica answer for herself," he said. "The procedure followed by the police was, from what you tell me, perfectly correct, and you were present at all interviews. But it is Monica's voice we want to hear."

Monica looked pleasantly surprised at hearing her mother being told off; it was a rare occurrence. As a result she was kindly disposed towards Franklyn Davey, and more open in her answers than she had been to the police.

He intuited that her friendship with the dead girl was not all it had been cracked up to be by both sets of parents. There was some girlish spite in the way she talked of Elinor, and plainly there had been envy. This was understandable; both girls had inherited their mothers' looks.

Monica stressed that she was older than Elinor, even though it was only a matter of months, so that when they arrived at the school she had tried to protect Elinor from the influence of what she called "the rough element". Mrs Hodge gave a nod of approval at the phrase. But, despite Monica's guiding hand it seemed that Elinor was soon whisked off to join an older set. Through them she began going to the youth club after school rather than take part in the activities provided by the school itself. In time, but reluctantly, Monica said that she had followed. No, she didn't like it much. She hated pop music, and a lot of the boys were from the council estate.

"Not what Monica's used to," put in Mrs Hodge. "She takes lessons from Mr Higgins, the music master – classical piano, you know."

Monica went red, but whether at her mother's evident snobbery, or the mention of Mr Higgins, Frank couldn't be sure. Anyway, he wasn't interested in the girl's musical talent.

"Can I ask you again, Monica, about the night Elinor went missing. How did she seem when you left her house to go to the youth club?"

"Off-hand, as usual. That's what she was like." Monica moistened her lips; this was her party piece and she had it word-perfect. The more she told the story of what happened the more it became relief for her resentment and anger, the more frustrated because she had no one to be a target for such feelings. Had she been younger, Monica

112

would have stamped her foot and cried when she told how Elinor had left her almost as soon as they'd got to the club.

She hadn't even bothered to change into her sports gear, she never opened her locker where it was kept. She'd just tossed her head, and told Monica: "I'm not going to play in any silly old team, you can go and find someone else." Then Elinor had just stalked out of the door, and Monica never saw her again. At that point in her story Monica did suddenly seem to realise a deeper feeling within herself, and she stopped, her voice quavering as it died away.

Frank waited a second or two. "I understand how you feel, Monica. Just a few more questions. Did anyone go out at the same time as Elinor?"

"Not that I saw. But then I had to find another team member so I wasn't really looking. We never really got a game going that night. A lot of the others left later and we all knew where they were going."

"You mean to the Drill Hall?"

"Yeah." She leaned forward as if to take Frank into her confidence. "The school rock band should never have been allowed to go there, Mr Davey, those people who run raves like that – that's what they call them – they bring drugs down from London." She nodded her head vigorously to stress the importance of her information. "Ecstasy pills, or worse." She sat back, satisfied she had made her point, and Frank could almost hear Mrs Hodge's silent applause.

"Is that what they say?" He made the comment levelly. "Tell me, Monica, did you ever hear Elinor talk about a friend she had who worked at Bernes?"

"The factory on the industrial estate? Good lord, no. I don't think she'd be friends with a factory girl." Monica gave a little laugh. "That wouldn't be Elinor's style at all. She liked . . ." – she searched for the words – "the high life, like what you see on the television, excitement I suppose you call it. I think that's why she went with this gang."

"What gang was that?"

"The police know all about them, Mr Davey," Mrs Hodge

said, as her daughter seemed loath to answer, "and of course Monica never had anything to do with them."

"Did the police ask you about them, Monica?"

"Yeah, but I said I didn't know any of them."

"But you knew that Elinor was going around with them?" She nodded.

"Hooligans, they are, that's what Inspector Hopkirk called them. They're well-known in the town, and should have been locked up long ago." Mrs Hodge seethed in her smart tweed costume but it was her daughter on whom Frank was concentrating.

She had gone red, she kept moving her legs as if she was uncomfortable. "Yes, Monica?" he prompted.

It was to her mother she turned. "Mum? D'you mind if I speak to Mr Davey alone?"

Mrs Hodge reared up like an endangered cobra. "Of course I mind. I wasn't going to leave you on your own to answer police questions, and I'm not—"

"Mother." Monica's voice was surprisingly sharp. "I mean it . . . Mr Davey is different from the police, and anyway this has nothing to do with their enquiries. It's something confidential and, no, it's not to do with me."

Franklyn intervened. "Mrs Hodge, perhaps I should listen to Monica, and you allow me to be the judge of whether it should go any further."

"Please, Mum. It's important but I can't tell you because you'll only go and tell other people. I don't see why you can't just trust me for once."

Torn between a desire to know and showing in front of a third party that she didn't trust her own daughter, Mrs Hodge had no choice. Frank held the door wide open for her as she swept out.

"Thanks," said Monica as he came back to his chair. "This thing, it's been worrying me. I didn't tell the police because it was private, see, to someone else."

"That's all right, Monica, take your time. Is it about Elinor?"

She nodded. "The last few weeks, she'd been worried. That wasn't like her, usually she never worries, she sails through

everything, school work, parent rows, all that – even exams.
It all came so easy for her." She stopped as if looking back at
what she'd said. "But lately she was different, she was really
bothered about something – and I don't think it was herself.
Only the day before she disappeared I asked her what was
wrong. And she told me. Mr Davey, Elinor was worried about
her mother . . ."

"About Mrs de Lisle?"

Monica nodded her head, and sat back looking at him with
serious eyes. "She said, as if she was talking to herself – well,
that's sometimes the way she was with me, as if I wasn't there
– she said, 'I don't know what to do about my mum. I'm
really anxious for her.' So I asked her what she meant but
she wouldn't tell me, just said, 'I think she's in some kind of
trouble.'"

Frank had taken a note; it might be important to take
down exactly what the girl was saying, though it seemed
inconsequential.

"Can you remember anything else about this conversation?
How did it start for instance."

Monica thought hard. "I think it was about her grandmother.
My mother thinks the world of her – a real lady, she calls her."
She suddenly remembered. "Oh, I know what it was. I said I
thought she was sensible because she didn't believe in taking
lots of pills like some old ladies, and Elinor said something
like, 'I'm not worried about *her*, it's my mother who has to keep
going to the doctor.'" Monica's mouth formed a round O. "You
don't think Mrs de Lisle's got cancer and Elinor suspected it?
It's always happening on the telly, people getting cancer and
their loved ones not knowing." For a moment she was caught
up in the familiar scenario.

Franklyn thought about it, too. "Well, thank you for telling
me, Monica. I think I agree with you that it should go
no further. It's not something the police need to know, and
it wouldn't be wise for it to be spread about. I shall assure
your mother that it is a personal matter concerning someone else, and that you are wise to keep it to yourself. And now
before you go I'd better get back to why she brought you here.

Were you upset by the police questions?"

"Not really." Monica seemed to have become less the dutiful daughter, more the independent girl in the last few minutes. "It was more Mum who objected, not me. And when I thought about Elinor I nearly cried." Suddenly she blurted out: "I really am sorry about Elinor and it only gets worse when I think about her. We don't know the truth about each other till something happens. I don't know what to say . . ." She was crying now, her eyes filled up with tears. Frank handed her a tissue and waited.

"Can I tell you something else, Mr Davey, but don't tell Mum." She didn't wait for any assurance from him, so anxious was she to let it all out. "That gang she was in, she said she'd ask if I could join but they wouldn't have me. And if they did do drugs Elinor said she never would, she was against them."

Plump and not very pretty, it wasn't in Monica's nature to be other than honest. Frank came round his desk and gave her shoulders a squeeze. "You're all right, Monica – and I won't tell your mum. Come on and we'll assure her we've got no evidence here of police brutality. Compared to NYPD the Newtown force are gentlemen."

She gave him a weak grin. "I don't think I'd mind being questioned by the one with the ginger hair – I think he's cute."

Sixteen

Lennox Kemp was listening to the sad tale of Darren Roding, and getting a strong feeling of déjà vu. It must have been a dozen or more years since he had faced the father, Ted Roding, and now here was the son. But he reminded himself that Ted Roding, having got his younger brother Kevin into trouble, had done all he could to get him out of it. Unfortunately Kevin had mixed with players out of his league and paid for it with his young life. Ted, feeling let down – he would never have phrased it so civilly – by the forces of law and order, resumed his life of crime but he'd married a good 'un, who had the sense to divorce him and light out for a new life in Newtown with Grandma Margaret Roding.

Kemp had felt almost a part of this family saga, and for a time indeed had been their only lifeline out of the submerged depths of East End crime. From what he had now learned from this young scion of the Rodings it was the women who pulled for the shore . . . But despite his mother's efforts here was Darren on the brink.

He had not yet been charged, but all the noises being made between Sergeant Martin and Inspector Hopkirk signalled that charges were imminent. Kemp was going to wait until he'd talked to John Upshire before forming any opinion. For the moment, he wanted a clear field, knowing nothing, so that he could assess the truth or otherwise of what Darren himself had to say.

He had told the officers concerned that he wanted to see his client alone and had been given this interview room, slightly refurbished since the station was built in the fifties but not by much. Despite the introduction of new electronic equipment and strip-lighting the scratched table still wobbled, and bore the stains of a thousand cups of tea. Nothing really changes, thought Kemp, there are rooms like these in police stations all over the country where people sweat and swear and think up all manner of fancy fables. I just hope this isn't another of them.

"There's no use my being here if you don't come up with the truth, Darren," he'd told him at the outset. "I can spot a lie a mile away so don't try any on me. I don't give a damn what tales you've spun to those officers. What I want is the truth or I'm not going to listen."

The young man gulped. I hope he knows the difference between falsehood and verifiable fact, Lennox thought, the little lies and the big ones – his dad never could, which is why he spent so much time in jail. Darren had Ted Roding's build but his features were more delicate, not so much the bruiser type. He also had better manners – perhaps there was something to be said for the comprehensive school system after all.

On the other side of the table Darren was sussing out the situation. He'd been all right at first when they took him down to the nick, kept his cool, if he said nought they'd get nought. But now they were talking witnesses, and he knew he hadn't been exactly inconspicuous when he'd panicked that Tuesday night and fled the woods. Worse, they were talking DNA. He'd read about that, it meant they could trace bodily fluids. And he'd been sick all over the body. Even thinking of it made his stomach heave.

His gran had talked a lot about this lawyer, Lennox Kemp, how he'd helped the family that time his Uncle Kevin got killed. Legend had it the rozzers were to blame for that, least that's what his dad said, and that this Kemp hadn't gone along with them. Mebbe he wouldn't be in cahoots with them now. That's why his grandmother had gone to see Kemp when the police came pestering. But there was no way to get them off his back now they had witnesses – or were they only bluffing?

Darren admired his dad – but only up to a point. That part of Darren's brain which Thornton Comprehensive had educated, even if inadequately, told him the reason Ted Roding was a loser was because he didn't think things through properly and the Bill were always a step ahead of him. Darren didn't want to go down that same road.

These lengthy cogitations had taken up the hour or two while the officers waited for the solicitor to show up. By the time Darren was facing Kemp in the interview room and even before the warning about lying, Darren had come to a decision: he would tell the truth to this Kemp bloke. After all, he'd done nothing wrong, so the truth shouldn't hurt him.

Kemp listened as the whole story was blurted out. The only bit that Darren kept back was his real reason for going out to look for the den. It didn't really matter. Kemp was still one of the few people who knew that a cache of Ecstasy tablets and some cannabis all neatly wrapped in plastic shopping bags had been found at the back of the cave. He guessed it was more than curiosity that had led Darren to explore Emberton Woods.

All he said was, "So you'd never been to this cave place before, Darren?"

"I heard them talk, like. Said they used it in the summer, and it was all kitted out with a bit of carpet and old chairs."

"And was it?"

"Was it what?"

"Kitted out with carpet and chairs?"

Darren snorted. "I never got to look, did I? She was there, right at the entrance like I told you."

"And did you recognise her?"

"Well, not really. I didn't know her if that's what you mean. Didn't know her name, f'rinstance."

"But she was someone you'd seen before?"

"Mebbe once or twice I'd see her at Lily's place. I think she hung around with Lily."

"Ah, yes, Lily's place. What you've told me about that is a bit sketchy. Can I have some more information?"

He waited while Darren sorted through a few things in his mind. They'd been crafty, these coppers, never letting on where the gang met but acting like they knew. None of the group had got back together since the body was found. Word had got around – it came to Darren via Jeff Coyne – that they should lie low a while. And – this was a definite order – not go near Lily's place.

"Come on, Darren," said Kemp, "you ran to this Lily person after you'd stumbled over the body. Now why would you do that? Why not go into Newtown Police Station on the way home, or go straight home and phone them. Wouldn't that have been sensible?"

He did make it sound reasonable but nobody acts that way when it happens, certainly not in any cop series Darren had seen. He couldn't explain just why he'd panicked, nor why the house of Lily Egerton seemed like a refuge that night.

He did his best to tell it like it was, stumbling over the words as he tried to cover the guilt he felt. By revealing all he knew about their HQ he was not only betraying Lily Egerton but the whole gang.

"She was a sort of leader, like. Even the older boys . . . they did what she said. I thought because it was their place, that den, she ought to know about the girl being there. I had to tell somebody, Mr Kemp, I was in a right stew." He paled as he remembered it. "As for going to the police – you've gotta be joking. Me and them, we've never really got on."

Kemp hadn't really been serious in suggesting that Darren should have reported the discovery of the body like any worthy citizen might have been expected to do; Darren's relations with any police force, whether the Met or local, would be bound up with the experiences of father Ted, so that a police station would be the last place he'd run to.

"And this Lily person – when you saw her that night, she didn't suggest it would be better to call the police?"

"I told you, I never even saw Lily. It were her sister that took me in, and told me to clean myself up. But I know she told Lily because when I was in the downstairs shower I heard Lily go off on that motor bike of hers. It didn't half roar as she went up the road."

"And what happened then?"

"Well, like I said, I did as the woman told me, shoved my muddy clothes in the washing machine and hung around in the sitting-room watching the telly till it was dry – actually it was still a bit damp but Lily's sister said I could borrow some gear from the hall closet to go home in. Lily keeps a lot of stuff for the ga . . . for the group in that closet, sports stuff and that. Although she's only a girl, Lily is right on the ball when it comes to clothes, all the shirts and trainers are the big names, and she hands them out real generous."

"Did she come back while you were there?"

"No, I never saw her. Her sister says for me to just leave quietly when my stuff's dry and I never saw her again neither. I think she'd gone to bed. She was probably getting ready for bed when I got there. She's heaps older than Lily and a bit of a frump but I'll say this for her, she cleaned all the mud off my anorak and left it hanging in the hall for me."

"She certainly looked after you like a mother . . . I wonder why?" Kemp was more or less talking to himself.

"Had you met her before, this sister of Lily's?"

"I might've done. She wasn't the sort you'd notice. Not like Lily, now she's a real go-er, terrific looks and great personality. It's no wonder the other members of the group have been following her around for yonks. I only came into it in the last few months."

Asking about the activities of the gang, which he noticed Darren had changed into a group as if to distance himself from any hint of nefarious doings, Kemp employed some tact. Aware that the young man had not wanted to betray his cronies nor their female leader, but had had no option, Kemp wasn't all that interested in the gang's former pranks – it would all be in a police file somewhere while the local constabulary waited for enough evidence to pounce. But he was interested in the possibility of wider, less innocent proclivities than spraying graffiti on garage doors, heaving bricks into people's gardens or shouting abuse through letter boxes. Having got young Roding into confessional mood, there was a chance to find out.

"You say the girl Lily is responsible for kitting out her team or whatever you call it. Does she also supply the drugs?"

Taken by surprise, Darren could only feign horror, and splutter: "Whoever said anything about drugs? Just because

121

I had a little run-in with the fuzz. Is that what they're trying to do, fit me up on a drugs rap?"

"Calm down, young Darren. Nobody's going to fit you up with anything while I'm around, so long as you stick to the truth with me. Now we'll come back to the question of drugs later. What I want to know before we have to go in front of those men next door is what you've told them to date."

Darren had of course given Inspector Hopkirk and Sergeant Martin the shorter version of that Tuesday night, simply that he'd been home all evening watching the telly and had never been beyond his own front door, that he certainly hadn't been wandering around in Emberton Woods.

"I suppose they took a good look at your bicycle?"

"They've still got it – tests, they said."

"And you tell me you pushed it into some bushes near the forest road?"

Darren nodded. "It were too muddy to ride it down that slope to the den."

"And I'll bet those bushes have maybe a wee scrape of paint on them. Oh, they know very well you were up and about in the woods that night, and they're not bluffing when they say they've got a witness or two."

"It's that bloody jacket of mine," said Darren, miserably. "Bright yellow – even Sergeant Martin remarked on the colour. Jesus!" He stopped suddenly. "I've just remembered . . . Something Lily told us. That Harry Hopkirk, he lives opposite her house in Marshall Avenue. He's been watching her for months, she says, either him or his missus, and she used to be a cop."

"Sounds as if you walked into a goldfish bowl that night. You'd been seen going in and seen going out, not to mention your bike was up in the woods. I think you're going to have to come clean with everything. If it's the truth, and you've told me everything, then you've nothing to fear. Now we have to talk about those nasty illegal substances. Have there been drugs handed out in this gang of yours?"

"Not to me, I swear it. I've had to stay clean because of that little spot of bother back in Hackney. If I was caught again I'd go down. I promised my mum."

"OK. But what about the others?"

"I think they got them when they wanted them, like. That's the way they talked anyway. When we'd all be sitting around at Lily's place they'd hand round a joint. Nothing serious, you know, not crack nor heroin. But they talked like they could get that too . . . I dunno, might have been just talk, making them sound big, you know. I heard someone say Lily could get bags of stuff when she went up to London – she knew some guys. Least that's what I heard, but you have to believe me, Mr Kemp, I stayed clear, I didn't want to take the risk."

"Hm." Kemp scratched his nose. "I think we'll go easy on any question about drugs. Just say you don't know what the others got up to, but you stayed clear. What you've told me is simply what you overheard and doesn't count, so there's no need to repeat it." He was thinking that it was up to Inspector Hopkirk, who seemed to be in charge of the case, to find out if individual members of the gang were into drugs and whether such a finding was relevant. He did not know Hopkirk personally but had heard of him. A keen careerist, with no imagination, he was an officer for whom promotion was the name of the game: that had been an off-the-record comment from John Upshire whose ranking as Chief Superintendent had come late because he had never sought it.

Kemp wondered if what the lad had said about Hopkirk keeping an eye on the house opposite were true.

"This girl, Lily – what's her other name?"

"Egerton. I don't know her sister's name."

"What did you mean about Inspector Hopkirk watching her? Why would he do that?"

"He's out to get her, that's why. What I heard from Jeff Williams was that when he were only a sergeant about a year ago, he starts asking Lily out and she gave him the brush-off. Not surprising – he's a right ugly bloke. Now he's married, and he's got this vendetta thing going about Lily. She gets a kick out of stringing him along, you know – she's quite daring, for a girl." She obviously had Darren's full admiration.

In view of the forthcoming interview Kemp thought it better to temper the lad's enthusiasm with a word of caution.

"If this Miss Egerton is already the subject of Inspector Hopkirk's displeasure, then the less you say of her the better. I want to get you out of here, Darren. Tell the truth about your own actions that Tuesday night, including your visit to her house. You may yourself be puzzled as to why her sister should help you, and you may wonder why the police weren't called. But these are matters beyond your knowledge."

Not far beyond it, of course, Kemp said to himself as he went off to inform the waiting officers that their victim was ready for the slaughter. Darren knew, just as he did, that things were not looking good for the Dick Turpins. It was in their den that the body had been found, she had been a friend, or at least an acquaintance of their leader – the repercussions would reach out and touch them all.

And I must be careful, thought Kemp. I must tread softly. This was the daughter of Alys and George de Lisle, their grief outweighs everything else.

Seventeen

About the time that Darren Roding was coming clean at the Newtown Police Station, Frank Davey was parking his car at the rear of the health centre, largely deserted at this time of night. The premises at 14 Bolton Street had once been the house and garden of a sole general practitioner, becoming a group practice with the advent of the NHS and eventually the present health centre occupied by four doctors and their attendant staff. Dr John Sutherland had been there longer than anyone else and, in his quiet way, had imposed his own ethos on the practice which was well run and user-friendly.

It was this latter quality which struck Frank as he approached the reception desk. The young lady was preparing to shut up shop, but she turned on Frank a pair of warm brown eyes which welcomed him into her immediate vicinity as if he were a long-lost puppy. "May I help you?" she breathed, letting her glance slide from the top of his head to the toes of his shoes.

"Er . . . I've an appointment with Dr Sutherland."

"You must be Mr Franklyn Davey?" Her tongue lingered on the syllables of his name even as she got it wrong. He guessed it was deliberate and made no move to correct her. "If you will just take a seat he'll be with you presently."

Even as she buttoned up her coat, and threw a scarf round her neck, she kept looking over at him with little smiles, and flutters of eyelashes. "Is it cold out?" she asked him across the intervening space of the waiting room. "It's freezing," Frank responded, which was true, "you'll need your mittens." Her laugh was a burble of delight as she went out of the door. Frank could not help staring after her; she was enough to make anyone a regular patient of the practice. He looked at the name on the desk: Crystal Stephens, receptionist. It hadn't only been her friendly manner which attracted him, she had that unusual combination of brown eyes and very pale blonde hair, which always gets a second glance. And she wore her hair short as Dinah did, so that it swung out from her head when she turned as she had done, prettily, just before she closed the door. Since he had become engaged, Franklyn was finding himself more and more interested in the looks of girls – at first he had been shocked at the tendency, but then accepted it as perhaps natural. He was comparing all females of a certain age with his one and only choice.

His thoughts were interrupted by a door opening along the corridor and a voice raised: "Is that you, Mr Davey? Would you like to come in?"

John Sutherland was in his early sixties, grey around the edges but as yet unbowed by the demands of his work.

"I gather you wanted to see me about a patient, Miss Egerton," he said once Frank was seated. "You're a lawyer, you must know there are limits to what I can tell you. First, though, can I ask why you want to know?"

Frank was prepared for that one.

"She asked me to act for her in the matter of a police summons."

"And the case was subsequently dropped."

"Was it because of her health, Dr Sutherland, or were there other reasons?"

"Why do you need to know? Surely the matter was over as far as you were concerned?"

"Miss Egerton still comes to see me. She's worried about the police attitude towards her – harassment, she calls it. I have to assess her veracity."

John Sutherland chuckled. Frank looked at him in surprise.

"You're a clever lad and no mistake," said the doctor. "You know I can't discuss a patient's medical condition with you, but you've thought of a way round that . . ."

"Her complaint about police harassment is real enough, but whether it's valid or not depends on—"

"Whether our Lillian's telling the truth or indulging in fantasy, eh?"

Frank sighed. He knew the doctor had got the upper hand but he had to pick up on any scrap of information. "She does seem to fantasise," he said. "I wondered if it was normal for her, I mean whether she does it all the time."

"Don't we all? Young people more than most, as they try to come to terms with a world perhaps not to their liking." The doctor was adept at avoiding the issue, as he no doubt had to be in practice. But Frank was determined not to be side-tracked.

"I've seen Miss Egerton three times in my office, and at each interview she's suddenly changed in the middle of it. Becomes someone different, I mean, in a short space of time. Then there's this file the police have on her, it's full of her alleged misdemeanours but also full of her own fantastic stories, stories which can't possibly be true . . . And yet . . ." He knew he was floundering, but at least he had the doctor's attention.

"You're puzzled and you're curious, am I right, Mr Davey?"

"I can assure you my curiosity isn't idle," said Frank.

"I didn't say it was. You may well have her best interests at heart, as I do . . . Oh, come on," he continued briskly, "I'll give you facts if that's all you want. I've known Lillian Egerton since she came here as a child to live with her grandparents after her parents were killed in a car crash somewhere in London. She got a decent upbringing: went to local schools and now she's got a good job at Bernes. The grandparents left her the house which they'd bought from the council years ago. Mr Davey, I've seen Lillian through childhood infections and injections, as well as the minor traumas of teenagers, and I find her a normal, cheerful girl with no health problems that I know of apart from slight anaemia."

Slightly anaemic was how Frank would describe this word-picture by the good doctor.

"Then why on earth would this normal girl hurl a brick through your surgery window on a Saturday night and then spin a fantasy tale of not being there?"

Rather than laugh outright, Dr Sutherland nevertheless gave a full-throated chuckle, which had the same effect. "Why, to show off to her mates, of course. That little gang of hers she goes around with when she gets bored. I bet some of the boys dared her to do it." He became more serious. "Naturally we had to report the break-in to the police because of insurance and all that. But when Dr Parfitt and I discussed it we decided not to take it any further."

"You didn't think she was trying to get in to get drugs?"

This time the doctor did laugh. "Everyone seems to think that doctors' surgeries are stuffed with exotic and illegal substances. Any young hooligan who broke in to raid our cupboards wouldn't know the difference between amyl nitrite and Epsom salts – and long live that ignorance . . . Lillian Egerton certainly didn't break in to get a supply of her anaemia pills! She did it for a lark – egged on by the boys."

Frank couldn't help feeling somewhat deflated after this perfectly reasonable explanation. Dr Sutherland kept reminding him of a kindly but stern schoolmaster trying to keep the young Davey's imagination from running away with itself.

But Frank could be stubborn.

"You don't see anything psychologically wrong with her behaviour, then?"

"Ah, if you want to talk psychology, I'm afraid I'm not the right man for that. I'm a bit of an old fogey when it comes to matters Freudian. It's my assistant, Dr Parfitt, you should be speaking to – he's our expert on psychology. And, as a matter of fact, Lillian is more his patient than mine lately. Would you like a word with him? I'll see if he's still about." Dr Sutherland reached for his buzzer.

"You still there, Gerald? Could you spare a minute?"

The man who came in was tall – well over six feet, Frank reckoned – and rangy, with an untidy crop of red hair. He had the pale skin and freckles that often went with the colour, and bright, very blue eyes. He didn't take a seat but straddled it and gazed at Frank with friendly interest as Dr Sutherland made the introductions.

Gerald Parfitt held out his hand, and gave Frank's a firm shake.

"Glad to know you," he said, with an unmistakable New Zealand accent. "You work at Gillorns, don't you?"

"Mr Davey acted for Lillian Egerton in that little matter of the break-in. He has become rather intrigued with her personality. I thought you might be able to help him out."

"Sure. I'm not surprised you're interested, Mr Davey. I'm not going against any professional ethic, am I, John, in discussing Lillian with her lawyer? I bet he's found her just as difficult to understand as I do."

John Sutherland chuckled in what Frank had decided was a mannerism intended to show avuncular wisdom, or a method of dismissing other opinion. The older doctor looked at his watch. "I must be off," he said. "I'll leave you two to your psycho-babble. Lock up when you go, Gerald, and, no, I trust any discussion you have about our Lillian will be for her benefit rather than otherwise."

"Oh, sure, John. You know my interest in her case, and that I want to help her in every way. I'm glad of the opportunity to meet someone else who's on her side." He turned to Frank. "I get mighty tired," he went on, "hearing all that stuff about her from the police. They sure have it in for her."

"Well, no more bricks through our windows," said John Sutherland as he put on his coat. "That plate-glass cost a fortune to replace."

Once alone, the two young men studied each other for a moment, and both liked what they saw.

"Care for a drink?" asked Gerald, opening one of the filing cabinets. "John keeps a good old malt – and not for medicinal purposes." He took out a bottle, and two small glasses. "Real glad to meet you, Franklyn Davey," he said, again.

"Frank, please."

"And it's Gerald – but for some reason never has been Gerry . . . Now, what's your real opinion of Lillian?"

"I haven't got one. Or, rather, it's not formed yet. What worries me are these changes in personality – sometimes before your eyes."

Gerald Parfitt took him up eagerly. "That's what I keep telling John. But I don't think he's ever seen her during one of these abrupt changes. In fact," he lowered his voice as if the senior doctor was still around, "I don't think he sees the present Lillian Egerton at all. To him she's still the kid he treated for chickenpox and measles."

"That figures," said Frank. "Dr Sutherland put the window-breaking episode down to a schoolgirlish prank. Showing-off, he said. Is that how you saw it?"

Gerald ran his fingers through his carroty hair. "It wasn't completely out of character. Lillian and that little gang of hers have been known to heave some pretty heavy stones around on the estate, dumping them on the properties of people they don't like. On at least one occasion, garden gnomes were said to have been injured."

The two young men roared with laughter. They were getting along famously in what looked like a budding friendship, helped by the pure peaty taste of Dr Sutherland's good malt. They found that they had other interests in common besides Lillian Egerton. Gerald was keen to know what courses Dinah was following at college, and knew some of her psychology tutors. He himself had taken his medical degree at Cambridge, and Barts, and had taken the assistantship in the Newtown practice while he had a go at an MD.

"I've enjoyed my year in this town, and would probably be tempted if they asked me to stay on permanently, but psychology's my real interest. That's why coming across someone like Lillian Egerton has been a real incentive to get on with my thesis. You know there was all this buzz about multiple personality back in the States, then it all died down. Well, I think I've got a real case here."

Frank told him how Dinah had poured cold water on the idea.

"I know it's no longer as popular a theory as it was. But at least Lillian's behaviour struck you with the possibility – and you're not even a medical man! You see, with Lillian there are all the classic symptoms: the traumatic event in her childhood . . . Did you know she was in the back seat of the car when her mum and dad were killed? I had to do a lot of careful probing to get that out. At first she wouldn't talk about it at all.

She was five at the time, and she seemed to have blocked the memory out pretty effectively."

"These personalities of hers," said Frank, conscious of venturing into unknown territory, "they seem to be poles apart. One so vivid, larger-than-life, the other so dull . . ."

"And you've not met the one in between?"

Frank thought for a moment. "Perhaps, yes, but only for short periods." That time she'd asked about missing persons, she'd seemed normal then despite the oddness of her enquiry. "Did you know she was friendly with the dead girl, Elinor de Lisle?" he asked Gerald Parfitt.

The young doctor's colouring was such that he could not hide sudden emotion. Now a tide of red swept up his face until lost in the roots of his hair.

"What?"

"She told me they were friends."

"For God's sake . . ." Gerald took up his glass with an unsteady hand and took a mouthful before he went on. "Do you think the police know this?"

"Not from Lillian herself, certainly. I think she's got a game going with the police, not to tell them anything but fancy stories she makes up as she goes along. Why's it so important the police shouldn't know?"

The New Zealander had calmed down, but he was still serious. "Because they're out to get her, and this might just give them the lever they want. When did Lillian tell you about this friendship?"

"When she came in to see me this afternoon. I can't see why it's so important. Lots of young people in Newtown must have known Elinor de Lisle."

"Look, Frank, this is confidential but you are, after all, Lillian's lawyer. She gets dope for her gang, someone she knows in London. It's what holds her gang together and keeps her as its leader. We're talking here of an inadequate personality who tries to compensate. It's all to do with power, I think, and the bolstering up of her ego. The one personality of hers that always seems to come out on top is the brash one, the leader of the pack."

Frank wasn't sure he was getting hold of the jargon, so he stuck to facts. "How'd she get the money to buy dope? Bernes don't pay that well, surely?"

"The one good thing that came out of the crash that killed her parents was money. There was some kind of insurance settlement. Lillian got it when she was eighteen, and then the house left her by her grandmother. Don't you see the position she's in on that estate? There's a whole trible of disaffected kids, there's poverty, there's little scope for any activity except hanging around making a nuisance of themselves to the neighbours – and the police. Then Lillian comes along not only with a place to go but with dope for the asking."

"How'd you get to know all this?" Frank asked, his curiosity genuine.

The doctor was rubbing the freckles on his forehead as if trying to wipe them out. "I'm not proud of it," he said, "Don't get me wrong . . . But I was really studying the girl closely and making notes for my thesis. Then I've had one or two of the youngsters from the Thornton Estate in here as patients, stomachaches and things like that, and of course I soon realised they were on dope. The rest wasn't hard to wheedle out of them – at the same time giving them the kind of stern lectures they ignore from their parents or school."

"You never told the police?"

"Good God, no! What do you take me for?" He seemed genuinely upset.

"Sorry. Of course you wouldn't." Frank felt that he had to apologise to Gerald to whom he had taken a liking. "As a matter of fact," he confessed, "it's no surprise to me. Lillian herself told me the gang smoked dope. Did she ever tell you?"

"No, she never did. You seem to have got more out of Lillian than I did. I think she was wary of me and I can't blame her. But don't you see, if the police get hold of this friendship of hers with Elinor they'll tear her place apart – and they'll pin a drugs charge on her whether they find anything or not. That little gang – they're not of the brightest brain – they'll grass on her as soon as a cop touches their collar."

"And she'll spin them another of her unbelievable tales."

"But this time it's too serious a matter for that. I tell you, Frank, there's a lot of folk on that estate who want the whole gang banged up. Once they get the whiff of a drugs charge she'll have more people after her than the police. There's some very sad families on that estate, Frank. Just because they're out in the country here and not in an inner-city tower block doesn't mean they don't have the same problems. Frustrations build up and it only needs a spark of hatred to turn them into a lynching mob."

Frank regarded his new friend with a quizzical eye. Gerald responded with a grin. "You think I've got a fiery temperament to go with my hair," he said, ruefully. "It's not often I shoot off my mouth like that, but you're a sympathetic listener. Maybe I'm exaggerating the danger to Lillian, but I just hope she's got a better story this time if the police haul her in."

"You think it likely?"

"Believe me, they're going to interrogate every youngster on that estate if they make a link between Lillian Egerton's gang and the dead girl. They've got to arrest somebody soon – anybody will do – before the media starts pointing them out for the idiots they really are."

Franklyn had been doing some quick thinking during the doctor's outburst. Somehow the episode of the garden gnomes seemed less funny now.

"I can see why you weren't keen for Lillian to be prosecuted for the brick-throwing."

"It wasn't difficult to get John Sutherland to agree to drop the matter. He, too, feels responsible for Lillian – even if it's because he still thinks of her as a child. It was pure luck that I was here that night – a patient phoned my digs complaining of heart trouble and I stopped by the surgery to pick up the necessary medicine." He gave a rueful grin. "You read my statement – the brick landed by my feet, and I saw our Lillian climbing in at the window. She saw me, and left – but not in any particular hurry. She was obviously doing her leadership thing and the rest of the gang would have been impressed."

"And all the more impressed when the charge was dropped," said Frank, thoughtfully. "But I agree with you. She can't keep this thing up for ever. Some day Harry Hopkirk is going to get his revenge."

"Is that his name? She once told me she had some policeman by the balls, if you'll pardon the expression. She said he'd fancied her and she gave him the brush-off. I doubt he's the forgiving type. I think she's heading for trouble. This murder case has everyone on edge. It changes things . . ."

Frank thought Gerald Parfitt looked suddenly washed out. "It's time I went," he said, getting to his feet. He'd had a couple of tots of whisky, but the other man had had more. "You've been very good entertaining me this long. Isn't it time you went home?"

"I'm on duty, either here or in my flat where my landlady takes the calls. But you're right," he got up, stretching his long length, "time to go home. Sorry I let off steam. I've got a lot on my plate at the moment. I've other patients besides Lillian Egerton, and one of them is Mrs de Lisle."

"Oh, I'm sorry." Frank really meant it. "Here am I bothering you at a time like this. I didn't know."

"No reason why you should. As a matter of fact, you've been good for me tonight, Frank. I needed someone to take my mind off things, and I've really enjoyed your company. We must do this again some time."

"Come out for a drink some evening," said Frank, heartily. "Give me a ring at the office and suggest a time when you're off duty. I shall look forward to it."

Gerald responded with alacrity. "Bring your Dinah. I'd like to meet her – and find out what that college of hers is teaching these days . . . Might bring me up to date." He gave Frank his rather charming boyish grin as he opened the outer door. The two men parted on the amicable note that they would meet again soon.

Eighteen

As Franklyn Davey drove out of Bolton Road, he glanced at his watch: a quarter to ten. It seemed much later, perhaps because his visit to the health centre had covered so much ground, and given him so much to think about.

The impulse that took him in the direction of Marshall Avenue was not sudden, it had been slowly growing in his mind all evening. His rational argument – and he badly needed one – was that he must warn Lillian to be careful what she said to the police, and it was only right that he, as her lawyer, should be the one to convey the message. What he had heard from Gerald Parfitt only confirmed him in his opinion that she needed legal support, should she be questioned. He thought, once again, of the dossier already compiled on her activities, and her reputation as a spinner of tales. That hadn't mattered when it was vandalism or abusive language against people on the Thornton Estate, but this was murder.

Frank knew, of course, that Lillian couldn't have had anything to do with the death of Elinor de Lisle, although at the back of his mind there stalked the unanswered question of how she'd come to know about Elinor's disappearance before anyone else. But the friendship between she and the dead girl, once it became known to the police, would bring the full force of the enquiry down upon Lillian, her house, and her pathetic little gang. Where would she run for cover then? Behind which personality would she hide?

As he drew up outside number 24, he saw there was a light on downstairs; well, at least he wouldn't have to get her out of bed. Glancing across the street, he noticed that Inspector Hopkirk's house was in darkness but, even as he looked, he caught a faint glow from a lamp in one of the bedrooms.

At his ring, Lillian herself opened the door to him. She peered out as he was standing in the dark. "Don't be scared, Miss Egerton. It's only me, Frank Davey."

"I can see it's only you, Frank Davey." She came out on to the step and switched on the porch light. "And I hope that old hen over there gets a good peek at my late-night gentleman caller." She waved an arm vigorously, and hooted like an owl. Turning round, Frank could have sworn he saw the twitch of a curtain in the house across the way.

"You really shouldn't do that," he told Lillian, as he followed her indoors. He wondered if there was an aspect of police harassment which covered surveillance by the wife of a serving officer. He doubted he'd ever see a judicial review of that one.

Lillian's place had been described to him as a gang hide-out and a drug scene, so that he was not sure what to expect as she led him down a narrow passage to the sitting-room. He automatically sniffed for the sweet scent of marijuana, but without effect.

It wasn't like he had envisaged a council property to be. He had not visited many, since his had been a sheltered middle-class life and little boxy houses owned by local authorities hadn't entered the grand feudal territory of the Chancery division in which he'd worked. This particular little box was light and airy as if the walls had been pushed back to give more space. An arch led to a darkened dining-room, and beyond to a glassed-in conservatory full of plants. Furniture was minimal, a couple of sofas and armchairs covered in rough calico, a scatter of beanbags, cushions and rugs on the bare wooden floor. There were no ornaments, no fripperies, even the curtains were unbleached linen and severely tailored.

"Welcome to this ole pad. I hope that bitch over the way is satisfied I run a brothel, so she can go happy to her bed. Sit down, only Frank Davey, and tell me why you've come."

Apart from the cheeky wave at the watcher across the street, this seemed to be the "normal" Lillian – the "one in between", as Dr Parfitt had called her. "You asked my advice about police harassment. I'm just checking it out."

"At ten o'clock at night? You must be barmy. Can I get you a drink? Just coffee or Horlicks. I don't go in much for alcohol."

"Coffee sounds fine, Lily." In fact it was just what he needed now that the effects of the malt and the excitement of listening to Gerald were starting to fade.

"Make yourself at home while I get it." She was wearing a very short skirt, not leather but some clinging fabric from which her legs, in black tights, emerged like liquorice sticks, ending comically in scuffed pink bedroom slippers. The whole effect was clownish but to Frank, in his present mood, rather endearing.

He heard her filling a kettle in the kitchen and rattling cups, so he took a look round this strangely anonymous room. It gave nothing away. True, there was a small set of bookshelves beside the radiator, but the books were boys' stuff, football and laddish magazines – nothing to suggest that Lillian could even read. Pushed into a corner, however, there was a Penguin paperback. Frank took it out and read the title: *Sybil* by someone called Schreiber. It was from Newtown library, and long overdue. As if to emphasise carelessness as to its source, there was a card stuck in between the pages threatening fines. Frank hastily shoved the book back on the shelf as Lillian appeared with a tray.

Frank found it oddly peaceful to sit back on her sofa with a fairly decent mug of hot coffee in his hand. It seemed harsh to have to break the calm but looking at him over the rim of hers – clearly marked "Lily" – she said, "You didn't come for a cozy chat, did you? What's up?"

"Lily, what did you actually say to the police when they asked you – as they've asked every young person from round here – if you knew Elinor de Lisle?"

"Like I said . . . What would I be doing with a posh kid from the Coverley Drive set?"

It wasn't what she'd told him before; possibly with so many stories going around in her head, she wouldn't remember which she'd used.

"They'll find out you did know her. One of the Turpins at some time is going to say she was in the gang."

"I never said she was." Lillian was spitting mad. "You made that up. Anyway, nobody in the gang's going to tell the rozzers anything."

Frank drained his coffee, and set down the mug. He leaned forward.

"Lillian. This isn't a game, this is a murder enquiry. It'll blow everything apart, there won't be any secrets left. Your little gang, they'll spill the beans. Even if Elinor was only a hanger-on, they'll have seen her with you, and they'll tell—"

She looked at him with furious green eyes. "They don't know nowt about Elinor and me . . . Anyway, lots of others knew her – what about her own lot, the boys from the comp?"

"I'm only concerned with you, Lillian. What did you and Elinor get up to, anyway?"

She lowered her eyes, turned away. "She liked the woods," she said, dreamily, "like me . . . Sometimes we'd just walk among the trees. She liked to get away."

"Well, there's no harm in the police knowing about your friendship. Why're you so stubborn, Lily?"

She didn't answer. She put her mug on the tray and reached for his. She got up and carried the tray through to the kitchen. He followed her.

"Remember, Lily, I've read that dossier the police made on you. Now I don't say all of it's true, but there were complaints from a lot of older people on the estate about your Turpins. You've made enemies and that's not good when it comes to finding a scapegoat."

She crashed the mugs into the sink and turned the tap on at full power so that it splashed out on the floor. "Now look what you've made me do."

"And that's not all," he insisted, even though he was talking to the back of her neck. "There were a couple of complaints from motorists in the woods about the activities of some your lads."

"Motorists!" She hissed the word as she turned to him. "You

mean them that goes courting in cars? If you call it courting. Fucking in the back seat more like!" She dried her hands on a dishtowel and went back into the sitting-room. She's trying to gain time, thought Frank as he followed her.

"Is that what your little lot get up to? Spying on couples in cars?"

Something of the disgust he felt must have sounded in his voice for she went red. "No harm done," she muttered. "Some of the boys, they liked to rap on the windows and shine a torch, like. Never saw folk pull up their pants so quick."

Frank was surprised at the sudden loathing he felt. Before Dinah had got her flat, and he himself was in digs with an inquisitive landlady, they had often gone to Emberton Woods in the car . . . His face felt hot, and he was conscious that Lillian was staring at him. She gave a guffaw, and there was relief in it, as well as genuine merriment. "You too, only Frank Davey, I bet you and your girlfriend—"

"Shut up." He strove to keep calm, to find the right words. "Lillian, I'm beginning to understand why there are people on this estate, and in Newtown itself, who would like to see you and your gang punished. These games you get up to, they are dangerous."

"Huh! These complaints, they were just moans to the police 'cos some of the boys came a bit close on their bikes. You think they'd come forward and admit to snogging in the back seat of their cars? You gotta be joking."

"So the boys would be out there on their bikes on the look-out for couples in their cars?" Frank knew there were many places in Emberton Woods where cars could run off the road and be partly screened by trees and bushes. He felt sick at the thought. "And you and the girls you'd have a look too, tap on the windows, shine a torch?"

"Only a bit of fun." The way he'd described it, he knew she was ashamed. "There's a lot worse goes on in Newtown."

"Maybe, but I'm only concerned about you. Now I'm going to ask you something very serious and I want you to be truthful, if you can. Did Elinor ever take part in these spying games?"

"No! Never. I wouldn't let her. What d'yah take me for?"

139

"But she might have heard of them through the others."

Lillian didn't answer. She had slumped down in one of the armchairs, her face drawn and sallow, her eyes lacklustre. "I'm going to bed," she said slowly, slurring the words. "Please let yourself out." It was Miss Egerton speaking, the woman who worked at Bernes.

Nineteen

Early morning light moved slowly over Newtown. The frosts of February had died with the month, and March had come in mild and lamblike.

Mary was up before six; in fact she had hardly slept for she had been watching over a restless Alys. Mary drew the curtains of her own room, which faced out towards the woods, and opened the window. A breath of spring in the air, she thought, how very inappropriate. She looked over at the line of trees, their trunks faintly reflecting the light from the eastern sky, their tops gossiping as the breeze shook them like rumours.

George had been home for a day and a night but now he had to leave early for London to receive the plaudits and the criticisms of the media now that the conference had been well and truly analysed. Although he had not said so, Mary felt he could take brickbats from any quarter of the globe and hit them for six but, faced with his wife's despair, he was helpless . . .

So rather than talk of Alys last night, they'd discussed the conference report. "The intransigence of my own country made things difficult," Mary remarked. "The great USA doesn't understand poverty."

"One can see why. They took the labouring poor out of Europe and built a nation. Looking at its power, now, we mustn't forget it came from the shaking free of religious contention, and the cruelty of tyrants."

"It certainly gave my mother a choice, something she never had in Ireland. I can't blame her new country for the fact that, when it came to the bit, she chose the wrong man to look after her."

George was deep in thought. "It's always difficult to know when it comes to making choices," he said, heavily. "If I hadn't taken this London job I'd have been here in Newtown to look after Alys and Elinor instead of halfway across the world."

Mary shook her head, as she gathered the coffee cups and made for the kitchen. "Go and get some sleep, George, I'll look in on Alys."

Dr Parfitt had left sleeping tablets, but Mary was pleased to see that he doled them out sparingly. Last night it had given Alys at least a few hours of rest before she woke in time to say goodbye to her husband. But there was no warmth in the cheek he kissed, no spark in the beautiful eyes, nor answering pressure from the hand he took. She tried to smile, and the effort she put into it came close to breaking George's heart.

Mary watched the car drive off, then turned back into the house of mourning. None of her past experience had prepared her for this – the awful lethargy, the bleak surrender of someone who had no wish to go on living . . .

Lennox Kemp had not had a good night either: he missed his wife on the other side of their double bed, and the thought of her up in that house on Coverley Drive troubled him. His young client, Darren Roding, would not have slept much either for the officers down at the station had decided he must endure their hospitality for another twelve hours.

"He's a material witness," they had explained to Kemp, who didn't need to be told; Darren had not only found the body, he'd literally fallen over it and been sick. More to the point he had not informed the police but had run to this mysterious leader of the gang, this young woman on the Thornton Estate about whom Kemp was hearing for the first time.

"It weren't her I told, not Lily," Darren had insisted, "it were her sister there."

But Inspector Hopkirk, who was doing the questioning at the time, had laughed at him.

"Lillian Egerton hasn't got a sister. There's only one person lives at 24 Marshall Avenue, and that's Lily Egerton."

"It didn't look like her, I swear it," Darren mumbled.

The other officer in the room, Chief Inspector West, had answered Kemp's query. "She lives there alone, this Miss Lillian Egerton; this gang – they call themselves the Turpins – meets at her house. That much we know for fact, Mr Kemp."

The events of Tuesday night had been gone over till they were threadbare. Darren stammered – evasive at first – but once into his stride he became more articulate and sure of himself. "It's the truth," he kept saying and, as the story was much the same as he had already told Kemp, there seemed little reason to doubt it. Kemp was aware all through the officers' questioning that they had plenty up their sleeves. They knew, for example, exactly when Darren, bright in his yellow anorak, had arrived at Lillian's house, and they also knew when he had left. He had been "observed by a credible witness", he was told, but Kemp gathered that, in respect of timing, the boy's version was corroborated by this unseen witness. Darren was in his own house by ten o'clock when his mother arrived, having finished her late shift.

His mother. That had been one call Kemp had had to make before going home that night. He saw both Mrs Rodings to tell them the bad news: Darren was still at the police station. "He's acted foolishly," he told them, "but essentially he's done nothing wrong. He was just unlucky. He went out to that den the gang talks about, and it was there that the girl's body was found. He panicked, I'm afraid, and didn't report it as he should have done."

The younger Mrs Roding was quick to understand the workings of her son's mind. "Were there drugs involved?" she asked.

"Not as far as Darren is concerned," Kemp replied, as truthfully as he could. Only through his conversations with John Upshire did he have the knowledge about the stuff found at the back of the den; the news had not yet been released while the authorities made certain enquiries. On the other hand, although Kemp suspected that Darren's curiosity about the gang's summer hide-out was fuelled by a suspicion that it was the place where they stashed their dope, he believed the lad when he said he'd not participated in that branch of their activities. Having been charged once – it was on his record – he was too scared of being caught a second time.

"I told him. I said, 'Darren, if you ever try that game again, I'll turn you in myself.'" His mother was in earnest. "That's what I told him, Mr Kemp, and he knew I meant it."

The elder Mrs Roding said, "I shouldn't have complained about the police asking him all those questions. But how were we to know? Why'd he go to this young woman, then? Why not tell the police?"

"You know the answer to that one, Mrs Roding. Ted's his dad, and Ted wouldn't share the time of day with a policeman if the two of them were stranded on a desert island."

Darren's mother sighed. "It's true. All he heard about from Ted was how the police stitched you up. Half the time, I think Darren was just scared of them. That gang he was in, Mr Kemp, they're all local lads from the Thornton Estate, but they were his mates. He'd mates like that back in Hackney and he missed them. As for this girl, well I've heard things down at the store – they say she's a proper hellcat and ought to be put away."

"I've not met her, Mrs Roding. I agree with you about the gang, I think Darren had some ideas about being loyal to them, and telling the police about the body and where it was lying would seem like a betrayal. One thing I'm sure of, though, is that Darren didn't know her. He's not implicated in her killing – just his bad luck he found her."

He tried to reassure the two women that it was unlikely the boy would be charged with any offence; even his failure to report his find did not look so bad when it was revealed that the police dogs had discovered Elinor's body within two hours of Darren having been there.

As he left the Rodings, Kemp went over in his mind the crucial timing and why the police went over it again and again: the silent watcher obviously confirmed that Darren had arrived at 24 Marshall Avenue just before eight o'clock. Darren himself had said he'd set out for Emberton Woods about quarter to seven, and, although too upset to be sure of the time, he'd thought that he'd found the den by about half-past. Apart from being sick, he'd then lost no time in scuttling back downhill to the Thornton Estate.

His time of arrival seemed to have coincided with what the witness saw. Naturally they had been interested in what he said about the motor cyclist leaving the house; there was no doubt in their minds that this was indeed Lillian Egerton. At this point Kemp had intervened in the questioning.

"This watcher in the wings," he said, mildly, "seems to have been assiduous, almost like a police surveillance on the house."

It wasn't so much a question as an observation. The more junior of the two inspectors, the ugly one, looked at Kemp from hard, black eyes and said nothing. The other, Chief Inspector West, whom Kemp knew slightly and recognised as an old friend of John Upshire's, hastened to correct any wrong impression. "No, nothing like that," he said, "witness was a woman who also lives in Marshall Avenue and who heard the motor cycle."

Kemp had questioned Darren closely about this incident. The boy had been in the shower when he heard the roar of the motor, and he worked it out that the time must have been about half-past eight. Kemp knew from Upshire that the body had been found at about eight o'clock. If indeed this Lillian Egerton had driven her vehicle up towards the den at that time, she'd have found the place swarming with police and dogs. If her object had been to retrieve the drugs she would have been too late.

Kemp would have liked to have spoken to John Upshire before leaving the police station but he was told by Inspector West that the super was in London. "He's up seeing the Met – there's aspects of this case where there's a common interest."

I bet it's the drugs side, thought Kemp, and wondered how relevant it was. Darren had admitted that the gang used dope – it seemed to have been made freely available by this Egerton woman – and there was no doubt that the officers at Newtown Police Station were out to get her. The ugly one, the one with the eager black eyes, positively bristled every time her name came up in the questioning. In Kemp's view, they were playing it close to their chests because the process of gathering evidence was not complete. One of the reasons, no doubt, for keeping Darren in overnight was probably so that he didn't contact this legendary queen of the gang.

As Kemp tried to get to sleep, one incident at the police station worried him. At one point, Hopkirk's line of questioning had come down hard on young Darren. "You know very well it was Lillian Egerton you saw at that house on Tuesday night. It was Lillian Egerton who told you to wash your clothes. You did what she told you because she hands out the dope, doesn't she?"

"I never . . . No, it weren't Lily . . . I thought it was her sister." Darren was not only confused, he was scared at the mention of drugs.

"Come on, lad, admit it – that's the house you all go to to smoke hash, and she's the one supplying—"

"Hold on a minute," Kemp had interjected at this stage. He rarely bothered to use legal language unless the occasion called for it; this one didn't. "You're asking my client a lot of questions here. He has told you he has no personal knowledge of drugs at this locale, and badgering him the way you're doing is going to get you a lot of wrong answers."

He had been interrupted by Inspector Hopkirk's rapid movement. "Record suspended," he snapped, giving the time and switching off the machine. "A word with you outside, Mr Kemp, if you please."

Completely baffled by the man's behaviour, Kemp had followed Hopkirk out into the corridor. Putting one hand on the wall close to Kemp's face so that he felt hemmed in, the inspector barked, "Your Lillian Egerton might hoodwink all the doctors and lawyers in this town, but she can't fool me. She's involved in this murder up to her neck and I'll prove it. You legal johnnies run around in circles trying to protect her, but this time it's not going to work."

Kemp had been more amused than angry at Hopkirk's outburst, which, in any event, he didn't fully understand. It is always galling to a police officer – when about to nab some rogue or other – to be restrained by an anomaly in the law which allows his victim to escape scot-free, but this inspector's rant had seemed unnecessarily personal . . . Kemp had considered trying to disillusion the man about his own involvement with Lillian Egerton – of whom he had heard for the first time today – but he'd thought better of it. At this moment, speaking rationally to the inspector would be as stupid as talking to a steam kettle about to blow its lid.

Kemp had merely turned on his heel and re-entered the interview room where Inspector West and the usual attendant sergeant had been holding the fort. As he came in, Kemp caught a flicker of sympathy out of the corner of West's eye; perhaps the new Inspector Hopkirk was a cross the whole station had to bear.

Kemp finally got to sleep in the small hours, and woke not altogether refreshed. Darren Roding hadn't been the only one confused last night in that interview room.

Twenty

Y our ears are supposed to tingle and go red if people are
talking about you. Lillian Egerton's were well hidden
under her working cap, but there was no hint that they were
anything but normal. She bent over her desk, intent on the lists
before her, occasionally mouthing numbers as she checked
item against item, and entered them on the keyboard before
her. This was a mid-week job and she was doing it as she
always did, concentrated and careful. If she heard the murmur
of the other girls talking more than usual, she took no notice.
She didn't appear to realise that her name was on everyone's
lips or, if she did, she didn't care.

The newspapers were having a field day. As if in revenge on
the local police force for being so cagey about how the murder
case was going, the press had decided this was one for them.
Somehow the juxtaposition of a schoolgirl and a youth gang,
with the hint of a drug connection through what was now being
called a "rave", set a lot of journalists off on ego trips of their
own into juvenile delinquency and under-age sex, only just
stopping short of gang rape. The fact, confirmed by the home
pathologist's report, that the dead girl had not been molested
robbed them of the ultimate sensation, but, they hinted, she
was mixed up in something, so the spotlight settled on the
Dick Turpins.

People on the Thornton Estate gave them plenty of material,
a lot of it shoddy but all of it the kind of thing their editors
told them readers would die for. Hordes of hooligans sniping
at old age pensioners, walls defaced, gardens vandalised – the
gnomes popped up more than once to prove modern youth had
no respect for property – driveways and flower-beds gouged

by motor-bike tires, folk scared to go into the streets because they'd be jeered at, sworn at or even mugged by roving bands of lawless youth . . .

And this gang was being led by a young woman – they were careful not to name her – who was clearly unstable (probably through drug-taking) and ought to have been properly dealt with by the police long ago. All the things that should have been said to the police (who would never pay for it) were being joyfully spilled out to newspapermen who everyone knew kept rolls of cash in their back pockets for citizens who could tell the tale.

The whispers of the girls at Bernes must have reached Lillian's ears but she carried on with her work – much to the approval of Alex Bexby who still could not believe all this talk had anything to do with his prized employee.

Now when he watched the chattering girls who were doing everything but point a finger at Lillian, Alex decided to get in touch with Franklyn Davey. After all, they'd agreed to have that drink together some time.

They met in the Cabbage White at lunchtime, Frank glad to have someone to share in what he gloomily considered to be his obsession with Lillian Egerton. She seemed to stand between himself and his work, between himself and Dinah. He had phoned her last night on his return from Marshall Avenue. They usually spent some quality time in pillow talk if they had not seen each other during the day.

He told her all about Gerald Parfitt. "He's a clever chap, and he genuinely thinks that Lillian may be suffering from split personality. You remember I thought of that?"

"Indeed you did, and I told you to stick to your job."

"But now I know that her doctor is on the same track as me. He's been studying Lillian for months as a very interesting case."

"If it's attention she's after, she's certainly getting it." Dinah's tone was distinctly chilly, and it might have been better if Frank had dropped the subject but his head was too full of it for that.

"I went round to see her tonight, and caught her in what

Gerald calls her 'in-between self'." He went on to enthuse about Lillian's house and lifestyle. "Not a bit like the hell-raiser that that policeman has dubbed her, and he's encouraging the media to see her in the same light. In her own home she's any normal girl, sitting there with a cup of Nescafé in carpet slippers – it was quite cosy . . ."

"Franklyn, have you been drinking?"

"Oh, that was ages ago – a glass of malt whisky Parfitt gave me at the surgery."

"Don't you think going round to see Miss Egerton at ten o'clock at night is taking the solicitor-client relationship a bit too far?"

"I have to see this client in her home surroundings because I fear she is being made a scapegoat," he said, huffily, "and I'm proved right. She's suffering from multiple personality syndrome, and one of them is an ordinary girl with a nice home and bookshelves like anybody else."

"Oh, this personality can read? That's an eye-opener. Anything interesting on these bookshelves?"

Frank thought it best not to mention the comics and the football books. "Well, she goes to the local library . . . There was a Penguin paperback called *Sybil* or something."

There was a grim silence the other end, then Dinah blew her top. "You idiot," she said, "she's really got you fooled, all of you, including that expert doctor friend of yours. That's where Lillian's got it from, that book. It's by a writer called Schreiber and the subject is a woman with real multiple personalities. Lillian's read that book, and pinched the idea. She's conning you all, and I for one am sick of hearing about her. Goodnight." The phone was slammed down.

Naturally, Frank said nothing of this to Alex Bexby. "You say she's at her bench every day as if nothing had happened?" he queried.

"That's it. She's carrying on as if it had nothing to do with her."

"But the papers are full of tales about this gang. And you could almost say a hue and cry is out for her, Lillian Egerton, even though they don't name her."

"I still think there's a mistake."

Frank shook his head. "I'm afraid there's no mistake, Alex. I understand the police have had members of her gang in for questioning. With all these reporters after them as well, it's only a matter of time before they catch up with Lillian herself."

Alex Bexby wasn't being much of a help. He had only seen one side of Lillian. Frank tried another tack.

"Is she friendly with any of the other girls at work? She must at least talk to some of them."

Alex looked uncomfortable. "Well," he said, "since she got that promotion, talking with the others wouldn't have been encouraged. Hold on a minute, I've just remembered someone . . . but she left."

"Who was that?"

"A girl Lillian asked me to find a job for about a year ago. I'll remember her name in a minute. We tried her for a few months but she wasn't really suitable. She was a bit rough, not very intelligent. The job might look rather mechanical, Frank, but really it does need a modicum of brains." Alex was obviously defending the type of girls they kept on. "She was a friend of Lillian's, lived a bit further up the estate. "I've got it, Teresa Cane. I think they called her Terry. As I said, she didn't last. She was the only one, so far as I know, who was what you might call a friend of Lillian's. Though now I come to think of it, I was a bit surprised at the time – she didn't seem Lillian's sort, somehow."

"Any idea where she might have gone?" Frank remarked, casually.

"I've seen her in a shop. That one by the station, sells sweets and newspapers, doesn't it?"

That was enough for Franklyn. His first afternoon appointment wasn't till three; time to buy a magazine and some chocolates for Dinah, who was coming to his place tonight. He hoped by then she wasn't as snappy as she'd been on the telephone last night. Was it simply that she was exasperated by his non-professional approach to psychology, or was she actually jealous of Lillian Egerton? Frank found the possibility rather pleasing.

There was only one person serving in the shop who was not of the family – and rather obviously not for she was fair-haired with large blue eyes of absolute candour. Not even when Frank asked her if she was a Miss Cane did she show any suspicion of him.

"Sure, I'm Terry Cane," she said as she took the box of Black Magic from him and looked around for a plastic bag.

"I wonder if I could ask you something, Miss Cane."

"Sure, go ahead."

"Do you know Lillian Egerton who works at Bernes?"

"Sure I know Lily. Why'd you want to know?"

"I really can't talk to you here, I'd be keeping you from your work."

"I'm having a break in a few minutes. I usually go round the corner to the café for a cup of tea. That be OK?"

"Sure." Frank had caught the habit from her. "I'd be very obliged if you could spare me the time . . ."

"Sure. See you there. I'll just check with the boss."

Frank bought a cream cake for her while he waited at the little table in the corner by the kitchen door with a coffee in front of him. Terry wasn't long in joining him.

"That for me? Great. I know I shouldn't . . . Fattening, aren't they?"

"You don't have to worry about that," said Frank, gallantly. "Not with your figure."

"Sure, it's OK now but it won't be if I go on eating the things. What's this about Lily? Who're you?"

"I'm a solicitor, Frank Davey. I've done some work for Miss Egerton."

"She's always in trouble, isn't she, but she'll come out all right, won't she?"

"I don't know. That's why I may need your help. You're a friend of hers, aren't you?"

She came out with the inevitable "sure" and a lot more besides. She'd known Lillian for about a year, and lived near her on the Thornton Estate. Terry had even been a member of the gang . . . "Not any more," she said, sliding her hand across the table towards Frank. A small diamond twinkled on her ring finger. "Not since I got engaged."

Because she was now out of the gang, Terry saw no reason why she should not talk about it to Frank. For her it was all in the past, and for Teresa Cane there was now only the blessed present and a future wreathed in white tulle.

Terry had enjoyed her time with the gang, and spoke highly of Lillian. "Got me a job, she did, at the place she worked. But I'm afraid I didn't suit them, I hadn't the skills." No attempt to make out that the job didn't suit her; Terry was candid about that, as about everything else. "When you've been nothing much at school it's nice when somebody takes a bit of notice of you. That's what Lillian did, made them folks on the estate sit up and take a bit of notice, like." She gave a giggle which was so infectious Frank had difficulty keeping his face straight. "All those old biddies turning round in the street when you used the f-word out loud. And the things that got written on their doors – and on the top of their garden gnomes!"

But what had given her the biggest kick was the game played out in the woods with what she called "the car people". She made Frank realise that, to this bunch of aim-less boys and girls, labelled failures by the time they'd left the comprehensive, people with cars were from a different tribe. On the estate itself, the only cars were owned by parents – in themselves also a different tribe – and a lot of them were second-hand rust-buckets unlike the suave and sexy Porsches and Rovers which crept into the woodland glades at nightfall.

It had all started, Terry told Frank with that candour which was as much part of her as the wide blue eyes and the blonde ringlets, with a joke being played on that policeman who'd been pestering Lillian for a date. "Wouldn't take no for an answer, though how could anyone even think of going out with such an ape? Anyway, Lillian thought of getting her own back when she found out he was courting a policewoman from London. When he was doing a stint at Newtown in the autumn, she'd seen his car in the woods – up to no good."

Unrestrained giggles from Terry almost blotted out the story, but what emerged was that the gang had targeted the car, shone a torch in the back, and hoopla – caught him with his trousers down . . .

After that it had become more or less a ritual game, down to the woods in the twilight, the boys on their bikes or skateboards, the girls usually in Lillian's beat-up old van, spotting all the best cars, then the stealthy approach through the undergrowth, and the final assault, rapping a twig on the car roof and shining a torch through the windows. Then they were off scrambling through the trees whooping with laughter. Terry nearly fell about at the memory. Frank felt queasy. At one point he was forced to ask: "Didn't you feel you were spying on them? You wouldn't like it if it were you and your young man."

She turned her candid blue gaze on him. "We don't have a car," she said, "besides, we'd never go down to the woods for that . . ."

He asked her if they weren't afraid someone would turn on them, or put in a complaint. "We'd scarper before any of them were out of their cars. And who'd they complain to? If they were up there, they weren't home, were they? They'd be with somebody they shouldn't."

"Did you know any of them?" Frank asked, somewhat diffidently, for he was finding the subject repulsive.

Terry shrugged. "Not often," she said. "I never hung around long enough. I once spotted that young doctor from the health centre but Lily, she said leave him alone, he'd only be with his receptionist and as neither of them was married it weren't adultery. She'd a thing about adultery, Lily had, called it a crime. Anyway I never shone a torch in on the doctor and his girlfriend, didn't need to, there was a moon. Quite romantic it was, her long pale hair in the moonlight. But I left them alone, like Lily said. There were plenty of other courting couples anyway. The boys got quite a kick out of catching one of the teachers at the school. That gave us all a laugh."

Frank couldn't bear to hear any more, he already felt like a spy. He got Terry back to other pursuits of the gang.

"When you met at Lillian's house, did you ever see Elinor de Lisle there?"

She shook her ringlets till they bounced round her head. "She never came when I was there. I think Lily took up with her after I'd sort of left. That was when Robbie and me started going seriously. I told Lily I wouldn't come so often, but she didn't mind. But wasn't this Elinor just a kid? She's the one that got killed, right?"

Frank nodded. Terry's eyes clouded over. She was ever so sorry but there were bad people about in those woods. "I'd never go there alone," she said, "too scary." Obviously she'd been all right with the rest of the gang around her. Frank came away from his talk with Teresa Cane as if their woodland pranks were as innocent as a teddy bears' picnic.

Although he'd questioned her about the changeable nature of her friend, she said she'd found nothing strange in Lily's behaviour. "Sure, Lily has her moods, don't we all? When she's at work at Bernes she wouldn't carry on like she does with us. Stands to reason. And she's careful with the law. Has to be with that Paul Pry living opposite. She even keeps her old van properly licensed – he'd catch her out on the least thing." Terry had giggled. "Sure he would after she'd caught him that once with his trousers round his ankles."

With another ringing peal of laughter, Terry went off, back to selling sweets and dreaming of white wedding dresses.

Twenty-one

Newtown Police Station had been built in the fifties – a penny-pinching time – when the planners, fresh from the knowledge of the real crimes of war, thought that new residents might leave their nasty habits behind when given green grass and spacious woodlands, and that a small building would be enough to hold the forces of law and order. Unfortunately human nature reasserted itself, rogues came out from the City trailing their "previous" like clouds of glory, and a rising generation simply put a new face on old crimes so that the police station had to be enlarged several times to hold its own. There was still hardly a room big enough to contain all the officers engaged on the de Lisle case on this March day when Superintendent Upshire addressed them.

Everyone knew he'd been up with the Met and it was rumoured there'd been a breakthrough on the drugs side, and it was this report he was about to give them. First, though, he went over the main features of the murder despite the fact that he knew they were already all too familiar with them. He had found that constant repetition served to remind them of small details which might get forgotten; it also brought together the several lines of enquiry which individual officers were following. John Upshire thought of this exercise as "pulling the strings together", and emphasised that he wanted his men to remember they worked as a team. This, he felt, was essential at this juncture for he knew that there had been discord at the station on several issues arising from the case.

Elinor de Lisle had gone missing on Saturday the twenty-fifth of February. The police had not been officially informed until the following Tuesday evening when an intensive search of Emberton Woods had led to the discovery of the body. At first, many of the officers, particularly the uniformed branch, had been disgruntled that the search had got off to such a slow start. They said that, given a chance, they'd have found the girl by Sunday. It was only when the pathologist's report came in that they were satisfied, for it confirmed what the original police doctor had surmised: the murder had not taken place at Dick Turpin's Cave, the body had been moved there after death and possibly less than a few hours before it was found. Moreover, the girl had been strangled some time in the early hours of Sunday. The ligature was probably her own school tie, confirmed by her family as having been in the pocket of her anorak when she left home for the youth club where she had been expected to play table-tennis. She had left the club soon after arriving, and no one had yet come forward who had seen her since.

A search of the hollow – Turpin's Cave – and the surrounding woodland had produced a welter of objects, most of them destined for the rubbish bags, but two were significant. At the back of the cave, hidden under an old chair, the officers found two plastic containers, one full of Ecstasy tablets, the other cannabis resin. It was not a large find of drugs but sufficient to alert the Drugs Squad. The other discovery was of a torch lying under a bush in another part of the woods, a fair distance from the cave, but not far from the Drill Hall where the musical event was taking place the night Elinor disappeared.

It was this event which provided the link. For some time the drugs branch in the Met had been taking an interest in a man called Simon Marco who, among other activities, arranged for London groups to play at out-of-town concerts. There was a suspicion that Mr Marco had a sideline in drugs, the music business giving him a ready-made market.

The superintendent paused at this stage as Inspector Hopkirk popped up like a jack-in-the-box, and took the stand. He fiddled with his papers, cleared his throat and announced that he would give them the full account of what had been said by Lillian Egerton in the course of a recent interview he'd had with her. "You've all heard of her," he said, with a knowing smirk, "now

157

you'll see how important she is to this case. It took me hours of tiresome questioning to get this out of her, I can tell you . . . She's pulled the wool over the eyes of many in this room but never me."

A murmur came from the room. "Get on with it, Harry," whispered John Upshire.

But his new inspector was set on justifying himself. "I've had to listen to a lot of criticism from all quarters. Now you'll see I was right all along, because Lillian Egerton mentioned the name of this very man, this Simon Marco, in the course of my interview. She told me that on that Saturday night, when the concert was on at the Drill Hall, she went up to London with Simon Marco and was at his club until the next morning."

"Which she wasn't," said Superintendent Upshire, briskly. "Marco has been picked up by the Met and charged with various drugs-related offences, some of which he's already confessed to. One of them concerns Newtown. Marco's been peddling his illegal substances to someone here for at least six months. Of course he blames the bigger boys – the syndicate the Drugs Squad's really after – he's only the courier. It's what they all say, they were just taking orders . . ."

"How come this Marco talked so freely?" asked DS Martin.

"Abduction of a minor, possible murder charge," said Upshire, grimly. "Remember the papers were full of it, Marco was scared he'd be lynched. He'd been up at the Drill Hall early that evening just to check out a couple of gigs he'd arranged, and the small matter of his commission . . . At least that's his excuse for being in Newtown, but when pressed a little further it transpires he also made the drop – dumped the drugs at the back of Turpin's Cave according to the plan."

And a very simple plan it was, too. Marco would get the message by telephone about once a month or every six weeks. Yes, it was a woman's voice, and yes he knew who it was. He was told to leave the drugs at the back of the cave and take the money, which would be waiting for him in a wooden box. No, in all the months he'd been doing the run, the money never failed to turn up, so he always left the dope as ordered.

It was never more than a few hundred pounds' worth, which was why he regarded the whole enterprise as chickenfeed but it was regular, and the delivery ground near enough to his place of business in London. Simon Marco made it all sound as easy as ordering groceries on the internet.

"The method of delivery and collection sounds just like something dreamed up by that freaky girl," said PC Andrews. "I've spoken to Lillian Egerton several times in the course of this investigation, and she tells things as if they were fairy stories." He mimicked her high voice, and made not a bad shot at it. "There's these dark woods, and a white Mercedes, and a dark man bringing treasure."

A ripple of merriment went round the ranks.

The superintendent put up a hand. "We've got a better identification than that," he said. "You don't think for a moment that Marco's bosses would let him run an operation with an anonymous woman, do you? They told him early on to stay and see who picked up the packages, and he's given us a good description of someone remarkably like our Lillian Egerton. He's certain he could identify her."

"How do we know this Simon Marco wasn't involved in the death of Elinor de Lisle, if, as you say, he was in Newtown that Saturday?" There had not been time for John Upshire to report the result of his London visit to Inspector West. "When I interviewed Miss Egerton at her place of work she said she didn't know the dead girl and was surprised to be asked about her. She struck me as a quiet, subdued kind of person and not the sort to get mixed up in drugs."

"She got you fooled then," Inspector Hopkirk snorted. "I think I may say I know Miss Lillian Egerton better than anyone else here." He glared as a snigger came from one corner of the room.

But it was to Inspector West that John Upshire turned. "Sorry I couldn't fill you in earlier, Peter but I've only now received confirmation from the Met. Simon Marco has an unassailable alibi for all the hours when Elinor was in danger. Yes, he was at the Drill Hall about six in the evening, the doorman who knows him has confirmed that, then he left for London – making a detour through Emberton Woods to stash the drugs and lift the money – but he was certainly in his Leicester Square club by eight o'clock. He walked into a crisis involving his team of bouncers who were – you won't believe this – demanding less hours and more pay! The fracas grew into a minor riot and the police were called . . . It was well into Sunday morning before things got sorted out and, as a result of accusations thrown about and insults exchanged, the Met boys were well pleased with the information they obtained about the workings of the syndicate they'd had their eye on. Simon Marco dropped into their hands like a ripe plum."

"And now we've established the connection between Egerton and Marco, who's a self-confessed drug dealer, I'm all for bringing her in." Inspector Hopkirk was having difficulty curtailing his enthusiasm at the prospect.

John Upshire demurred. "At present the only identification we have on her is Simon Marco's, and he's a tricky customer. All right, he spilled the beans about where he was that Saturday night, but only because he was scared. Once the cave had become a murder scene, who knows what forensic evidence might link him to the place? He wasn't taking any chances. As for the Egerton girl, we may have got her link to the drugs found there, but we still don't know of any connection between her and the dead girl. All we have is Roding's statement that he saw her at the Egerton house. It's not much to go on."

Inspector West agreed. "Someone dragged, or carried that body down into the cave – Miss Egerton certainly doesn't look strong enough for that."

"She'll have had accomplices," snapped Hopkirk, "and she's got a van among those old vehicles in her garden. I'm getting tired of people making excuses for her. What about the other side, eh? We're inundated with complaints from the Thornton Estate, they're telling us to arrest the whole gang and lock them up."

"I've seen the dossier, Harry," said John Upshire, mildly, "but I still don't see juvenile delinquents changing into murderers overnight."

160

"You'd be surprised." Hopkirk muttered. "I'd not put anything past that lot."

John Upshire and Peter West put their heads together. They agreed that perhaps Hopkirk was taking too personal an interest in the girl when there were other aspects of the case to be considered.

The arrest of Simon Marco had provided much-needed impetus to the Newtown team. They had up till then been disappointed at the absence of leads and the fact that any they'd had led nowhere. The media, on the other hand, had taken over their role – journalists speculating on why a nice girl like Elinor should have become mixed up in small town hooliganism (this without proof that she even knew members of the gang now well known to the press as The Dick Turpins).

"I think it's time for another press conference, John." Inspector West was unhappy about the position being taken up by his successor. It really shouldn't have worried him, but West had been proud of serving under John Upshire for many years, and hated to leave him with discord in the ranks. He himself would be retiring in a couple of weeks as the chemotherapy he had had to undergo was taking its toll.

"Let's take things in order," said Upshire, proceeding to give out instructions. If it meant going over old ground, the family, the school, the youth club, the whole background to the dead girl it still might mean someone somewhere remembered, something forgotten would surface – at the moment it was all they could hope for. He knew Inspector Hopkirk had other ideas – in fact just one idea – and was not surprised to hear his harsh voice raised.

"I'm for bringing her in . . . Let's see what she says about her Simon Marco now."

"Very well. But only for questioning, mind. Go easy. What was it that chap Bexby said about her health, Peter?"

Inspector West looked back at his notes. "He was concerned that the attention she was getting from us was upsetting her. He inferred that she was delicate."

"Delicate!" Hopkirk exploded. "Delicate as a pig's arse!"

The new inspector was known to have his weaknesses in

161

addition to his one obsession, but profanity was not one of them. The room was hushed in astonishment. Chief Superintendent Upshire decided it was time the meeting was brought to a close.

"Peter West and I have decided to let the Roding lad go. We feel he has nothing more to give us. His finding of the body and his lack of disclosure will of course be put up to the CPS but in the meantime we are not charging him."

John Upshire conveyed this news to Lennox Kemp on the telephone. He was brusque about it. And when Kemp asked for more information on how the case was going, and whether there was anything he could tell George de Lisle, Upshire was even more taciturn. This isn't like John, thought Kemp, persisting with his questions.

"I shouldn't even be talking to you," growled Upshire. "And if you don't know the reason, then you've got your ethical knickers in a twist."

The call was abruptly terminated, leaving Kemp staring at the receiver in disbelief. He had been getting some very strange messages from the Newtown Police Station in the last few hours . . . It made him wonder what he was doing wrong.

Twenty-two

Frank Davey was once again in the Cabbage White at lunchtime; it was becoming a habit. Gerald Parfitt had telephoned him at the office in the morning and suggested lunch. "Just a snack," he said, "with a large pint or two. It's my afternoon off, so I'm allowed more than my quota of alcohol."

At Frank's suggestion, he picked Gerald up at the health centre. "Then you don't have to worry about driving," he said. "I've got clients to see late, so, sorry, can't join you in a binge."

"Why is it that drunken doctors and lawyers are always seen to be far worse than inebriated bank managers or tipsy tailors?" Frank enquired as they settled over their respective drinks, and the pub's limited edition of a ploughman's.

Gerald laughed. "It's something to do with the public's view of our jobs, life and death, liberty or its opposite . . ." He seemed in a good mood, indeed he had been since they left the surgery. Frank had had to wait five minutes or so for him, which he hadn't minded in the least as he spent the time chatting up the receptionist. Crystal seemed ready to go along with that. Chatting up girls was new to Frank, it was something he would never have done before getting engaged, and he couldn't account for the phenomenon that he now did it with ease.

Crystal had been having an animated conversation with the practice nurse when Frank walked over to the desk. "I'd never have long hair," Crystal was saying, "because my hairdresser tells me I've got a beautiful nape." The nurse hooted with laughter. "Aren't you the conceited little miss," she said as she disappeared into her own sanctum.

163

"I agree with your hairdresser," said Frank, "I think your nape is perfect."

Crystal Stephens dimpled. "You are Mr Davey, aren't you? Gerald is expecting you. He'll be with you in a minute."

"I don't care how long it takes," said Frank, "so long as I am in your company." It was funny how getting engaged to Dinah had made him bold with girls in a way he'd never been before. Now that he was "taken", as it were, it was safe to graze the meadows. He enjoyed talking to Crystal, watching the warm brown eyes widen and slide away, the play of her features. What a pretty girl. He remembered what Terry Cane had said. Well, he couldn't blame Gerald Parfitt for fancying his receptionist, Frank fancied her a bit himself.

Both men were in the mood for some light-hearted banter, and it was some time before Frank broached the subject of Lillian Egerton. "I went round to see your patient Monday night, he said.

"My patient?" Evidently she was not in the forefront of the doctor's mind as she was in Frank's. "Oh, you mean Lillian. How was she?"

"I think I hit on the middle one – somewhere between the other two."

"Now I find that interesting. She's rarely like that with me. I either get the hot-pants or the frump. It's usually the frump who calls round for her pills. I see Lively Lily occasionally in the street with her mob, or even in here." He looked a trifle apprehensively through into the main room of the pub. "Anyway, it's night-time they come, she buys them all drinks and eggs them on to scandalise the customers."

"Gerald, are you serious about this multiple personality thing? Shouldn't she be seeing a psychiatrist?"

"That would certainly drive our Lily up the wall. I honestly don't know. At first she was just an interesting patient, then I'd see that quick change – like the ones you noticed – and it set me thinking." He gave a laugh. "You know how it is with doctors, they're studying something and, hey presto, before they know it, they've got it! All medicos go through that when they're students – it's a great relief to the males when they come to gynaecology, I can tell you . . ." He paused, and then went on, more seriously, "As I told you, I'm trying to get an MD in psychology, so I've been getting in deep with the subject. Although there was a cluster of multiple personality cases in the States during the seventies, there's never been any over here. So I took to observing our Lillian pretty closely because she does have a lot of the classic signs."

"And they are?"

"Oh, I can't be specific, Frank. But you must have noticed how she kind of goes blank just before a change? It means she's in a state of fugue, you understand?"

Frank didn't, but he nodded just the same. He asked another question: "If she was being one person, would she remember what she was doing at the time she was being another?"

Gerald took time to answer. "If she does truly have multiple personalities, then no she wouldn't remember. She would have periods of lost time. That's the danger."

"How do you mean?"

"One of the personalities might go somewhere, do something, which the real Lillian wouldn't know about."

"But that's serious," exclaimed Frank. He saw the look on the other man's face, and knew this was where they were on common ground.

Neither of them wanted to voice the unthinkable. At last Frank took the plunge. "If Lillian really is mixed up in this murder, she's going to get a roasting from the police if she doesn't tell them the truth about where she was on that Saturday night the girl went missing," he said, slowly, "and maybe she can't because she doesn't know herself."

"Have you asked her?"

"Oh, yes, she says she was in London, clubbing with a gentleman friend called Simon Marco."

Gerald Parfitt sighed. "That sounds like our Lily. I wonder if he drives a white Mercedes. What's the betting he doesn't even exist?"

"I'm worried for her."

"So am I."

Gerald was on his second pint, and he stared into it. Frank

drained his coffee. He was about to tell the doctor about the book he'd seen at Lillian's house, but he looked at his watch. "Hell's bells! I should have been back in the office ten minutes ago. I must fly."

"We must do this again some time. Lucky me, I don't have to rush off anywhere." The doctor looked smug. "And it's our receptionist's afternoon off as well." He grinned broadly.

"You've got good taste," said Frank, in the spirit of male bonhomie, as he dashed for the door.

He was met in the corridor by a very angry Joan. "Where on earth have you been?" She glared at him, and almost pushed him into his office. "I've doled out enough cups of tea to your waiting clients to launch the Titanic, and if you haven't a decent explanation for Mr Kemp you'll be sunk."

"Has he been asking for me?"

"Asking? He's been yelling – and you know how rare that is . . ."

"Oh dear. Will you tell him I'm back, please."

"I'll tell him in my own good time, Franklyn Davey. But your clients come even before him. First, Mrs Smithers about her will, second Mr Horrocks about planning. Here are the files. Get your coat off and look busy at your desk while I prise Mrs Smithers off the curtain rail in the waiting room."

It seemed that it was business as usual at Gillorns that afternoon.

By half-past five Franklyn was feeling rather pleased with himself: two clients satisfied, all his mail signed, his filing cabinets tidy and his brain more or less in order, he was preparing to go out to supper with Dinah who was coming out from town. His buzzer sounded. He picked it up. "Oh," he said, "yes, Mr Kemp – I quite forgot . . . I'll be with you right away."

Twenty-three

Lennox Kemp's anger had been working up to something all day. First he had been irritated, then cross, now he was in a cold, furious rage.

The strength of it stopped him in his tracks – literally – for he had been pacing his office for a good half-hour. He sat down abruptly and took stock. He had always considered himself to be the mildest of men, tolerant of other people, and amenable even in the most trying circumstances. I must be getting old, he thought, but that did nothing to help his bad temper.

It had started that morning when he had gone up to Coverley Drive to talk to George and bring Mary home, her duty to Alys suspended at least for a few days as George was taking some leave to be with his wife.

George and he had sat in the kitchen – it was not a house to have nooks and crannies, nor even a study in which to be away from others, all was open-plan, open to the light of day.

It was only gradually that Kemp realised that George knew far more about the police side of the case than he did. Of course, that was as it should be; George was the father of the victim, he was an intelligent man and, although deeply grieved by the tragedy, he could still take a dispassionate view. John Upshire had been to see him several times to bring him up to date with such progress as had been made. This in itself was remarkable to Kemp for the superintendent was not a visiting man and usually left that side of things to others.

"There was never any question of our appearing at press conferences, and certainly not on television," said George. "We are very private people and we must deal with our loss in our own way. Superintendent Upshire agreed, he didn't think it would help to find the killer anyway. Besides, Lennox, how could Alys have faced such an ordeal?"

Kemp gathered that it had been George who had dealt with the investigating team as much as possible, to spare his wife, particularly over the possibility of collecting forensic evidence from Elinor's clothing. Both her grandmother and her mother had been able to confirm what she had been wearing that Saturday night: black anorak over a dark blue tracksuit, underwear and black tights. She would have pushed her school tie into her pocket, as she usually did, to wear later with her table-tennis blouse and skirt kept in her locker at the youth club – they were still there, she had never changed that night. The clothes she had worn were the clothes she was found in, rumpled, and dirty from forest soil and leaves but, in the opinion of the scientists who worked on the body, only the anorak had been removed – and that had been placed under her head in Dick Turpin's Cave.

George had recognised the torch found by the search team as belonging to Elinor. "She usually carried it if she was out at night," he said, uneasily. "She got a kick out of coming in the house through the back way to see if she could fool the garden lights, even when someone brought her home." He blinked and looked away; he was remembering his stepdaughter.

The torch had been found a long way from the body, in quite a different part of the woods, near to the Drill Hall, but they both knew that Elinor must have been there at some time in the evening. The police had told George it strengthened their opinion that the murderer had been someone connected with the event – possibly a complete stranger down from London who had tried to abduct her. She had fought him off and in the struggle she had been strangled. The post-mortem had shown strangulation to have been manual; the school tie had been placed round the neck afterwards as if it had been the ligature. This was news to Kemp who had not had the benefit, like George, of the full report.

Kemp felt a twinge of disquiet. "As if trying to throw blame on her contemporaries?"

George shrugged. "An amateurish attempt, don't you think?"

He went on to say that Superintendent Upshire had told him that they were keeping all of their options open; if it had been a complete stranger – someone in the woods at that time but otherwise unconnected with Newtown – then solving the case might be difficult, he had been frank about that . . . On the other hand, Upshire had hinted at a suspect nearer home, someone the police were keeping a watchful eye on, but he would say no more about it until they had more evidence.

As he listened to his friend Kemp's thoughts became more and more troubled. He had not seen John Upshire since the early days of the investigation when the super had indicated that he would appreciate any help Kemp could give, particularly as he knew the de Lisle family. Since then Upshire had been almost incommunicado as far as Kemp was concerned. Efforts to reach him on the phone proved useless and, when Kemp asked any of the officers about the case, he had been fobbed off. He knew he had no right to this feeling of being deliberately kept in the dark yet it irritated him. In the past he and John Upshire had worked together in other cases – now he began to think that the superintendent didn't want him on this one.

Determined to find out what the problem was, he went to Newtown Police Station after taking Mary home. "Unlike you to be irritable, Lennox," she'd told him, "but you were a bit snappish up there with George. Whatever it is, you'd better get it out of your system before tonight. Remember I asked your young man, Davey, to bring his new fiancée to dinner? When I knew Alys wouldn't need me, I confirmed it."

Well at least I'll get a decent meal, thought Kemp. He hadn't liked fending for himself, it reminded him too strongly of his solitary days in a cheap flat, living out of tins.

Sergeant Cobbins was at the desk sorting papers. He looked up briefly at Kemp then went back to whatever task was engaging his not very superior intellect. No greeting from the sergeant, who knew Kemp well, meant that the freezing-out ran through all of the police hierarchy.

"Is Superintendent Upshire in?" Kemp asked.

Cobbins did at least look up, but his gaze was diverted to someone else who had just come out from the back.

"Not to you, he isn't." It was the voice of the ugly one with the small black eyes. Kemp decided that in the face of this rudeness nothing was to be gained by matching it. "Inspector Hopkirk," he said, pleasantly, "I gather you're in charge of the de Lisle case."

"I am."

"I've just come from the de Lisles. I wonder if there are any new developments."

Inspector Hopkirk came round the desk and thrust himself so close to Kemp that the solicitor had to take a step back.

"You're the last person should be here asking . . . I don't give a damn that you and John Upshire were buddies in the past, Mr Kemp, but I think you've got a nerve trying to wangle information out of us." He turned on Sergeant Cobbins, and barked: "You didn't tell him anything?"

"I never even spoke." Cobbins was surly with both of them.

"I don't understand what this is all about," said Kemp, as peaceably as he could. As before, he was mystified by the inspector's behaviour.

"You understand only too well," said Hopkirk, darkly, "but I'm on to your little game. You get the run of all our investigation so you can make sure your client keeps one step ahead of us. Sending that young whippersnapper of yours round there at all hours of the night."

Kemp tried to keep both his temper, and the sequence of Hopkirk's words. "What do you mean, my client? Darren Roding's out of it."

The inspector gave a low growl in his throat. The kind of noise a hungry tiger might make on approaching its prey.

"Trying to make out you don't know your own firm's clients? Your Mr Franklyn Davey acts for Lillian Egerton. Don't he, sergeant?"

Cobbins nodded, keeping his head well down.

Kemp noted that, when really angry, Hopkirk betrayed his origins by a drop in grammar. It was an idle thought put into his

170

mind to cover up embarrassment. He exited the police station with as much dignity as possible.

Now, back at his office, it was five o'clock and he was still waiting for Franklyn Davey.

When a very flustered Frank Davey finally edged into the room, Kemp sat down but left the young man standing. "Shut the door," he said, coldly.

Forty minutes later he said, "How do you feel now?"

"Gutted," said Frank. "Like a filleted flounder. Can I sit down?"

"Yes. I think you've learnt your lesson. Sorry I had to use a knife but I had to get to the bones of what you knew – and without your notes or whatever you've written down. I wanted the sequence straight out of your mind in the order the things went in. See?"

Frank was exhausted. Kemp had taken him through every minute of the time he had spent with Lillian Egerton from the first moment of her appearance in the office on that Monday, the twentieth of February, to his last sight of her on the doorstep of her house two nights ago, putting two fingers up at the neighbourhood watch. Behind it all, he sensed his employer's purpose, to get a picture of the person and of the events in which she was concerned, all in the correct order. Clarity had been needed and, although Frank knew he had a memory trained to remember, there were times when only Kemp's sharp questions had brought things into focus.

"Of course, I know I should have come to you with all this . . ."

"Of course you should. Particularly what she asked about missing persons." He had made Frank go over and over that episode, getting the correct words used, her attitude when speaking, her reaction to his suggestion of the police.

"On that Monday morning," said Kemp, "only the two ladies up at the house, Mary and myself, knew that Elinor was missing. And of course John Upshire, but he was playing it very close. I think he simply told one or two of his officers to keep a look-out for truants from the school – the patrol cars were out on the roads on the council estate, and of course they searched the woodland area near the Drill Hall. Surprisingly, that was when the torch was found but at the time it had no significance." He glanced up at the clock on the wall of his office. "You and I are going to be in trouble with our respective mates if we don't get a move on. Go home and collect your Dinah. I think Mary said seven thirty."

"I feel such a fool." Frank was still trying to come to terms with his inadequacies. "And I've got you in bother with the local police."

"Not for the first time, Frank. I'm afraid we're going to be talking shop tonight, but I'm glad you're bringing Dinah. I could do with her opinion on all this psycho-babble your friend the doctor has been filling you up with."

Dinah was flattered that the senior partner of Gillorns should want her opinion on anything, so she was sympathetic to Frank's tale of woe, and even listened patiently to his enthusiasm for Dr Parfitt's ideas.

"He's doing his doctorate on the subject. I think he knows what he's doing."

"Researching Lily Egerton seems the fashion in Newtown," observed Dinah, drily. "The doctor's doing it in the interests of science, you're doing it in the interests of the law, and this nasty Hopkirk creature's doing it in the interests of justice."

"Wrong. Harry Hopkirk's doing it to get his own back. Sheer malice."

"That book you saw in her house," said Dinah, "it makes it obvious to me what she's up to. I think I hear our taxi outside. Come on, Franklyn, you don't want to keep your boss waiting again, do you? Sounds as if he already skinned you alive at the office."

When they were comfortably seated in the Kemps' drawing-room, Mary apologised to Dinah. "I'm afraid it's going to be shop-talk tonight at dinner. I hope you don't mind."

"Well, it takes in some of my shop too," said Dinah. But it was not until the coffee stage that Kemp brought up the subject of the book.

"Is it the kind of thing you would expect to find in the home of a nineteen-year-old checker in a factory?" he asked her.

"With brains enough to be made supervisor," Frank added.

"Or simply got promotion because she curried favour with the boss . . . I don't know as I've never met her. But the paperback, *Sybil*, is certainly of interest to students of psychology – I've a copy myself, which I've brought for you to read. But of course it's available in any public library. I'm interested in the fact that she's kept it so long – Frank says it's long overdue. As if she keeps going back to it . . ."

"So she might just have got it out like an ordinary book, then found it so intriguing she kept it," said Mary.

"What's your opinion, Dinah?" Kemp asked.

"The book only confirms what I've been thinking all along, that this Egerton girl is spoofing. Most cases of so-called multiple personality have been found to be faked. There may well be a psychotic background but there is also malingering – the desire to escape the consequences of some act. There was a rush of cases after that film was made, *The Three Faces of Eve*, but there were few found to be authentic, at least in this country; in America psychotherapists were more gullible. Perhaps I shouldn't be saying this, I'm only a student."

Dinah stopped. She was aware that her tongue was running away with her; there was also the little matter of her personal view that the Egerton girl might be taking up too much of Franklyn's time.

"Say someone wanted to pretend to have multiple personalities," Mary wondered, "all they'd have to do would be to read up the symptoms in this book, and fake them."

Frank disagreed. "I don't think you could hope to fool a doctor, particularly one with an interest in psychology."

"I'm not so much interested in Miss Egerton's psyche," said Kemp, rather impatiently, "as in her timetable. Let me put it this way: nobody has come forward to say they were meeting Elinor that night, and yet it's clear that she *was* meeting someone at or near the Drill Hall. I think it was Lillian, and the meeting had been arranged beforehand. Either Elinor didn't turn up, or they separated sometime later, and Lillian lost her – hence her reason for asking you about missing persons. Perhaps Elinor had already spoken to her about doing a bolt, getting her own back on an interfering grandmother by a disappearing act. It would explain the phone call, setting up the Hodge mother and daughter as a temporary alibi."

But Mary was shaking her head. "I don't see Elinor doing that to her mother." She sighed. "But then I don't know the girl. Young people can be needlessly cruel sometimes."

Frank repeated what Monica had told him, that Elinor was worried about her mother and thought that maybe she was ill.

"I've been with Alys a lot, and I've seen no signs of any physical illness but I'm not a doctor. She's altogether stunned by grief, grief and guilt. Says she shouldn't have been out that night."

"To be strictly logical," said her husband, "it would have made no difference. Elinor would still have been killed."

"Oh, logic," said Mary, sharply, "there's little help in that. The sorrow of Alys is beyond logic."

"If she had been ill, as Monica Hodge suspected, at least she's got a good doctor in Gerald Parfitt."

"You've met him?" Mary asked. "Yes, he's been very attentive and understanding. She needs a lot of that. She's not at ease with George, the guilt seems to get in the way. So it's to strangers like myself and Dr Parfitt she turns to when she wants to talk."

"Perhaps he could try some of his psychotherapy on her," said Dinah, and then realised it sounded a snide remark. Could she possibly also be jealous of this man Frank had taken to so enthusiastically?

"I only meant that he's interested in the subject," she went on, hurriedly, "and that's why he's been studying Lily Egerton, of course." She turned to her fiancé. "Despite what I've said about this book called *Sybil*, do you still seriously think she really has multiple personalities?"

"Yes, I do," he said, stoutly, "because I don't think she could fool someone like Gerald Parfitt. He's a smart young man with a good career ahead of him, and great taste in women."

"Indeed. And how do you know that, Frank?"

"He's courting the pretty receptionist at the health centre, and she's very like you – blonde, bobbed and beautiful – so there . . ."

"You got out of that one nicely," said Kemp, "we'll make a lawyer of you yet."

"I don't see why Frank has to be the one to interview all the girls in this case. Let me see, there's Lillian of course, all dark and spiky, then this Crystal with the big brown eyes, and what was the name of the one in the sweet shop with the ringlets?"

Frank felt himself go red. He didn't want to discuss Teresa Cane, for he lacked the nerve to tell Dinah about the gang spying on courting couples. He'd had to tell Kemp, of course, but with Dinah there would be memories of intimate moments, spoiled now for him and, if he told her, spoiled for her too.

He changed the subject. "That tale Lillian gave the police about being up in London clubbing, I don't believe a word of it. She goes off into these fantasies when she wants to hide something. It's just another of her Mercedes Benz stories. I wonder where she got the name Simon Marco from? Sounds like a film star."

"Or a drugs dealer," said Kemp. "The police will have chased it up by now, and if she's lying they'll have her down the station in the wink of an eye."

"I wonder which of the Lillians they'll get?" said Frank when he and Dinah were in the hall, putting on coats and saying goodbyes.

"And which of you two lawyers will defend her?" Dinah laughed, but looked at her host for reassurance.

"Don't fret," he said, "I wouldn't let any of her personalities within a mile of your young man."

Twenty-four

W PC Peggy Pollard was disappointed with Lillian Egerton's appearance on the doorstep of 24 Marshall Avenue at eight o'clock in the morning. On the way there she had been well entertained by DS Martin and his stories of this feisty lady, and of course she had listened to the legend circulating the station that Harry Hopkirk had had an affair with her – the legend, recently revived, grew with each telling. Even PC Andrews, who was a bit of a wet as far as Peggy was concerned, had given a blow-by-blow description of his last visit to the Egerton house when, accompanied by Hopkirk, he had listened to a tirade of what he described, primly, as sexual filth. It was no wonder Peggy Pollard was eager to meet the lady.

The timing of what Inspector Hopkirk called "pulling her in" and the more correct "asking her to accompany them to the station" had been fully discussed the night before at the big meeting of the investigative team. Hopkirk had been all for picking her up at work, regardless of the effect on the rest of the staff at Bernes; the other two senior officers, Upshire and West, had favoured an early morning call at her house before she left for the factory, and this plan prevailed.

WPC Pollard couldn't believe they'd come to the right house. "Miss Egerton," she said to the woman who answered the door, "I'm WPC Pollard from Newtown police and this is my colleague, DS Martin. We have to ask you to come with us to the police station to help us with our enquiries into the murder of Elinor de Lisle."

Lillian Egerton was pale of face, and wispish of hair. She had on a faded pink jumper and a tweed skirt down below her knees. She already had a dark duffle coat in one hand.

"But I'm just going to work," she said peevishly. "I have to be there by half-past."

"We will inform Bernes that you will be late this morning," said DS Martin, helpfully. He would have sworn this must be a sister of Lillian Egerton, there was some resemblance to the harridan who had been here on his last visit, but not much . . . "I must ask you to come with us."

"No," she said, flatly, "this is the morning I check the returns. Mr Bexby expects me to be there."

"Your absence will be explained, Miss Egerton." While she was talking, Peggy had been taking a good look at the woman who for days had been at the centre of discussion at Newtown Police Station . . . Surely it couldn't be this mouselike creature, her face unmade-up, her clothes dowdy to the point of total drabness, her stockings wrinkled and her feet carelessly pushed into shapeless slippers.

"I suppose I could come for a little while," said the creature, as if it was a social event she wasn't keen on attending, "but the foreman won't be pleased, he'll have to do the checking himself."

She awaited the response of the two police officers; when none came, she withdrew into the doorway. "I'll have to change my shoes," she said, disappearing.

Although they had not been invited in, Sergeant Martin thought it wise to follow her into the hall. Peggy went in, too, anxious to get a look at what she had heard was a den of vice. But the place was tidy, there were no youngsters lying half-doped on beanbags in the sitting-room, and the packet of white powder on the dresser in the kitchen was Persil. DS Martin stuck a finger in it, licked it and grimaced. Lillian Egerton was scuffling her feet into shoes that were in little better shape than her slippers, and took no notice of him.

She followed them out of the front door which she carefully locked, at the same time grumbling away in a querulous tone about the foreman's ignorance of the work she should be doing that morning, and how she'd have to make up for lost time when she got into work later. She showed no curiosity about the reason why she was being taken to the police station, though she did turn at one stage to Peggy Pollard and say, "I've never seen you before." She made it sound like another complaint.

The interview did not go well from the various officers' points of view. It started off badly by Lillian Egerton saying that she'd no idea why she should be there because she'd never had anything to do with the dead girl, and she'd been told that the murdered teenager was what it was all about.

Inspector West reminded her, quite gently, that she had already been questioned about her movements on the Saturday night the girl went missing. Since then they had tried to verify her story of being up in London with a man called Simon Marco; Mr Marco had denied seeing her.

Lillian simply looked bewildered. "I don't know anyone of the name of Marco," she said, "and I never go to London except maybe on my day off to do some shopping. I'd never go on a Saturday night."

"Where were you then?" This was Inspector Hopkirk who was sharing the honours today with Peter West.

"When was that?" She peered at him with dull eyes.

"Come on, Lillian," he said, roughly, "last time you were in here you were only too anxious to tell us all about your visit to a London club with Mr Marco – only it wasn't true, was it?"

"Where was I?" she repeated. "On a Saturday night? I always wash my hair on Saturday nights so I was home, wasn't I?"

It was hard going, interviewing Lillian Egerton. "Like pushing a pram through mud," grumbled DS Martin, from experience; he had recently become a father. "If I didn't know better, I'd say it was a different girl."

"It's uncanny," agreed Inspector West, "she even looks different, and yet there are sometimes flashes of the girl who was in here before. But her whole attitude has changed."

These officers were having a breather, leaving the interview room to John Upshire and Harry Hopcroft. Superintendent Upshire had not seen Lillian Egerton before, although he had all the reports on her, and her own statements in front of him. His first impression of her was that she looked crumpled, and tired out.

"Has Miss Egerton had any refreshments?" he asked, sharply.

WPC Pollard was at the back of the room. She came forward. "No," she said.

"See to it." He turned to Lillian. "I think we'll have a break now, Miss Egerton."

She drank the tea, listlessly, and ate two biscuits. She gave a little smile. "It's just about now we get our tea at the factory," she said to the inspector. "I was ready for it."

Inspector Hopkirk took over after the break, and tried to be a little less brusque, as John Upshire was seated beside him.

"Miss Egerton," he said, leaning forward, "we have a witness who says that Elinor de Lisle has been in your house, that she was a friend of yours. She might even have been a member of your gang?"

She brushed wisps of hair from her forehead. "What gang is that?" she asked in a puzzled tone.

"They come round to your house, Lillian," said John Upshire, "almost every week. You know all of them, Kevin Williams, Jeff Coyne, Darren Roding – they're in and out of your house a lot."

"I've got friends, yes," she said, sulkily. "What's wrong with having friends?"

"And Elinor de Lisle was one of them," Inspector Hopkirk snapped.

"I don't think so . . . Mebbe she came with one of the others. They do come in sometimes for tea and a chat when there's no place else for them to go."

"Where were you on Tuesday night, the twenty-eighth?"

"I'd be home. I'm always home in the evenings. I get tired after work. I'd have a bite of supper, then wash up, mebbe watch the telly. I generally go to bed about half-past ten. It would be the same that night. Why're you asking?"

"Darren Roding came to your house that night about eight o'clock and stayed for more than an hour. During that time you went out on your motor bike, didn't you?" Harry Hopkirk, when he was on firm ground, could sound quite staccato – he

179

liked to think of his questioning as the rattle of a machine-gun. Here he didn't get quite the reaction he expected.

Lillian turned her pale greenish eyes on him. "Oh, Mr Hopkirk," she said, "I think you should tell your wife there's a gap in her bedroom curtains, looks like they needs sewing up . . . I thought I should tell you for you never know who might be looking in. Sorry about that," she turned her attention back to the superintendent, "it was just something I suddenly remembered."

John Upshire was more amused than anything else by his junior colleagues' discomfiture; it also made him study Lillian Egerton more closely. "You are not giving us satisfactory answers, Miss Egerton," he said. "I think I should warn you of the effect that such evasiveness has on our investigation. This is a murder enquiry and not to be taken lightly."

To his surprise, although the eyes remained expressionless, tears gathered in the corners. She blinked.

"Of course I'm ever so sorry about the girl. She was only young, wasn't she? But I can't help you."

"Oh, I think you can," said Inspector Hopkirk, with rising anger. "You have told us lies, and that is suspicious in itself. Now you are refusing to answer our perfectly reasonable questions." He paused as if to allow his message to get through. "And there's another matter . . ." He glanced at John Upshire who gave him a nod.

"Did you know that Simon Marco is a self-confessed dealer in drugs?"

"This is the man you asked me about before?" She was back to her lifeless tone. "And I'm supposed to know him?"

"I have your statement here, made at this station when you were last in for questioning, Miss Egerton." Upshire read it out. "Lillian Egerton stated that on the evening of Saturday the twenty-fifth of February she went to a nightclub off Leicester Square in the company of one Simon Marco, and was there between the hours of nine and three the next morning."

"And that was a tissue of lies!" barked Hopkirk, taking the paper from Upshire and waving it in front of Lillian's face. She shrank away but only, it appeared, to keep the document out of her hair. "Did I say all that?" she asked, "for I don't remember any of it."

"You know what I think?" Hopkirk adopted his most menacing stance yet, his face barely an inch from hers. "I think you brought Elinor de Lisle into your snug little circle of wrongdoers, it pleased your crazy sense of humour to try to corrupt this innocent girl . . . I think Elinor wouldn't play your game. She would have nothing to do with drugs, but she saw you at it . . . I think she saw you, on that Saturday night, taking your delivery of drugs . . . What would a well-brought-up girl like Elinor de Lisle do? She would tell, wouldn't she? She would want to go to the police . . . So you killed her. And you and some of your gang tried to hide the body in the den, didn't you?"

Superintendent Upshire had been warned by Hopkirk that he would attack when he thought the time was ripe. It was vicious when it came, but Upshire could not object; they were making little headway on the case, all other leads had stalled, and this obtuseness on the part of Lillian Egerton had to be broken. Carefully, he watched her response to the onslaught of accusations.

"Could I have a glass of water?" she said, and in the same level tone, she added, "and a solicitor?"

"You were offered one when you came in," said Upshire, realising it wasn't clear which. "But you said you didn't need a solicitor."

"That was then." She cleared her throat. A carefe and a glass were brought and she swallowed the water greedily.

The recording was switched off, and Upshire and Hopkirk left the interview room.

Hopkirk wiped his forehead. "I've never met anyone so . . ." He was at a loss for words.

John Upshire went to the phone. "She says she wants that chap at Gillorns, the one she had before."

"Franklyn Davey. She's got him eating out of her hand. Talk about eating, I need my lunch."

John Upshire relayed the message to Gillorns that a client of theirs required the services of Mr Davey down at the station,

181

then he too joined his inspector in the canteen.

It was left to WPC Pollard to watch over Lillian when a tray was brought in to her. Peggy was astonished to see the girl eat heartily.

"Not as good as we get at Bernes," she told Peggy, "but I was hungry. I don't know what kind of a mess my foreman has got the checking in, I'll have to sort the lot out when I go in."

Surprisingly, Peggy found herself caught up in a quite ordinary conversation about their respective jobs, their hours of work, the perks, and even the pay. After forty minutes, Peggy was seriously considering training as a supervisor at the optics firm.

Twenty-five

It was half-past two when Lennox Kemp reached the station; he hadn't hurried. He found both John Upshire and Harry Hopkirk looking rather grumpy, and realised that, whatever their objective might have been in questioning Lillian Egerton, it had not met with any great success.

It must have been the first time in their long relationship that John Upshire had scowled at him, but Kemp ignored it. "I want," he said, briskly, "all the documentation you have on my new client, whom I have not yet met. And I want a room where I can talk to her free of you lot."

"You can't," began Inspector Hopkirk, with a mutinous look.

"Oh, but I can . . . Even a dock brief gets a few words alone with his client."

"All right," said John Upshire. "It's a deal, so long as you play fair with us. Which you haven't, to date."

"I did not know that my assistant solicitor acted for Miss Egerton until last night. I remained in ignorance of this connection all the time I was talking either to you, John, or George de Lisle about the case. Naturally I take full responsibility for my young man's actions but, as I understand it, he too was acting in good faith."

Harry Hopkirk gave a snort of derision, but the superintendent gave a half-hearted apology. "I'm sorry," he said, gruffly, "I just took it for granted you knew. We'll let you have a room where you can see your client."

Kemp took a good quarter of an hour on the papers – reluctantly produced by Inspector Hopkirk – before saying he was ready to see his client.

The first things she said was: "I don't know you. Where's Franklyn Davey?"

"Submerged in the law reports. I'm Lennox Kemp, his boss."

He took a good look at her. She was dressed in dowdy clothes, the kind that would not draw the attention, her hair straggled on her shoulders, a dullish brown and, as she sat in the chair opposite him, she dropped her shoulders so that the dirty-pink jumper flattened her chest. It's all deliberate, he thought. This is one clever little lady.

"I'm here to represent you as your solicitor," he told her, pleasantly. "I've been reading your file."

She said nothing, simply looked at him with eyes which reminded him of the thick greenish glass at the foot of cheap wine bottles.

"You tell a lot of lies, Lillian. May I call you Lillian?"

She shrugged. "I didn't ask for you, Mr Kemp. I don't think I can get on with you."

"I'm not sure I can get on with you either," said Kemp, equably, "but the system decrees we're stuck with each other." He paused while she gazed at him blankly. He stared back at her, with a look not unlike hers, opaque, giving nothing away.

"I've learned a great deal about you, Lily, from my young colleague, and of course from the police whose hospitality you're now enjoying. I also have some scanty reportage of your medical condition from your doctors. All this at second-hand, which isn't the best basis for a correct assessment of you, Lily." Again he threw in the diminutive at which she blinked, but said nothing.

"I'm going to tell you a story, so just sit back and relax. Do you want a cigarette?"

"I don't smoke."

"I thought perhaps you did, Lily."

"Don't call me Lily."

"OK, Lillian. Now for the story: there once was a little girl of about five or six, and she was in a car accident with her mum and dad who were both killed. The little girl had a wonderful time, she was given all kinds of presents: toys and sweets and little bicycles, dolls and prams, and lots of lovely clothes. Everyone felt so sorry for her, they wanted to console her for the loss of her parents. For the first few months, even at school, she got all the attention she'd never had before. But of course the memory of most folks is short, and soon the public forgot all about little Lily Egerton, the heroine of the tragedy. She came out to Newtown to live with her grandparents, and she went to the local school. She became just one of many, an ordinary girl growing up, neither good nor bad, not remarkable in any way. But she never forgot those heady months when she had been showered with attention, and loved every minute of it. She evolved a fantasy world for herself, alone in which she was back there being the heroine of the moment. It was such fun that she gradually spread it out into the everyday world, and found that she had quite a talent for getting noticed, and getting noticed was the first step towards that centre stage she'd enjoyed when she was six—"

"Five, actually, I was five and a half." The voice was different, she was sitting up straighter, which made her jumper fit her figure, her eyes were a deeper green.

"There's all kinds of ways to get noticed, aren't there, Lillian? Wearing dowdy clothes when you don't have to is one of them, talking like a tired rabbit is another, playing dumb in fact . . . The role you play at Bernes, although you couldn't quite hide the fact that you are actually quite bright, so you got noticed – and promoted . . ."

She made a gun of her first two fingers and shot him in the eye. "Bingo!" she said.

Kemp pressed on, relentlessly. "Then you happened to pick up a book in the library about someone with multiple personalities, or the term was mentioned to you – I don't know which came first, the chicken or the egg – but it gave you an idea you could exploit . . . How am I doing?"

She grinned. "Right on."

"You got a certain doctor interested – not the older one at the centre because he'd known you too long and he'd have spotted your little game – a harmless little game, Lily, until now."

"That's a great book, that *Sybil* . . . Jeez, sixteen separate personalities. I could only manage two or three. I think I got the red-haired doc fooled, though. He began to give me lots of attention – oh, not in the way all you men think – I'm not into that kinda thing. No, it was just he'd always see me if I rang up, and he'd want to talk for ages. Kept the old tabbies waiting outside, you should've seen the looks I got. Yeah, he treated me special, like."

"So you hurled a brick through his window."

"That was a great feeling. He'd let his attention wander for a week or so. Know what I mean? When the blonde bimbo started work as receptionist. So I thought I'd let him know I was still around, like."

"Seems to have worked. He's writing a thesis on you."

"Gee, that's cool. A book about me. Shows what a girl can do when she gets a bit of attention."

PC Andrews came into the room, and stood smartly to attention. "Inspector Hopkirk wants to know how long you're going to be."

"Wants to get home to his missus, does he?" Lillian turned and looked at the young constable who blushed. "Does he give her one afternoons as well?"

"Another ten minutes," said Kemp, snappily. "Then your inspector can have her."

When Andrews had left Lillian turned on Kemp. "Aren't you going to get me outta here? That's what lawyers are for . . ."

"Only when you've answered some questions. You're in deep trouble, my girl, and it's time you came out of your fantasy world and faced facts."

"Such as?"

"I want to know about your relationship with two people because that's where the officers are going to nail you. One is a man called Simon Marco—"

"I've told them over and over I don't know any Simon Marco."

"Oh, cut it out, Lillian, he's the man who supplies the dope, the runner who takes the money . . ."

"I don't know what you mean."

"I see, we're back to the rabbit talk. You know what I've figured out? There must have been money in trust for you until you were eighteen, then it went to your head. It's what you had over the other teenagers on the estate, so you gave them all the fun of free drugs and in return they made you Queen Bee. But it's all going to come unstuck, Lillian. The police have got Simon Marco, and he's landed you right in it."

She thought about it. "I've never actually met him," she said. "All I did was phone a number and order the stuff, and leave the money."

"The night Elinor went missing, was there a delivery?"

She hesitated. "Yes."

"And you went to the den to see if it had come?"

Kemp hadn't expected the tears, the outburst of pent-up feelings.

It was some time before she regained some composure. "So that was it," said Kemp, leaning back in his chair. "It's that you were hiding. That's why you made up that ridiculous story about going clubbing." She had been sniffling into a torn tissue. "Here," he said, handing her a large clean handkerchief.

There was a lot of heavy stamping of feet out in the corridor; the wolves were getting impatient. Kemp decided to ignore them. "Take your time, Lillian, and tell me exactly what was supposed to have happened that night between you and Elinor, and what actually did happen."

She blew her nose which by now was quite pink. She wiped the last of the tears from her eyes, faced him stolidly, and told him.

It was simple enough. Elinor and she had been friends for some months, the younger girl intrigued by the gang, the older one genuinely fond of the impulsive young schoolgirl. Elinor wanted to show a spark of rebellion by spending a night away from home, going to stay with Lillian at Marshall Avenue in order to share in whatever gang activity was going on. Elinor would go to the youth club with Monica Hodge, then ditch her and meet Lillian who was outside with her motor bike. They would then go up to the Drill Hall to the forbidden concert. From there Elinor phoned her grandmother to say that she

187

would be spending the night at the Hodges. All went according to plan, and Lillian watched the phone call being made. She even reproduced much the same giggles when telling of it. "Gran'll be so sozzled," Elinor had remarked, "she'll never remember the time . . ."

"She'd never have got away with it if her mother had been there," Lillian remarked. "I don't think she'd have tried it on. She was very protective about her mother – it was her gran she took the mickey out of."

"Did you ever meet Elinor's mother?"

"Good lord, no. That was never on the cards. But, well, I did imagine what she was like, so pale and lovely, with all that long golden hair . . . like the one in the fairy story that lets down her hair." There was a far-away look in Lillian's eyes, perhaps she was imagining the mother she'd love to have had. Kemp must bring her back to unpleasant reality.

"What happened next, up at the Drill Hall?"

She was reluctant at this point; only persistent questions from Kemp finally got the facts from her. Lillian had to check out Turpin's Cave to make sure the delivery had been made, and the money taken. She could be there and back on her bike in twenty minutes, but she daren't take Elinor . . . Never – and she was vehement about this – had any hint been dropped about drugs within the gang when Elinor was about, Lillian made sure of that. Elinor was against drugs of any kind, she'd never experimented with them, and vowed she never would; she simply thought that those who did were stupid.

"But you did go to the den?"

"Yes," said Lillian, miserably, "and now I'd give anything . . . I'd give my right arm." She struck the table hard with her fist. "I wish I'd never gone."

But she had. She'd told Elinor to stay at the Hall, listen to the gigs going on, maybe talk to some of the boys from school, while Lillian had to go and meet someone. She promised she'd be back in no time at all, and they arranged where they'd meet, just by the phone box . . .

"I was hardly fifteen minutes away. There was the start of a frost and the ground was hard, so I got the bike down to the den, had a quick peek in, saw the stuff was there, and raced back. I never touched a thing, there wasn't time. Anyway, I'd meant to leave the stash there – wouldn't have it in the house because Elinor was coming to stay."

"When you arrived back at the concert Elinor wasn't to be seen?"

"I never saw her again . . . I'm telling you this, Mr Kemp, like it really was. I hunted around for her. The concert was still going on but she wasn't inside the hall. I searched everywhere, hung around the toilets and by the phone box for at least another hour. Then I decided she'd got the wind up, chickened out, like, and gone home. So I got on my bike and did the same."

Kemp felt a wave of pity for both of them, the dead and the living. A perfectly innocent small friendship between two young girls who liked each other, and were filled with inexpressible yearnings for things they couldn't name and a restless discontent with things as they are.

But he must stay with practical matters. Why hadn't some-one seen Lillian Egerton at the Drill Hall? She was usually pretty conspicuous.

"What were you wearing that night?"

"Clobber I wouldn't be noticed in. It had to be secret, like, the fact that Elinor and I were pals . . . So I couldn't ask around for her up there. All I could think of was that she'd cried off the whole thing. But she didn't phone me Sunday which was what she always did – it was kind of a pre-arranged signal we had. Nor was she at the youth club where I'd call for her if she'd not been on the phone . . . Then I starts to think, mebbe she did want to go through with it, mebbe she'd taken off on her own Saturday night. She was that sort, once an idea was in her head, she wouldn't give it up. And that's when I began to worry."

Kemp told her where Elinor's torch was found. George had described the place to him.

Lillian's eyes widened: "What did she go up there for? That's lovers'-bloody-lane, what was she doing up there? I told her we'd dropped all that, too much hassle from it, all that swearing. Only the lads still kept on with it, but I told them I didn't approve."

"Quite right, too." Kemp shook his head at her, as he got to his feet. "That was a nasty little game your gang was up to, spying on parked cars."

She had the grace to go red, but she tried to blazon it out just the same. "I don't approve of adultery," she said, primly.

Kemp got to his feet and went over to the door. "You now must tell the gentlemen in the back room exactly what you've told me, all of it . . . Do you understand?"

"I thought you were going to get me outta here?"

"No chance, I'm afraid. There's bound to be a drugs charge, but we can deal with that later. What you should have been scared of was a much more serious matter, but if you've told me the truth – and I think you have – then I am convinced you had nothing to do with Elinor's death."

She started up from her seat, and almost shouted at him: "Who on earth would think I could harm the girl? She was my friend. How can anyone think—"

"Oh, but the police do, Lillian. All they've had from you to date is lies and more lies. Now you must tell them the truth."

"Surely they can get to the truth without my help," she said, wildly. "Why should I help them? Isn't it their job to get to the truth?"

Kemp shook his head at her. "My poor child," he said, "you're under a delusion. The job of the police isn't to establish the truth but to present a case that can be proved beyond all reasonable doubt through the provision of legally admissible evidence."

The change in him startled her. She had taken him to be sympathetic to her plight, now there was a new seriousness in his tone.

Then he smiled. "Tell the truth, Lillian. Surprise them."

He opened the door, and Inspector Hopkirk almost fell into the room. "About time," he grumbled. "Do you think we could have the pleasure of Miss Egerton's company now?" He hadn't the voice for heavy sarcasm, being more the barking type, so the remark fell rather flat.

"I think my client could do with some refreshment, it's more than two hours since she had anything to eat. And while you're taking care of that, I'd like a word with your superintendent."

Twenty-six

Superintendent John Upshire was unhappy. "We kept the drugs element from the media to give the squad in the Met a chance to get on to that syndicate, they'd been after them for months. They didn't want anyone getting warned – and then your young man gets mixed up with one of their pushers."

"She's not a pusher. She's just a silly kid who only got into drugs to show off to her mates. I say go easy on her, and in return she'll give you vital information on the real issue – who killed Elinor de Lisle."

"I don't do deals," said Upshire, but he listened all the same.

"You mean Lillian Egerton is willing to retract her statement about being in London that Saturday night?"

Kemp nodded. "She'll tell you why Elinor went missing, what the two of them had planned, and what actually happened."

Upshire glowered. "How do we know it's not a lot more lies?"

"You don't, but you have to listen and make up your own mind. Believe me, John, what she has to say may be vital in catching the real killer, so you can't afford to ignore it."

"You trying to teach me my job? You get back to yours and let me handle this."

It must have taken some time for the superintendent to persuade other officers that the suspect they were holding at the station should be given the chance to explain herself. She wanted to change her story about her whereabouts on that Saturday night; she had not been up in London clubbing, neither had she been at home all evening washing her hair.

In the meantime, Kemp had managed to get some work done in his office, and he had also a word with Frank Davey. "I never told her drugs had been found at the scene," he protested.

Kemp shrugged. "You didn't need to, she knew it. She went out there on the Tuesday night after Darren had been to the house, but she didn't get far into the woods before she saw the place was swarming with police. She said she just stopped somewhere at the side of the main road out of Newtown, and cried. She was actually very fond of the girl."

"You don't think then that she could have done something during one of her transitional states – Dr Parfitt calls them fugues – that she doesn't remember? You say Lillian cries now – could they be tears of guilt which only her subconscious recognises?"

Fortunately Kemp's buzzer went off before he could answer. "Yes?" he said. "OK, I'll be right there."

"I'm wanted at the police station," Kemp told Frank curtly. "You take over signing the mail, and for God's sake keep your Freudian ideas to yourself!"

All the same Frank's words stuck in Kemp's mind as he drove to the station; the young man had got to know Lillian Egerton well, better perhaps than Kemp could have done in his short time with her. Frank and that doctor had their theory, he, Kemp had his . . . Was there much to choose between them as to the cause of the girl's deviant behaviour, or the outcome?

Nonsense, he told himself; I'm a reasonable man, the man on the Clapham omnibus, I believe only what is reasonable.

But even as he mounted the steps into the station, a little voice at the back of his mind told him he was not a medical man and he had never read psychology.

They were all waiting for him in the largest of the interview rooms – Lillian was obviously getting the VIP treatment. There was a WPC just inside the door, Upshire himself was in a chair to one side while Inspectors West and Hopkirk were at the table with their suspect, looking for all the world as if they were about to hold a seance. Kemp took the empty seat beside Lillian.

They let him hear the recording already made of the question and answer interview, in which Lillian said that she had originally lied about Saturday night but that now she was telling them the truth. Apart from the fact that she didn't sob and cry, her recital was very much as she had told Kemp, leaving out her more intimate feelings. She was asked, among other things, what Elinor had been wearing, and what frame of mind she'd been in. She gave them a rough idea of the time they had got to the concert, the time of the phone call, and the time she had left to go to the den.

At this point, Hopkirk had snapped in quickly with: "And you went there again the following Tuesday night, didn't you?"

Lillian's voice hadn't wavered. "No, I didn't get there. You people were all over the place."

"But it was you at 24 Marshall Avenue who took Darren Roding in?" Hopkirk again.

"I didn't want him getting into no trouble. Anyway, I wanted to see if what he said was true." She was silent for a moment. "I never saw her . . . Not after she was dead."

"You didn't get back till Darren had gone. Where were you?"

"I dunno. I was upset. Somewhere in the woods."

It was when the officers got on to questioning her about Simon Marco and the arrangements for receiving consignments of drugs that the tape had been stopped because Lillian had requested the presence of her lawyer.

"It's only right she should have her lawyer present," said John Upshire, gruffly, "since there could well be charges."

"On account of the drugs?" asked Kemp, sharply.

"Yes."

Kemp listened but said little as they took Lillian through her association with Simon Marco, and the bizarre plan she'd hatched for the drops at Turpin's Cave. She was at her most exasperating, at turns brash and boastful, at others sullen and uncooperative, her mouth a hard line and her eyes blank. Kemp could see the irritation her attitude was causing to the interviewing officers, and he was not surprised when Hopkirk eventually blew his top. He lumbered to his feet like a midget

Mussolini and, on a nod from the superintendent, he began the formalities of charging her.

By the time he'd reached the words " . . . but it may harm your defence if you do not mention", Lillian was under the table. She had slipped to the floor in one fluid movement like a Victorian maiden in a perfect swoon.

Kemp pushed his chair back and knelt beside her. Her face was very white, the colour of parchment, and there was a slight froth round her mouth. Above him Inspector Hopkirk was droning on with the end of the caution.

"Get a doctor," said Kemp to the WPC by the door, "and you, Inspector Hopkirk, can shut up. An accused is supposed to understand a caution, this one's beyond hearing."

The superintendent repeated, "Yes, Peggy, get the station medico and if he's not available ring the Newtown Health Centre. There's bound to be a doctor in the surgery. Jump to it, it's urgent."

Together he and Kemp got Lillian out from under the table as gently as possible. "She's breathing," said Kemp. "Perhaps it's only a faint and she'll come round in a minute."

"She ought to be made more comfortable," said Peter West. "I'll get a pillow from one of the cells and something to cover her with. Aren't you supposed to keep them warm?" He went off, thankful to be doing something practical.

Balked of his prey, Inspector Hopkirk disengaged the tape-recorder and shuffled the files on the table. "Is she coming to?" he kept asking, as if he'd hit her and she was down for the count.

She stirred, and blinked open her eyes. "Are you all right?" Kemp s
aid to her. "You seem to have fainted." There was saliva at the corners of her mouth, and her eyes had turned inwards so that all he could see were their whites.

"She looks pretty awful," said John Upshire, helplessly. He'd followed all the First Aid procedures in the book, but still wasn't happy. "God, this is the last thing we want at the station. At least you're here, Kemp . . . You can vouch for her not being bullied, there were no threats."

"Being charged is probably threat enough to someone like

195

her." He was feeling rather useless himself and was glad when West returned with a pillow and blanket, and they were able to make the girl at least look more comfortable.

The time waiting for the doctor seemed interminable, although it was a mere quarter of an hour. The trouble was, they didn't know what to say to each other. With Kemp in the room, the officers could not speak of the case, nor indeed refer to the charge against his client which Hopkirk had begun so zealously, and which in the end had trailed off into words meaning nothing. Of course Harry was only waiting for the suspect to get up on her feet before getting on with the formalities of arrest.

"Is this a sort of faint, or a fit, or is she spoofing?" he asked, but nobody wanted to take responsibility for an answer. Kemp himself was at a loss. He took her hand from time to time; there was a pulse, and she was breathing, though with a rasping sound. Was it a coma, he wondered, or was this what she would be like when in a fugue? Wasn't that what Frank had called it?

Peggy Pollard had come in to say that the police doctor was unavailable, but she'd phoned the surgery, and been told that either Doctor Sutherland or Doctor Parfitt would be on their way as a matter of urgency. Peggy knelt down beside Lillian with a glass of water, which she held to her lips, and the patient managed a sip. Peggy moistened a handkerchief and wiped the girl's forehead, and round the eyes which stared back at her blankly.

It was the red-headed doctor who came finally. He took one look at Lillian and said, "Miss Egerton is a patient of mine. I don't know what she's doing in a police station but I can tell you right now what's wrong with her. She's anaemic and has faints, but this is more serious. She suffers from a psychological illness which can lead to a changed state of consciousness – in short a fugue – and ten to one that's what she's in now." From his position beside his patient, he glared up at them. "It happens when she feels threatened, when people try to intimidate her – I don't like to use the word 'bullying' – but that would be enough to cause the condition."

Although he was down on the floor beside his patient, Dr Parfitt had nevertheless a position of advantage over the other persons in the room – he had a stethoscope. Gesturing to Peggy Pollard to help him, he got Lillian into a sitting position in order to loosen her clothing and examine her. Apparently satisfied, he rested her back on to the pillow and got up.

"Well obviously she can't stay here," he said, reasonably. "I'll arrange for her to be kept overnight in one of the amenity beds at the Cottage Hospital. To save an ambulance, I'll take her there in my car. Any objections?"

Inspector Hopkirk began to make noises of protest but was stopped by John Upshire.

"I think you should know the reason why Miss Egerton is at the station. She was helping us with enquiries into one of our cases when she collapsed. Naturally we are anxious she should completely recover before we question her again."

"So she's not under arrest, or anything like that?" Dr Parfitt was a very direct young man.

"That is correct," said the superintendent, just about drowning out Hopkirk's fervent, "Not yet, she isn't."

"All the same," Upshire went on, smoothly, "one of our officers should be on hand."

"That's all right with me. What about this young lady?" Parfitt waved a hand at Peggy Pollard. "Won't she do?"

The procession which left the police station consisted of Doctor Parfitt carrying Lillian Egerton still wrapped in the cell blanket, WPC Pollard with the handbag Lillian had brought with her that morning and a small overnight satchel of her own, while Lennox Kemp brought up the rear feeling useless.

He looked in at his client once she was lying on the back seat of the doctor's car, and was pleased to see some colour had come back into her cheeks. He stopped Dr Parfitt as he was opening the driver's door.

"As you may have gathered, I'm Lennox Kemp, Miss Egerton's solicitor."

Gerald Parfitt held out his hand. "Pleased to meet you," he said. "I thought Franklyn Davey was—"

"My assistant." said Kemp. "I took over this afternoon."

"Well, I'm glad she's got somebody on the legal side. I can only help her medically."

"That was what I wanted to ask you. This state of fugue. Could she do something while in it that she wouldn't remember afterwards?"

"It's possible. It's what I've been afraid of all along . . ." Gerald Parfitt got into the car and, with a quick wave, he drove away.

Kemp went over to his own car. He felt restless, dissatisfied. He must talk over these developments with someone who would help him to shake the bits into place. Frank Davey would be home from the office by now.

He found the young solicitor watching the six o'clock news while Dinah was in the kitchen preparing their evening meal. Once Kemp had given them a full report of the happenings at the police station, there was a divided response.

"It shows Gerald Parfitt was right – Lillian's really ill." This from Frank, but Dinah demurred.

"Not necessarily so," she said, "at least not in the way you're thinking."

Kemp gave her his own theory about Lillian Egerton, but with less assurance than he had felt earlier that afternoon. "It looked like a faint or a state of fugue, as the good doctor calls it, but I still have doubts. Is there a description of possible symptoms in that book?"

"Yes, there is. I've just re-read it because I was interested – it's all pretty explicit if you did want to fake the condition."

Kemp nodded. "And it came spot on, just when she was about to be charged with the drug offences. Either way, the girl's in trouble. I don't like what Dr Parfitt said about her not remembering . . . He'd been afraid of it all along."

"That was the impression he gave me. As if he knew she could do some act, even a violent one, and not remember it afterwards. Did he say this in front of the police officers?"

"No, I asked him about it when he was getting into his car but the policewoman who was there would have heard what he said. She's gone to the hospital with Lillian."

"That sounds like Harry Hopkirk's doing." Frank was indignant. "You say she's not under arrest, but he makes sure he's got a police presence in case she says anything, or even tries to bunk off."

"As an outsider," began Dinah, "I'm intrigued by the Hopkirk-Egerton thing. Do you think it's true he made a pass at her months ago?"

"Difficult to distinguish fact from fiction when Lillian tells it, but, yes, I think he did. Say she was out for an evening all dressed up in her gear, she would look both attractive and an easy lay. Harry could well have tried to pick her up, and she brushed him off – not particularly kindly either. She had quite a thing about his ugliness. Then she got her own back by following him and his girlfriend up to the woods . . ."

"You didn't tell me about that," said Dinah, turning on him. "Come on, what happened?"

Rather shamefacedly, Frank gave her a brief account of the Turpins' other nocturnal activity, the details of which he had wished to spare her.

But Dinah was made of more robust material than he'd expected. She hooted with laughter. "And you didn't tell me because we might have been one of the couples caught in the light of a torch!"

As she said it, the same thought flashed between them.

"But surely the police will have thought of that?" said Dinah.

"It's the one game the gang got up to that wasn't in that dossier on Lillian," said, Frank, picking his way through his memory. "I'm sure it's never been mentioned."

"Well, it wouldn't be, would it?" Kemp pointed out. "If one of the first of their victims was Harry Hopkirk himself . . ."

"Caught with his pants round his ankles . . . That's what Terry Cane said. He'd have been the laughing-stock of the station had that got out."

"This Terry Cane," Kemp queried, "did you make a note of what she said, Frank?"

"Yes, I did. I've got all my notes here." He read out the words used, so far as he had remembered them, in his interview with Terry. "I wrote up my notes on everybody as soon as possible afterwards," he explained. "I know you did a good job making me do a verbatim report to you à la Archie Goodwin when you were in your Nero Wolfe mode, but I did make proper notes as well – just to be on the safe side."

"Who the hell's Archie Goodwin?" asked Dinah, but the men were by now too engrossed in feverish discussion to answer her.

"It could be anybody . . ." Kemp finished, sitting back and sighing. "It throws the whole case wide open. So, what have we got? Elinor that night, waiting for her friend Lillian to return, gets bored with the concert. She remembers the talk of the gang about courting couples in cars down lovers'-bloody-lane – as Lillian calls it – so off she goes, torch in hand, to do a little spying for herself."

"And someone grabs her. Oh God!" Frank put a hand to his mouth.

The three of them sat in silence for some minutes.

"I don't think I can bear this thought," said Dinah, her eyes filling up with tears.

Kemp tried to keep his voice steady. "Let me see those notes you made, Frank. The ones of your interview with Terry Cane." Frank handed them over. Although they were brief, Kemp was still reading intently when the telephone rang. Frank answered it and handed the receiver to Kemp. He heard Mary's voice: "Lennox darling, I'm afraid I've some terrible news. Alys is dead. They think it's suicide."

Twenty-seven

"What happened?"

Mary Kemp hadn't cried when she met Kemp at the door of their house but her eyes were red. "I wasn't there," she said. "I know it sounds silly but if I had been . . . No, it would have made no difference."

"George was home?"

"Yes. It was George who phoned me just half an hour ago. He'd been with her all day, and she was up for lunch. Then she said she was tired, and went upstairs for her afternoon rest – she did the same each day when I was there. He looked in on her about four o'clock to take her tea but she was asleep, so he left her. Usually she would come down in time for the news at six. When she didn't, he went into the bedroom and found her. She'd taken sleeping tablets."

"I thought you said how careful—"

"How careful Dr Parfitt was? Oh, yes, I'm sure he was, but when you have someone determined on ending their life, they'll find a way. She must have been saving them up, only pretending to take them. I should have been more watchful. I should have stayed with her."

"Sshh, Mary, there was nothing you could do. Nothing George could do." Kemp put his arms round his wife and hugged her. "You were with her when she wanted you in these last days, you could have done no more."

"It was me she would talk to," said Mary. "Somehow she couldn't talk to her husband, always to me. Going over her life, remembering things. It's almost as if she was looking back for the last time. It was all about the past, never the future. She would never say next week or next year."

"She saw no future?"

"That was it, entirely. She never meant for there to be any future now Elinor had gone. I should have been thinking all that while I listened to her. Oh, my poor Alys, even I didn't understand. And I don't think George did either."

"She didn't leave a note?"

"He didn't say so. Where would be the need for such a thing? The doctor came – I think it was Dr Sutherland because Dr Parfitt was out. But she was beyond any help."

"Dr Parfitt had another patient this evening." He told her about the events at the police station.

Mary didn't speak for a while, then she said: "The saddest thing, that girl never knowing Elinor's mother, although she was Elinor's friend . . . Oh, those hateful barriers!"

"It's strange but Lillian seemed to have imagined Alys de Lisle the way you did, something out of an old tale – the maiden in the tower with the long pale hair." Kemp was thinking of the far-away look in Lillian's eyes. Something else came into his memory at the same time, but was gone before he could catch it.

"Perhaps I should go up and see George," he said.

Mary nodded. "I did think he wanted that. He'd tried to get you at the office. He does need someone. The papers will call it a double tragedy. The papers know nothing, they think what they give is what their readers want – it's all in the headlines . . ." She broke off.

Kemp leaned over and kissed her. "I know how you feel," he murmured, "and I only use words like that when I mean them."

He didn't want to go up to that awful house in Coverley Drive, he didn't want to sit with George again, sharing in, and yet not being part of, the wash of misery that sucked you under even as you tried to keep your feet on solid ground. There was friendship, there was loyalty . . . He had to go.

"Dinner's what I want," he said to Mary as he left her. "Dinner for two, with candles. Give me an hour."

"It's already in the oven," she said, "and it's the same as I'll be wanting. Tell me, before you go, what about your client? Will she be all right? She'll not be wanting you, too, I hope."

"Miss Egerton is in the Cottage Hospital where I'm sure the nursing staff will take care of her. She also has a woman police officer at her bedside who will take down any utterance she cares to make, and of course in the background she has her psycho-analytic doctor, Gerald Parfitt, who will, presumably, note down any interesting aspects of her various personalities."

Mary frowned. "Don't joke, Lennox. I know your views. I'm a little concerned about something, or somebody, but I can't put it into words. I have a notion that something's terribly wrong. I felt it those last days when I was up there in the de Lisle household. It was at the back of my mind, and now it's come to the fore." She gave herself a little shake. "A lot of blathers," she said, "off you go and comfort George. Poor man, he'll be needing that right now."

Lennox Kemp felt he had, once again, been given an impossible task. What more could he say to George de Lisle that had not already been said? What comfort could words bring to a man who had lost everything? They could only sink like stones to the bottom of a well.

But George did seem genuinely pleased to see him, and for an hour the two men talked gruffly of practical matters; the inquest (Superintendent Upshire had already called with his condolences and his assurance that the necessary formalities would be dealt with quietly), funeral arrangements for both the mother and the child now that Elinor's body had been released for burial, press announcements, and George's own responses to colleagues. Perhaps there was some solace in discussing these practical matters – they bridged the gap over the abyss. Even the disposal of Alys's car was on George's list, her inconspicuous blue-grey Nova sitting in the garage.

"I'll have a word with David Lorimer about a sale," said Kemp. "Is there anything else?"

"I think that's the lot for now. When it's over," and Kemp knew he was thinking of the funeral, "I shall never come back here. I shall take a flat in London near my mother."

Kemp could see how it would be. George would not be able to bear that house and its surroundings, those terrifying woods at the back – he wanted an end to that part of his life.

"To tell you the truth, Lennox, I don't care any more who killed Elinor. There's no point in knowing now that Alys is gone. While she was alive it was my duty to support and comfort her. Now that's finished, I want to draw a line under everything that has happened. I only want to know the murderer, so that I can close the account once and for all. If I sound like a banker, it's because I am one."

"I understand," said Kemp, realising that George was dealing with the aftermath of tragedy in the only way he knew; his work would become his life in the future. He might achieve an even higher status in the financial field but, in the meantime, he needed to balance the books.

As they stood under the pitiless light of the hall, Kemp asked him if Alys had been ill recently. "I think Elinor was worried about her," he said, diffidently. "Did you know that?"

"Alys hadn't been herself since Christmas. She thought she had caught the flu virus which was going about at that time. Dr Parfitt was treating her for it and she seemed to get better. But recently she didn't look well, according to her friends." He sighed. "I was away so much I didn't notice but people on the phone have mentioned it . . . You say that Elinor was concerned?"

"She mentioned it to Monica Hodge, who thought it might be serious."

"Oh, no, we were assured it wasn't. Alys was simply a bit run down, and she was a poor sleeper. She'd always taken sleeping tablets, that's why . . ." He broke off, then began again, "that's why it was easy for her to hoard them. I was amazed at the amount scattered about in the little drawer of her bedside table, and very grateful to Gerald Parfitt when he took them away." Gerge shook his head. "Perhaps being a doctor he suspected that I too might take that way out. But it's not my nature."

"Dr Parfitt took them?"

"Well, it was John Sutherland who came first, of course, when I found Alys, but later Gerald called to say how sorry he was. He asked about the tablets that he'd prescribed, so I took him into her bedroom and showed him what was in the drawer. He emptied it to take to the police, in case they would be needed as evidence."

"You say that friends of Alys had mentioned her not being well, do you think she'd talked to any of them about her health?" Kemp didn't want to upset George by asking more questions, but his mind had got hold of a line and would not let go.

"Several people I've spoken to said they'd noticed . . . The Finlays, for example, with whom she'd been playing bridge, they said Alys had to leave early as she was feeling ill. I think her health had always been delicate, Lennox, even my mother described Alys as frail."

Kemp turned on the doorstep. "Frailty, thy name is woman," he quoted, and could have bitten off his tongue. Why on earth had that sprung to mind? Fortunately he didn't think George had heard him.

Dinner was on the table when he returned to his own house and, throughout the meal, neither he nor Mary spoke much. It was at the coffee stage that he said to Mary, "Now I want to talk to you about sleeping tablets."

She nodded, calmly, and said to him, "And I want to talk to you about the colour of a woman's hair."

Twenty-eight

The dinner so carefully prepared by Dinah for herself and Frank went uneaten. The news of Alys's death left them strangely at odds with each other. Dinah could not accept that it had been inevitable, and she raged against the act. "That poor man," she cried, "how could she have made him suffer more?"

"I don't suppose she's been thinking straight since her daughter went missing. You can't blame her for taking the obvious way out. She simply could not go on living without Elinor. George will survive."

"Oh, you men . . . !"

As they talked Dinah found further reason to be indignant; Frank's thoughts were not in the same groove as hers. While she was overwhelmed by sadness for George de Lisle, her fiancé was more concerned with the other news that Kemp had brought.

"I think something has to be done for that girl," Frank said, finally. "What if she has another of these fugue states while she's in there and nobody understands what she's going through? That Cottage Hospital's a joke. Serious cases all go out to Emberton General. All you get at the Cottage Hospital is convalescent facilities, and there's no resident medico."

"For heaven's sake, Frank, she's got your pet Dr Parfitt on hand. According to you, he seems to know what he's doing."

"But he's not resident," persisted Frank. "He could be out on call, he could be off-duty for all we know."

"More to the point, Mr Kemp said there was a woman police officer with Lillian Egerton."

"A policewoman's the last person to understand someone

with psychological problems." Frank was sticking to his guns, although he knew he was rapidly running out of ammunition.

Dinah briefly researched her brain for a suitable retort. In fact she came up with something else, something which had been bothering her. "I think," she said without rancour, "everybody in this case has been too much influenced by theory. So much so they've stopped looking at ordinary human beings, not those with so-called psychological problems, nor those the police think are drugged-up, nor what the media loves to portray as the violence of youth culture . . . In this 'introvert' atmosphere, we're in danger of forgetting the essentials. I mean the actual characters, the lives, feelings and actions of the people involved."

But, even as she spoke, she knew that Frank was not with her. His thoughts were elsewhere . . .

"I have to go and visit her," he said, getting up from his chair. He knew he could not sleep easy tonight unless he'd checked that Lillian Egerton was being properly treated. He'd been horrified at the idea of her at the police station being interrogated by Inspector Hopkirk. Of course Kemp had been there, but somehow that wasn't enough. Only he, Franklyn Davey, could save Lillian Egerton from the violence of the mob or, perhaps worse, the vindictive malice of Hopkirk.

He was reaching for his anorak when Dinah said, quietly enough but with determination, "I'm not letting you do this on your own, Frank. I'm coming with you – even if all I do is sit in the car."

"I could do with the company," he confessed. "I've no idea of the visiting hours but I imagine they're pretty lenient."

When they arrived in the hospital car-park, which was almost empty, he reminded Dinah that they'd come here last winter when he'd had to interview an old man who had had a hip-replacement and thought he was likely to die of it. Instead he'd made a full recovery and many other wills since.

Dinah settled down in the passenger seat. "I'll wait for you," she said, "but don't be too long with your airy-fairy Lillian."

At present Newtown Cottage Hospital was a bone of contention between the local council, the Ministry of Health and a firm of developers bent on acquiring the land. Like any bone, the flesh had been gnawed from it by all parties, and it had long been stripped of any muscle. Frank stepped over the scuffed linoleum at the door, and went towards the dimly lit desk at reception. The only nurse on duty glanced at the clock.

"Visiting hours are till nine," she said, "so you could see Miss Egerton, but Dr Parfitt's with her now and he said he'd be some time."

"I'll wait," said Frank, cheerfully. At least she's got medical help, should she need it, he thought, as he took one of the worn plastic chairs in the waiting room alongside a scattering of slumped figures who were perfectly in keeping with the potted plants listlessly dying in corners. Faint footfalls echoed in a far corridor. Frank glanced around. The place was obviously in its death throes, it hadn't had a lick of paint in years. He figured the developers would win in the end, the folk of Newtown would lose their little hospital, and the council's millions from the sale would fund their new sports stadium. You couldn't grumble; it was survival of the fittest.

He saw a policewoman approach the desk, and the attendant pointed to the refreshment machines at the back of the room. Frank leapt to his feet. Here was an opportunity to find out how Lillian was.

"Excuse me," he said, "are you with Miss Egerton?"

Her eyes were not unfriendly. "Yes, I am. Doctor's with her now, so I've come out to get a coffee."

"Then allow me . . . I'm hoping to visit her, and I could do with a coffee in the meantime."

Peggy Pollard was fed up and bored. When Frank explained who he was she was only too thankful to sit down and be brought a drink while this rather nice young man chattered to her. She'd told him she thought the older gentleman was Miss Egerton's lawyer but was assured when Frank said he'd come out of hours, as it were, because he'd only just heard about his client's illness.

"I really can't say how she is," said Peggy, sipping her drink – she wouldn't have called it coffee, "because she's been asleep most of the time I've been with her. Anyway, that Dr Parfitt's with her now."

They agreed that the doctor's presence was for the best. "I don't know whether you'll be allowed in to see her, Mr Davey, but, so long as I'm in the room, I don't see any objection."

"Then we'll wait together," said Frank, cheerfully.

Outside in the car-park Dinah was not cheerful, and she hated waiting. She looked over at the grey shape of the low building. Down one side where overgrown shrubberies lapped the brickwork like waves about to take over, there was a lighted window. She knew the two amenity rooms were on that side and if one was lit then that would be where the Egerton girl would be. Talking to Frank by now? What would she have to say for herself?

Dinah got out of the car. She knew her reasons for doing what she was about to do were mixed, and not altogether commendable. Following her fiancé and spying on him were the actions of a jealous woman, and of course Dinah was not that. All the same, perhaps here was the opportunity just to get a glimpse of the girl who might possibly be twirling him round her little finger.

It was a mild night, for March had come in quietly, and many of the windows in the single-storey wing were open, including the one in the lighted room, halfway down the side. Thick ivy had made its home in the brickwork, the roots firmly set in the little mound of earth beneath the window. Even as Dinah pulled herself along with the help of the sturdy creepers, a figure crossed in front of the light, shaking something in his hand. She crouched below the sill, and heard his words come floating out into the night.

"Well, at least your temperature's back to normal, Lillian. How do you feel?"

The answering voice was thin and reedy but it could be heard plain enough. "Dunno. You tell me, you're the doc."

There was the sound of a chair being moved, and the shadow crossed the room.

There was a slight scuffing noise, presumably someone pulling up a chair. Beside the bed? That seemed to Dinah a reasonable guess. She knelt on the pile of earth, her head just below the level of the window.

"There's a lot I have to tell you, Lillian. I don't know whether you're strong enough to stand it." Although the man's voice was lowered it was still clear.

"Tell me, for starters, what the hell I'm doing in here?" The girl's voice was louder now, and harsher.

The next few words were inaudible; he must have bent over the bed, which seemed to be along the wall to the left of the window. Then his voice became clearer as he sat back in the chair. "We've been over this before. I warned you about the condition of fugue and why you'd not remember what you did when you were in it."

"You telling me I'd do summat and not know?"

"I'm afraid that is what it amounts to. I did tell you the last time you had this kind of faint. It's being in a different state of consciousness, personality dissociation characterised by amnesia and—"

"Hey, don't give me the long words, just tell me what I'm supposed to have done when in this what-d'you-call-it fugue thing."

"You remember the night of the concert at the Drill Hall, Lillian – you were going to meet someone?"

There was silence for a moment. Dinah suddenly was reminded of listening to a radio play; you could not see faces, but had to gauge the characters purely by their voices. Lillian's was now uncertain as if she was searching in her own memory.

"Yeah, I remember, I was meeting Simon, Simon Marco and we was to go clubbing."

"Are you sure, Lily? I think that's something you made up afterwards because you had to get away from what really happened."

"Was I up in the woods, then? Is that where I was?"

"You were with your new friend, Elinor de Lisle. You remember, you told me about her, how she wanted to join your gang. She was a bit of a rebel like you, Lily, and going to the Drill Hall that night would be a way of getting her own back at her parents, wouldn't it?"

210

"I remember now. She wanted to spend the night at my house, and I picked her up outside the youth club. We went up to the concert and she phoned her gran. That was a laugh." The voice stopped, and when it took up again it was hesitant. "I don't know what happened then. Oh, I remember, she got afraid of something, so I says we'd better hide in the woods. Then I lost her."

"What do you mean 'you lost her'– and what was she frightened of?"

"I dunno. You tell me." This was on a peevish note.

"I wasn't there, Lily. Only you and Elinor, no one else. Did you have a quarrel? Was it about the drugs, Lily? She wouldn't have anything to do with drugs, that's what you'd told me when you said she'd become your friend. Was that what the quarrel was about?"

There was a long silence. Dinah was getting cramp in her legs, and shifted her position on the mound of earth. From the direction of the bed there was a rattle as if something was pushed aside.

"Careful, Lily, you nearly had that lot over. Now, keep calm, and think again. Did you and Elinor have a tiff about your drugs?"

When Lillian spoke this time it was in a flat monotone. "I don't do drugs. Why do people keep on saying I do drugs? What am I doing in here?"

"Lily, Lily, come back." The doctor's voice sounded peremptory in Dinah's ears. "You can't keep on running away from it, you have to face it sometime. Were you collecting your usual supply that night? Did Elinor see you pick them up? Is that why you killed her, because she said she'd tell the police? You didn't mean to, of course," the voice softened, "it was really an accident. When you are being Lily you are quite strong, aren't you? You've had to be when men have tried anything on with you, you slap them down real hard."

There was a long pause, then a faint sobbing as the doctor spoke again, quietly, soothingly. "I'm sorry, Lillian, but I had to make Lily face up to what she'd done. Together you and I will see that she confesses to the police, I think they already know much more than they're saying. She'll be dealt with leniently, that I can promise you. I will give evidence of her several states of mind that I've observed over months, and there will be a lot of sympathy for you, Lillian, because you were not to blame for what happened."

Dinah held her breath; against all her previous scepticism she could have sworn there were three people in that hospital bedroom.

"I've just remembered something . . ." Lillian's voice – or was it still Lily's? – was strained. "What had frightened Elinor. She saw her mother's car. She thought that her mother had come out looking for her so she went and hid in the woods."

From another window Dinah could hear the sound of far-away music from a radio, otherwise the silence was deadly. When the doctor's voice eventually came, it was soft and full of regret. "I'm sorry you said that, Lillian, and sorrier still that you'll probably say it again. And I can't have that, no, I can't put up with that."

The shadow of his figure crossed in front of the window, and there came the sound of the opening of a briefcase. The doctor kept up a running conversation, although there was no response from the bedside. "I've just the thing for you, Lillian, since you've chosen to be silly. You need a sedative, and I'll have to inject it, but fortunately I have one ready. Then some sleeping tablets, that'll do a treat. And, again, I have some handy. I'll just get rid of the bottles, then I can give you a nice little meal of pills, and nobody will know where they came from. You probably pinched them from the hospital dispensary."

Dinah had to duck as three small pill bottles went sailing over her head, and landed in the bushes.

"Now don't move, Lillian, or I'll have to restrain you. The staff here will understand. You went a bit mad, didn't you, and I had to give you a sedative, isn't that the truth, now?"

This time the bedside table really had overturned with a crash. Lillian's voice came strongly over the sound of breaking glass. "I was only faking, Dr Parfitt, all along. But I got myself in so deep I couldn't get out. It's only now I remembered about that car. I told Elinor she must be mistaken, but I knew she

212

wasn't. We'd even seen the car in the area before. I think she guessed. But I never did. Not till now.

"I found those long blonde hairs in the back of your car when you carried me in from the police station. And do you know what? I kept them to give to Mr Kemp."

"You little fool, Lillian Egerton. After all I've done for you. Of course it was Alys up there with me that night when Elinor shone that torch. But Alys never knew. I told her there were hooligans fooling around, and sent her off double-quick to her own car to go home."

"But Elinor came after you. I'll bet she did. She was the one who had a thing about adultery. Her own mother . . . You bastard."

There was the beginning of a scream but he must have put a hand over her mouth. "Just a jab in the arm, Lillian, that's all. Then a mouthful of pills, I've got the really strong ones here. It'll all be over soon. You'll simply drift into unconsciousness."

Dinah could hear the sound of the struggle, and could bear it no longer. "No!" she screamed at the top of her voice.

She knew it had been a mistake to scream, as the tall figure was at the window in a second, threw wide the casement and jumped, landing firmly on two feet even as she was scrambling out of the ivy. She took to her heels down the passageway between the wall and the shrubbery but she felt him gaining on her with his long stride against her feeble attempt at running. Her breath was tight in her chest, she was never going to be able to keep up the pace, and she despaired of rescue.

Just when she was wondering which part of her anatomy would receive the fatal jab, she heard a shout. "You there . . . Stop."

There was a scuffle behind her and she stopped and looked back. Dr Parfitt had apparently been felled by a low tackle from a burly man in a trench coat. They were struggling at the corner of the building near the entrance where the light was better, and she could see both their faces. The burly man was the ugliest she had ever seen. As the doctor tried to get to his feet, he was recognised.

"Dr Parfitt? Sorry, I didn't know it was you."

"I was chasing a burglar, you stupid man. Let me go."

But another figure joined them, "I wouldn't if I were you, Inspector Hopkirk. Dr Parfitt's your murderer. Put the cuffs on him, and I'll phone Superintendent Upshire. He'll be well pleased with your good piece of police work tonight." Lennox Kemp turned to Dinah. "And you are a heroine, Dinah, I don't know how Frank is going to keep up with you."

Harry Hopkirk was still bemused by the turn of events, but as Gerald Parfitt sought to aim a kick at his legs the inspector didn't hesitate to knock him down again, and cuff him. You don't try resisting arrest with an officer like Hopkirk.

No one was ever to know what had brought the inspector so happily upon the scene that night. Like Franklyn Davey, he had been concerned, not with the well-being of Lillian Egerton, but with the possibility that somehow she would con WPC Pollard and once more subvert the course of justice.

He was not altogether pleased that, like Dinah, Lillian became a heroine overnight. But the congratulations of his fellows, and a commendation from the super for being the man who actually caught the murderer, sent Harry back to his Amy with all flags flying.

Epilogue

Lennox Kemp was pontificating. "Somebody once said, or wrote, that a skilled psychiatrist using his scientific knowledge and the experience gained in his consulting room is in a fairly good position to understand his fellow human beings, but less so if he allows himself to be influenced by theories. And that was what was wrong with all of us in this case, we had so many theories that we forgot to look closely enough at the people concerned."

"I was uneasy about Alys," said Mary, "but the ideas I was getting from the rest of you got in the way. And, because of George, I couldn't put into words what I'd come to believe – that his wife was having an affair and the only person who suspected it was her daughter."

"I should have listened to Monica," Frank admitted, ruefully. "And if I hadn't been so obsessed with my client's psyche, I might have looked more carefully at what Terry Cane had said. It was there, staring me in the face, the long, pale hair in the moonlight. There's no excuse for me for I'd met the receptionist, even compared her bobbed hair to yours, Dinah, and heard her say she'd never worn it long."

"I'd never met any of these people," said Dinah. "Only heard voices. Lillian was very brave telling him about the long blonde hairs she'd found in the back seat of his car. She, too, was a bit late in making the connection." She shivered. "He'd have killed her for those hairs."

"He'd have killed her anyway," said Kemp, briskly. "Sometime or other she'd have mentioned Elinor thinking she'd seen her mother's car up there in the woods. Gerald Parfitt is a creature of impulse. Nothing was planned, he just took events as they came and used them to his advantage. John Upshire tells me they've got a full confession out of him. It's rather like a re-run of what he was suggesting Lillian did. Once Alys was back in her car that night – she never saw who shone the torch in on them – and had driven away, he started up his engine but Elinor wrenched open the door, screaming at him. She clung on to the door handle and wouldn't let go. She shouted that she would ruin him for having an affair with a patient. John says Parfitt was incoherent at this point, kept asking how a girl of her age could be so knowing, so vindictive. Anyway, he got Elinor on the ground and was, he says, simply trying to stop her screaming. His hands were round her throat, he didn't mean to kill her, only to make her shut up. He bundled the body into the boot of his car. Oh, yes, the forensic experts have been busy – he'd not had time to clean it up."

"Too busy playing the good guy," said Frank, ruefully. "He certainly had me fooled. Did he kill Alys de Lisle too?"

Kemp shook his head. "He could never be charged with it. He simply left the means at her disposal."

"Pray God she died before she knew . . ." Mary used the words more as comfort to herself than for the others to hear.

It was not something they wished to dwell on. Frank changed the subject. "I understand Inspector Hopkirk is moving back to London."

"A side step," said Kemp. "Definitely not promotion. He may have been the hero of the hour when he collared Parfitt, but the gilt was soon off his gingerbread when questions were asked at the station as to why the gang's peeping Tom activities didn't get a mention along with the other misdemeanours in their dossier."

"And Lillian?" Dinah asked.

"It seems she's back at work, and has taken it all very calmly. Of course if she is charged on the drugs business, I'll act for her. I think she's worth it, as they say."

"I agree," Frank said, eagerly, despite a look from Dinah. "Now she's got over all that role-playing stuff she's quite an attractive girl."

"All she probably needs," said Mary, "is a steady relationship with a decent man." She turned to Frank. "That nice Mr Bexby, now, is he short of a wife?"